Louise Brindley was born in Darlington, County Durham, and at the age of four moved with her family to Scarborough in North Yorkshire. The moment she saw the sea and the sand, she knew she could be happy with the town and countryside destined to become her new home. All Louise Brindley's writings reflect her knowledge of, and deep affection for, the North East where she still lives. Her previous novels, TANQUILLAN, OUR SUMMER FACES and MOVING AWAY all deal with various aspects of life in North Yorkshire.

THE INCONSTANT MOON

Louise Brindley

CORGI BOOKS

THE INCONSTANT MOON

A CORGI BOOK   0 552 14193 3

First publication in Great Britain

PRINTING HISTORY
Corgi edition published 1991

Copyright © Louise Brindley 1991

The right of Louise Brindley to be identified as author of this work has
been asserted in accordance with sections 77 and 78 of the Copyright
Designs and Patents Act 1988.

This book is set in 11/12½pt Sabon by
Kestrel Data, Exeter

Corgi Books are published by Transworld Publishers Ltd.,
61-63 Uxbridge Road, Ealing, London W5 5SA, in Australia by
Transworld Publishers (Australia) Pty. Ltd., 15-23 Helles Avenue,
Moorebank, NSW 2170, and in New Zealand by Transworld Publishers
(N.Z.) Ltd., Cnr. Moselle and Waipareira Avenues, Henderson, Auckland.

Printed and bound in Great Britain by
Cox & Wyman Ltd., Reading, Berks.

For my friends Roy and Nora Knox, and Maisie Thompson, whose help in researching and typing this book has been so generously given.

Part One

I

She left the house early, taking the dog with her, and hurried through the quiet streets of home to watch the sun come up.

Home. Scarborough. The sea. The scimitar curve of the South Bay. The strong hilt of the Norman Keep on the Castle Hill, the blade of green-topped cliffs tapering to the gleaming point of the Flamborough Head lighthouse.

Light touched the waters of the bay to the ever increasing brilliance of a new day. It was going to be hot again, with scarcely a breath of air. No day for a long, tiring journey. She wished she could take Nell down to the sea's edge for a run along the beach, but barbed-wire barricades had been thrown across the slipways to the sands. Would those bramble-like strands of twisted wire really prevent a German invasion force from landing, Laura wondered. And now that France had fallen, the threat of invasion was all too real and terrifying.

Gazing at the shifting rays of light on water, she stood as an acolyte at some vast, blue-grey altar ashine with newly-lit candles. She had needed this little space of time to herself, but time was moving on. Her parents would be astir now, Mother starting to set the breakfast table, her father shaving. Another hour and a half and she would be gone, the leave-taking over and done with, all their goodbyes said. Whatever happened, she must not cry.

Her call-up had been a matter of time, waiting for that buff OHMS envelope to arrive. A girl with the sea in her blood, she had not wanted to join the ATS or the WAAF. It had to be the Wrens. And so she had volunteered for service.

'Well, we'd better be getting back.' The dog wagged its tail furiously as Laura bent down to fuss it – a smooth-haired fox terrier, white with black marking and two brown spots for eyebrows – a present from Dad on her tenth birthday; old now by human standards. Nell would not understand why she had left her, was bound to fret when she had gone. This was the cruellest cut of all, parting from everything she held dear. It seemed to Laura that her world had suddenly turned topsy-turvy. And what if anything should happen to her family during her absence?

Shivering slightly, despite the warmth of the sun, she thought about those sporadic hit and run raids when German planes crossed the coast by moonlight, following the shining ribbon of the Humber Estuary to drop their bombs and incendiaries, wrecking houses, shattering people's lives.

Hurrying home along the Foreshore and up through the Victoria Gardens into town, Laura thought of her coming journey with trepidation. Edinburgh seemed a long way from home, but Gran had said, with a kind of fearful relish, that 'they' always sent recruits as far away as possible. So where would she end up after her training? The Outer Hebrides? Land's End? John-O'-Groats?

Laura had never been away from home on her own

before. Holidays had always been family affairs. When Mum had finished with the summer visitors, Dad would close the 'Saloon' for a fortnight, and the Prentiss family, *en masse,* Nell included, would travel down to London to spend the first week with Aunt Marjorie, Uncle Herbert, and their sophisticated daughter Joanne, at their house in Walthamstow, the second week with Aunt Lally, Uncle Bob, and cousin Meggie, on Uncle Bob's farm in Wiltshire.

The pattern had existed, unchanged, until the out-break of war. Throwing a stick for the dog, Laura remembered the magic of those London sight-seeing excursions with Aunt Madge in charge, the aplomb with which she had guided them through the maze of the Underground system to the Tower, the Houses of Parliament, Westminster Abbey, St Paul's, Regent's Park Zoo where, as a child, she had fed nuts to the squirrels, thrown currant buns to the polar bears, and ridden nervously between the humps of a snarling camel. Remembered those damp cheese and tomato sandwiches they had eaten with such relish beneath the trees in Hyde Park; how, worn out but happy, they would catch the train back to Walthamstow for a slap-up high tea of ham and eggs, sausages and chips.

Then had come the contrast of Wiltshire with its rolling Downs and windy, cloud-chequered skies, where Aunt Lally would take them to visit Stonehenge and Salisbury Cathedral. The routine had not varied: walking round the cathedral – a never ending source of delight for Laura – followed by tea at an 'olde worlde' café where the hot buttered teacakes were served on willow-pattern china by genteel, elderly waitresses wearing starched white aprons.

11

She had loved every moment of those holidays, particularly the time she had spent with her favourite cousin, Meggie, who was mad about the cinema – the pictures, she called them – and would tempt Laura to the picture house in Devizes three or four evenings a week, often to see the same film twice if she happened to have a 'pash' on the leading man. Not that Laura had needed much tempting. There the pair of them would sit in the smoky darkness, gazing up at the screen with a kind of wistful intensity, revelling in Romance with a capital 'R', absorbing everything fed to them from the Hollywood soup-kitchen; believing in the validity of the fade-out embrace, that Romance meant happy-ever-after.

Laura had lost count of the number of handkerchiefs they had reduced to pulp. Even so, she had always been ready to come home, back to the sea, to Scarborough, to the streets of home shorn of the flocks of summer visitors who had arrived in May and departed in September, like migratory swallows, to the colours of changing leaves, and softly falling rain, the gentle folding in of the year before the onslaught of winter.

Home, a tall Victorian terraced house, overlooked a Corporation garden whose railings had been removed during the war weapons' drive, leaving the central half-moon looking rather like an indignant old lady robbed of her corsets by the powers that be, the mysterious 'they' whose word was law.

'They' had taken everyone else's railings as well, to Mrs Prentiss's annoyance, whose fine crop of flowering currant bushes and hydrangeas were left with no means of support. 'Well, if that isn't the absolute limit,' she'd cried in high dudgeon when she saw her precious railings being thrown pell-mell on to a Corporation lorry. Then she had calmed down a bit, and sniffed when Laura suggested that perhaps 'they' – the powers-that-be – were planning to attack the Germans with black iron spears stamped with a fleur-de-lys pattern. 'Trust you to think of something daft like that,' she'd said scornfully, marching out with pea-sticks and a ball of twine to tie up the bushes.

Entering the house, the smell of fried bacon hit Laura squarely in the nostrils. *Bacon?*

Mary Prentiss turned away from the cooker as her daughter hurried into the kitchen; a small, compact woman wearing a flowered pinafore over a neat blouse and skirt, with brown hair, greying slightly at the temples, finger waved in graceful curves on her forehead. 'Oh, there you are,' she said. 'About time, too! I've made you some sandwiches and a flask of tea for the journey. I know tea doesn't taste very nice from a thermos, but I daresay you'll be glad of it. Go and sit down, and I'll bring your breakfast.'

Laura went obediently to the living-room where the table was set with a starched white tablecloth, Grey Dawn china, neatly placed cutlery.

'All this bacon?' she protested, as her mother shoved a plate containing a week's ration in front of her, afraid to admit she wasn't hungry. 'But what about you and Dad?' Her grandma, she knew, never touched bacon, proclaiming loudly that she didn't like live pigs, never mind dead ones. Nasty pink things, with pale eye-lashes. Ugh!

'You'll need a good breakfast inside you,' Mary Prentiss said firmly. 'And I managed to get you a fresh

13

egg. Now where on earth has your father got to? He started shaving half an hour ago.' Hastening to the foot of the stairs, she called up to her husband, 'Will, do you realize what time it is?'

Staring at his reflection in the bathroom mirror, William Prentiss knew only too well what the time was. Almost time to say goodbye to his little girl, his Laura, who had grown from a child into a woman seemingly overnight, without his being aware of the fact. He had been dreading this morning ever since the arrival of that OHMS envelope containing her call-up papers and travel-warrant.

'Coming!' The razor slipped suddenly. Blood from the cut spurted down his chin. 'Oh, damnation!' he muttered, applying a piece of toilet-tissue to the wound, thinking that whatever happened he must not betray how much he dreaded the coming ordeal.

A gentle man who had always secretly liked poetry, he thought, dabbing at his chin, of the line of a poem he had learned as a boy, which had invaded his mind during a sleepless night: 'Since there's no help, come let us kiss and part . . .' He dashed his face savagely in cold water. Then, drying himself on a rough towel, he put on his collar and tie, eased the tissue from his cut, and went downstairs.

Laura's heart lifted as it always did whenever her father entered a room, and yet their love for each other made no outward display. It was simply a thing of shared laughter, a deep understanding of each other's need at any given time, as though the genes of father and daughter had not split, at her conception, to form a separate identity, but had somehow remained whole and indivisible.

The kitchen was long and narrow, like a railway compartment; hot on this airless August morning, even though the door to the yard stood wide open. The living-room, on the other hand, was big and square, with moulded cornices and a high ceiling rosette – a room filled with heavy old-fashioned furniture: solid oak sideboard, dining-table and six matching chairs; Gran's horsehair sofa with the curly, polished wood ends, her brass fender and fire-irons; the walls hung with framed reproductions of Landseer's 'Monarch of the Glen', Rembrandt's 'The Night Watch', and Millais' 'Bubbles', all of which Mary Prentiss found extremely depressing, which she could not very well get rid of because they belonged to her mother-in-law who had come to live with them five years ago. An oak-framed mirror hung over the brown marble fireplace. There were folkweave curtains in muted shades of brown and blue at the tall window overlooking the yard, the panes of which were covered with a lattice-work of gummed paper strips; a wireless set stood on a bamboo table.

Attempting to choke down her bacon and egg, Laura suddenly remembered that fraught Sunday morning almost a year ago, when she and her family had crowded round that set to listen to Neville Chamberlain's declaration of war against Germany; the utter weariness of his voice speaking the words which had changed all their lives.

'You'd better go up and say goodbye to your grandmother,' Mary Prentiss said, glancing at the marble clock on the mantelpiece, which reminded Laura of the façade of the National Portrait Gallery, 'only for goodness' sake don't let her keep you talking too long. We'll be on the last lap for the station, if she does.'

Bemused by memories, looking round the room at all the things which had never seemed particularly beautiful before, which now seemed infinitely dear and lovely to her, Laura went upstairs to say goodbye to her grandmother.

The curtains were drawn together, accentuating the stuffiness, the smell of old age and wintergreen lotion. Gran suffered from rheumatism. Her dentures reposed in a glass of water on the bedside table. She was sitting up in bed, wearing a slumber helmet, the ribbons of which were tied beneath her jutting chin.

'Ah, so you're off, are you?' Gran had a way of not beating about the bush. She had high cheekbones, deeply etched wrinkles about her mouth, piercingly blue eyes sunk deep in their sockets, a clipped, accusatory way of speaking. Her lips, minus her dentures, resembled the puckered up hole of a vacuum cleaner bag.

'I'm afraid so, Gran. I don't want to go but I have to. There's a war on.'

'Huh! No need to preach to me about war, young lady. I've been through all this before! I was here when the Germans bombarded Scarborough! Terrible, that was, in the winter of 1914! Your father had just joined the army, and there I was left all alone, not knowing which way to run for safety. Then my commonsense told me to stay where I was, not to go rushing about the streets like a mad woman, that if I was about to die, I'd best die in my own home with my own things around me.'

Laura had heard all this before, a hundred times

over. 'I know, Gran.' She perched on the edge of the bed.

'Ha, you *think* you know, but you don't! How old are you? Eighteen? Well, in my opinion it's high time you started to learn about life. I've no patience with folk who . . . Tell the truth, now. You didn't want to go into your Dad's business, did you?'

'No, I suppose not,' Laura admitted, 'but I . . .'

'You should have stuck to your guns, my girl,' Gran snorted, 'and your mother had no right to meddle. She knew your heart was set on that Art scholarship! Why didn't you tell her?' The old woman sucked in her lips disapprovingly.

'I did, Gran! You know I did! But Mum knew how much Dad wanted me to learn hairdressing, and I couldn't bear to disappoint him.' Laura's eyes filled with tears.

'Oh, come here, my sweetheart.' Leaning forward, Gran Prentiss clasped the girl to her heart. 'I'm sorry if I've upset you. But you see, love, I want you to go away with no regrets. To face facts. And the fact is, it's high time you flew the coop! You're too much under her thumb, and your Dad's far too soft with her. Oh, I know your mother thinks I'm just an interfering old woman nearing the end of my days. Well, that's as it may be, but I want you to have a life of your own, friends of your own age. Why, God bless my soul, I was married at eighteen, with a home of my own, and a baby on the way!'

'I'd better be going now, Gran.' Laura brushed her grandmother's puckered mouth with her tender young lips, making allowances for the old lady's outspokenness, pitying her role as a proud woman forced, by circumstance, to live under someone else's roof, understanding some of the reasons why Mother and Grandma did not always see eye-to-eye.

The old woman said fiercely, 'Now promise me you'll take good care of yourself, and don't forget to write to me once in a while.'

'I won't, Gran. I promise.'

'Oh, before I forget, here's something for you.' Gran Prentiss fiddled beneath her pillows with claw-like fingers stiff with rheumatism, and handed Laura a crisp five-pound note.

Laura drew back, in alarm. 'But I couldn't possibly . . .'

'Nonsense! I've been saving up! What does an old woman like me want with so much money? You take it, and welcome!'

At the foot of the stairs, Laura hesitated momentarily, then opened the door of what she and Dad had laughingly dubbed the Saloon, the generously proportioned front room which her father had utilised to his own requirements rather than renting a lock-up shop in another part of town. A home-loving man, he liked nothing better than to wander through to the living quarters between appointments to lend his wife a hand with the vegetables or the washing-up, or simply to drink a cup of tea with her.

A feeling of nostalgia swept through Laura at the intermingled scents of violet oil and green soft soap, the familiar sight of the snuff-brown chenille curtains at the entrance to the cubicles, the washbasins; wall telephone; trolleys filled with permanent waving equipment; hood dryers and perming machines; the high counter on which reposed the well-thumbed appointments' book, beneath which was kept the double pan in which the henna packs were cooked; cartons of Eugene sachets, carboys of .880 ammonia with ground-in stoppers, bundles of plaited crepe hair; piles of freshly laundered towels.

Gran was right in thinking that she had not wanted to take up hairdressing as a career, wrong in supposing that she had not discussed with her parents the matter of her Art scholarship, her starry-eyed ambition to become a dress designer. When Dad told her that it was up to her to decide, that all he wanted was her happiness, Laura had guessed his disappointment, knowing how much he had looked forward to her following in his footsteps, not that he had indicated his disappointment by a word or a glance. It was Mum who had taken her aside later and told her it would break her father's heart if she did not go into the business after all. Then Laura had known that she could not bear to cause him a moment's distress, that all she wanted was *his* happiness.

Glad now, in face of the coming separation, that she had known the joy of working alongside him, first as his apprentice, then an improver, gradually easing the work load from his shoulders, sharing the traumas of the Easter and Christmas rushes; the occasional perm which refused to take; sharing laughter too, and hastily snatched sandwiches when they were too busy to break off for a proper meal, she gave one last lingering look round the room, and closed the door gently behind her, wondering how Dad would manage without her. He seemed so tired nowadays; worried about her leaving. Perhaps she had done wrong in volunteering to join the WRNS, but she had discovered that only volunteers stood an earthly chance of getting into the Senior Service.

Mother insisted on taking Nell to the station with them. 'She'll create merry hell if we don't. Dogs always know when something's wrong,' she said in that decisive way of hers.

Laura felt she might have managed this leave-taking better without Nell, whose quivering wet nose poking through the barrier railings seemed a silent reproach almost too hard to bear. Was this the way prisoners felt awaiting execution? This terrible knowledge that nothing could prevent what was about to take place? She began to realize the meaning of bureaucracy, the powerful force and thrust behind top-level decision making.

A feeling of misery at the thought of saying goodbye; at the sight of her parents and Nell, lined up behind the ticket-barrier, welled up in Laura's heart. The ticket-machine, gagged with strips of gummed paper, the notice which read: 'Passengers only allowed on the platforms', seemed to her another facet of insensitive bureaucracy.

Mary Prentiss had bridled indignantly coming face to face with that notice, and rounded fiercely on the ticket-collector. 'You mean to say that we can't go on to the platform to give our daughter a proper send off?' she demanded.

The ticket-collector regarded her coolly. 'No use arguing the toss with me, missis,' he said. 'Regulations are regulations. Why not take it up with the Minister of Transport?'

'Don't fuss, Mary.' William laid a restraining hand

on his wife's arm, knowing the danger signals; flushed cheeks and pursed lips. 'We're wasting time.' He and Laura looked at each other, sharing a moment of complete understanding. Time. There was so little of it left now. Passengers were crowding through the barrier: eddies of steam from the seven-thirty train to York were billowing up from the engine. The guard, chatting to a porter, consulted his pocket-watch.

'Take care of yourself, love.'

'Yes, Dad. I will. You too.' How could she possibly express, in a few dwindling minutes, all that he and Mum meant to her? But there was no need. They already knew. Had always known. Especially her father. 'Look after Nell for me.' Tears were close to the surface.

'Now, Laura, let us know the minute you arrive,' Mum counselled. 'Don't talk to strangers, be sure to take a seat facing the engine, and remember you have to change trains at York.'

'I know, Mum. Don't worry, I'll be fine. Just fine.' Bending down to fondle Nell, feeling the dog's smooth tongue on her hand, the lump in Laura's throat felt like one of those bobbing celluloid balls in a shooting gallery.

Standing up, she exchanged brief kisses with her parents, turned away and hurried towards the train; heard, with a deep sense of relief, the slamming of the carriage doors, the blowing of the guard's whistle.

As the train began to move, she glimpsed, from an open corridor window, the blurred faces of her loved ones, seen through a mist of tears, and heard the shrill barking of a small, bewildered dog.

2

The Edinburgh train was late. Not that anyone expected trains to arrive on time nowadays. The well-worn phrase, 'Don't you know there's a war on?' covered every discrepancy from engine failure to the banana shortage. Porters uttered it as a subliminal exclamation mark to pithy reminders that it wasn't their fault if there'd been a hold up along the line.

On this sweltering hot day, the much lauded spirit of British camaraderie had been dispersed by the heat beating down on the roof of York station, creating a hot-house atmosphere of suffocating intensity. The travelling public appeared to be wilting visibly from heat and ennui.

Pushed to the back of the crowd lining the platform, Laura noticed that the railway lines, curving away into the blue distance, seemed to waver and shimmer in the heat-haze, for all the world like a mirage, as if they might suddenly dissolve beneath the sledge-hammer blows of the sun. She tried to think cool, and lifted her head in an attempt to rid her nostrils of the cloying smell of dust, engine-grease, and human sweat as a squad of airmen, hefting duffle-bags, pushed past her, stamping and jostling, jockeying for position at the far end of the platform where, presumably, the guard's van would halt when the train arrived – *when* it arrived, and she thought how hot and sticky they must feel in their scratchy uniforms on a day like this, their necks rubbed raw with their stiffly starched collars. No wonder they perspired so profusely.

With a sinking heart, she realized that, soon, she too would be imprisoned in a uniform, collar and tie, and be obliged to wear a hat. Laura hated hats, had never worn one winter or summer, preferring to feel the wind ruffling her hair. Mum said she would suffer for it later in life, a warning which Laura blithely ignored, laughing at her mother's overprotectiveness. In any case, an eighteen-year-old girl in the full bloom of youth and health could not readily envisage herself becoming old, needing to keep her head warm.

Poor Mum, always fussing over nothing, lacing her days with tiny fetishes and superstitions, fearful of spilling salt, dropping a glove in case of bad luck; forever uttering dire warnings, 'Don't talk to strangers.' But everyone she met from now on would be a stranger – and, 'Make sure you take a seat facing the engine.'

When the Edinburgh train steamed in at last, Laura thought that she would be lucky to find a seat at all. Carriages and corridors were jam packed. She would probably have to stand all the way to Waverley.

Now for it! No use hanging back. Using her case as a battering ram, Laura flung herself into the melée and boarded the train. Finding herself a square yard of space in the corridor, she heaped her belongings – gas-mask case, carrier-bag containing her sandwiches and thermos flask, and the heavy coat Mum had insisted she take with her in case the weather turned colder – on her upturned case, thinking that if she fainted from the heat of closely packed humanity in so limited a space, she would faint standing up.

Smiling to herself, she caught the eye of a young soldier sitting near the partition window, who winked at her, obviously thinking she was smiling at him. Of all the nerve. It wasn't the wink she minded so much as the fact that he appeared to be mentally undressing her.

Turning her head away to shut out the sight of his leering, acned face, she wondered if her new bra was making too much of her bosom, and tried folding her arms. Brassieres, like hats, had always seemed superfluous items of clothing to Laura, who hated restriction of any kind. She had bought this one for appearance's sake, to improve her shape. Now she wished she had stuck to the old, comfortable ones she wore at home.

She had never thought much about her looks before. Looks hadn't seemed all that important, walking along the seashore at home, feeling the wind in her hair, throwing stones for the dog. Hats and bras had been the least of her worries.

Relief flooded through her when, at Darlington, the soldier got up and offered her his seat. 'Know what, you've got a smashing figure,' he breathed in her ear as he pushed past her. 'Well, ta-ta, ducks.'

As the journey wore on, Laura reflected that, until this war happened, she had not thought it possible her world could change so abruptly. And yet, being young and idealistic, she must believe that her joining up would somehow preserve such beauty for coming generations of children. Her own children, perhaps? How strange. She had never pursued this line of thought before. Perhaps that was what Grandma meant when she said it was high time she flew the coop, to look to the future.

All very well to say. Laura wondered, in the heat, discomfort and loneliness of the journey, how it would be possible to ignore her upbringing without losing track of her identity.

As the train steamed northwards, she ate her sandwiches, drank tea from her mother's thermos, nudged a dozing RAF corporal's head from her shoulder, and thought about that future.

Waverley at last!

It was much like York Station, Victorian in design, sooty, dirty, with the same hurrying crowds and smells of trapped steam and engine-grease. But she was so tired she could scarcely lift her suitcase from the train. Her brain buzzing with half digested thoughts and impressions, the newness and strangeness of it all, she weaved unsteadily towards the exit barrier. Now what?

It was then Laura noticed a slim, dark-haired girl in Wren uniform: spanking white blouse with the sleeves rolled up to the elbows; navy skirt and black stockings, her Wren hat, broad-brimmed, sitting well back on dark, immaculately coiffed hair, scrutinising the passengers as they filed out between the railings of the ticket barrier.

'Your name Prentiss?' she sang out in a high-pitched voice.

'Yes.'

'Thank God! I'm Leading Wren Felix. The transport's parked over there. As near as I could get. Had a good journey? Fearfully hot, isn't it? Just sling your gear in the back. Better hurry or we'll be late for tea. Where are you from? Yorkshire? Oh, not too long a journey then. Well, hop in! We'll never get going at this rate.'

The environs of Edinburgh left behind, they were soon out in open country, speeding past trees in full leaf, past farm-houses and curving fields of grain – almost too golden in the glaring afternoon light.

'How far are we going?' Laura asked the question diffidently. It was stifling inside the transport. She felt ill at ease, awkward and lumpish sitting beside the super-efficient driver, clutching her shoulder-bag, holding her best coat across her knees, wishing that she had simply thrown it in the back of the vehicle along with her suitcase, but it might have got creased if she had, and Mum would never forgive her.

'About ten miles. Not far now. We're in a rather splendid country house. Must have been quite gorgeous before it was requisitioned. Actually, Daddy knows the people who own it – Sir Philip and Lady Westcliffe. They're in America now: Washington, lucky devils.' Leading Wren Felix spoke with a clipped 'county' accent. Laura noticed that her hands, on the steering wheel, were slim and elegant, that she wore a solitaire diamond the size of a pea on her engagement finger.

Laura, who had never come up against this particular type of girl before, felt more awkward and lumpish than ever. Glancing sideways, she noticed her companion's fine-grained complexion, wing-like eyebrows, sweeping dark lashes and full red lips. Above all, her air of supreme self-confidence, as if the world and everything in it revolved around her. Furthermore,

Leading Wren Felix drove extremely well and exuded, despite the heat of the day, the subtle, dry fragrance of lavender.

'Do you like being in the Wrens?' Laura blurted.

Felix glanced her way curiously, dropping her, it seemed, into some mental pigeon hole; summing up and dismissing her in a matter of seconds. 'It's quite fun, really,' she replied off-handedly. 'Actually, I'm due for a posting any day now: hoping for Ringley. Don't suppose I'll get it though. A bloody shame if I don't. I've been at Armley for simply ages. Dougal knows I want it like hell, the mean bastard, which is why she won't give it to me.'

'Oh, I see.' Laura, who didn't see at all, sat back in her seat, startled by her companion's easy flow of invective. 'Real ladies never swear,' was one of Mother's maxims, which was why Laura used 'blow', 'lousy', 'rotten', the occasional daring 'damn'.

The silence lengthened almost to the point of no return. Felix appeared to have forgotten Laura's existence. Lacking the savoir-faire to let the conversation die a natural death, feeling herself to be unmannerly, somehow lacking in charm and responsiveness, she said, 'My name's Laura. What's yours?'

'Look, Prentiss, this isn't a social club you're joining. The sooner you get that through your head, the better. You will refer to the commissioned officers as Ma'am, the petty officers as Chief. Christian names are used socially, of course, among friends, or those of equal rank, off duty. Understood?'

'Yes.' Laura's throat ached suddenly with unshed tears. Mum was right. Real ladies never swore. The silence continued.

Signalling left, Felix turned the wheels of the transport, expertly, between imposing gateposts. Gravel crunched beneath the tyres, the drive sloped upward between trees. Laura caught her breath at her first glimpse of Armley House, built of sun-washed stone, perched on rising ground. Her eyes devoured the symmetry of its walls; rejoiced in the perfection of the broad stone terrace; french windows standing open to admit light and air.

Felix pulled at the brake, impatient to be off, apparently desperate for tea. 'Do hurry, please, Prentiss, and follow me.' She watched, smoothing back a strand of hair with graceful fingers, making no effort to help as Laura fished her case from the back of the transport, and grappled with her coat and shoulder-bag. Then Felix turned and skipped lightly up the steps of the terrace and through one of the open windows, like a yacht with a barge in tow, thought Laura, finding herself in a magnificently proportioned room filled with long trestle tables in the process of being set for supper. The stewards, doing the setting, went on with their work, clattering cutlery, wheeling trolleys, talking among themselves, taking no notice of the intruders.

'Through here!'

'And Felix kept on walking, kept on walking still . . .' Laura laughed inwardly, remembering the words of the ridiculous song she had often sung to the rhythm of the 'bouncing ball' in the Singing Hall on the Foreshore at home, where the pianist had crashed out the chords on an out-of-tune joanna.

What a shame, she thought, following in the wake of the gracefully skimming Leading Wren Felix, that so lovely a house had been decimated by the removal of its furniture, carpets, pictures, curtains; that only the bare bones of its former glory now remained – the parquet flooring, panelling, moulded ceilings, and massive stone fireplaces.

What a magnificent hall! Glancing at the branching oak staircase lit with a high mullioned window, forgetting momentarily her heavy case, slipping shoulder-accoutrements, superfluous winter coat, tiredness and her long journey, Laura conducted her own love affair with this place, this house, reminiscent of her favourite book, Daphne du Maurier's *Rebecca*; imagining herself to be the luckless, plain and awkward new bride of Maxim de Winter.

'Prentiss!'

'Yes, Ma'am!' Romantic dreams shattered, Laura looked up, startled, into the eyes of the woman behind a glassed-in reception desk who had spoken her name abruptly.

'Not Ma'am. Chief, if you don't mind. I am Chief Petty Officer Allpress.' The woman smiled wearily, as if inured to dealing with fools. Even so, Laura's heart warmed to her. 'I'm sorry, Chief,' she apologized, 'I – I wasn't thinking.'

'That's odd. You appeared to be lost in thought! Look, this won't take long. I have a few papers here for you to sign, and I'll need your ration book, then perhaps you'd like a cup of tea? Afterwards, if you'll report back here, I'll get someone to show you to your cabin.'

Anxious to oblige, Laura leaned forward to sign the requisite papers, her bright golden hair spilling about her shoulders.

'You might manage better if you let go of your coat and shoulder-bag,' Allpress suggested drily, 'unless, of course, they are soldered on to your arm.'

'Yes, I mean no! That is . . .' Laura flushed crimson as she handed over her ration book.

'As a matter of interest, what were you thinking about just now?'

'*Rebecca*.' Laura's lips twitched upwards in an uncertain smile.

'Ah, yes. "Last night I dreamt I went to Manderley again . . ." But this isn't Manderley. A word of advice, Prentiss, the sooner you stop day-dreaming, the better off you'll be. If you wish to succeed in this women's navy, put day-dreams, the past, behind you. Face up to reality. You'll never make it otherwise.'

'Yes, thank you, I'll try.' But, Laura considered, how could she forget the past? There were bound to be tatters, remnants of the old life to flutter like waving handkerchiefs at a railway station.

'No need to worry unduly, you'll soon learn the art of re-adjustment.' Allpress scooped up the papers and the ration book, 'Now, go through that door over yonder, have your tea, then report back to me. Leave your case and your coat here, OK?'

'Yes. Thank you very much.'

What a nice child, Allpress thought, watching her go. Pretty, romantic, with a head stuffed full of dreams. A tender shoot, the kind that would not withstand harsh discipline, unless she stopped being so meek and mild.

Pushing open the door of the canteen, Laura almost turned tail and ran away from the noise, heat, and confusion, the sound of a hundred or so chattering voices which reminded her of the parrot house in Regent's Park Zoo.

Oh God, how would she be able to bear it? Homesickness flooded through her for the quietude, the peace of home. She badly wanted a cup of tea and saw, at the far side of the room, the trestle table on which rested the urn, a mountain of thick white cups and saucers and plates stacked with currant buns and wedges of fruit cake. She felt that her feet were rooted to the ground with fear, that she would far rather die of thirst than cross over to the tea-urn, clad in her cotton blouse and summer skirt, with her bust sticking out, her bottom too, she imagined, her hair a mess, her hands sticky with perspiration, her face devoid of make-up.

Suddenly she felt a hand on her arm and heard a friendly voice in her ear. 'Come over and sit with us,' the voice said. 'We're new here as well. My name's Grace Flanagan, by the way. What's yours?'

'Laura. Laura Prentiss.'

'Come on then, Laura. Squattez-vous! I'll go and get you a cuppa. Oh, this is Ruth Maple. We travelled from Manchester on the same train, arrived a couple of hours ago. Do you want a piece of cake?'

'Yes. Yes please.'

Laura's heart lifted. She was not alone after all.

3

The cabin which Laura would share with Flanagan, Maple, and three other girls was high up in what had been the servants' quarters in those pre-war days when the Westcliffes of Armley House had employed a small army of parlourmaids to do their bidding.

Grace and Ruth, by way of their two hour seniority, had already stowed away their belongings and laid claim to their bunks. When, after tea, Chief Allpress, seeing the three of them together, suggested that they might show Prentiss the way to the cabin, Grace complied with every sign of enjoyment. 'Don't worry, I'll carry your case,' she sang out. 'Here, Ruth, you take charge of the coat.' The coat had, by this time, become a deep source of embarrassment to Laura. Mum must have thought she was coming to the Arctic Circle.

Even the sturdily built Grace was puffing somewhat by the time they reached the top landing. 'Phew!' She grinned amiably, 'Well, this is it, our little nest under the slates. Not bad, eh? A bit Spartan but better than being in one of the big dormitories with a dozen or more bunks.' Flanagan's Cheshire cat smile lit up her plain, yet curiously attractive face, crowned with a thatch of dark brown hair cut in a chunky fringe. She possessed a laugh as infectious as influenza, a brogue as thick and warming as Irish stew, in direct contrast to Maple whose pathetically thin, white little face was framed by lustreless straw-coloured hair and whose pale blue eyes were red rimmed with weeping.

As Grace chattered on, Laura gleaned that she was the eldest of six children; daughter of an English mother, an Irish father, a Catholic – not a very devout one – that she had been a typist in civvy street, and possessed the knack of finding out things, keeping one jump ahead of events, rather like that clever-clogs at Laura's junior school who had always known exactly when to trade in her whip and top for a skipping-rope, her skipping-rope for marbles.

Grace already knew, for instance, that today's newcomers were required to attend a briefing session before supper. 'We'd better get a move on,' she said, hoisting Laura's suitcase on to one of the bunks. 'That's your perch, by the way, the top one. Ruth's in the lower. There's a lass from Liverpool over me, rejoicing in the name of Katie Boot, a bit of a rough diamond, but easy enough to get on with. I'm not too sure about the other two, though.' Grace wrinkled her nose distastefully. 'The one in the top bunk over yonder, is called Pat Armstrong, a suicide blonde with a refined accent you could cut with a knife, don't you know? And there's a red-headed Welsh girl called Blodwen Thomas, in the lower. She's engaged to be married, look you!' Flanagan kinked up with laughter, doing her Welsh impersonation.

At that moment, a steward of mature years, wearing an overall and suffering from a heavy catarrhal cold, poked her head round the door, glared at Laura's suitcase, and let fly. 'You ain't supposed to chuck

33

suitcases on the counterpanes,' she said hostilely. 'Huh, all alike, you newcomers. Five minutes and you think you own the place.' She was secretly jealous of everyone in a higher paid, more glamorous category than herself, bits of kids who came here to learn teleprinting, who would emerge from their training with a couple of crossed flags on the sleeve of their uniform, giving themselves airs and graces.

'I'm sorry, it's all my fault, so it is!' Flanagan's charm was irresistible. 'Say, that's a terrible cold you have there. What are you taking for it? Have you tried honey and lemon with a dash of Irish whisky? That's me father's sure fire remedy, though often enough he forgets all about the honey and lemon!'

The thin steward with the pinched nose and reddened nostrils, actually smiled.

Laura thought that Flanagan was laying on the charm a bit thick. She would later realize that whatever Grace said, she meant. Flanagan really cared about the people she drew within the orbit of her warm, sunny personality. But those she didn't like, had better watch out.

There was salmon for supper, of the tinned variety, backed up with lots of boiled potatoes, peas, and bread and marge, followed by a rib-bursting apple pudding in suet pastry, served with lashings of custard. Actually *salmon*, a luxury Laura had not tasted since the out-break of war. She wondered, wolfing down her meal, what her family were having for supper. Liver, most probably, with baked dumplings. Mum was a very good cook, unlike herself, whose Yorkshire puddings seldom rose properly. She might have joined the Wrens as a cook, otherwise, which would have saved her a lot of time and trouble.

The day at the Labour Exchange, when the Wren recruitment officer had told her that, apart from experienced cooks, only thirty-words-per-minute typists were required as teleprinter operators, Laura's heart had sunk to her shoes.

It was Dad who had suggested a crash typing course at a secretarial bureau. She had him to thank for giving her the time off from work to come to grips with a typewriter keyboard. At first she'd thought she would never get the hang of it, had despaired of ever reaching that thirty-word-per-minute standard.

Six weeks later, she had hurried back to the Labour Exchange complete with her typing certificate. And that, she thought, had been the most triumphant moment of her life so far.

Replete with salmon, and apple pudding, Laura imagined her family sitting round the table awaiting her phone call, not listening to the news in case they missed the shrilling of the bell in the Saloon.

Not that the news was uplifting. The Germans had shelled a Channel convoy, with heavy Allied losses, and there had been a savage air battle over Portland: Hurricanes in action against German Messerschmitts.

There were prolonged hiccups on the line before she managed to get through. Mum answered the phone, sounding strangely defensive: using her 'telephone voice'. Then her father took over, finally Gran. They all seemed so far away, their voices distorted by distance and atmospherics.

Mum seemed quite huffy that Laura had not managed to find a seat facing the engine, as if that was

35

her fault. Dad, sounding tired, said he'd been busy in the Saloon. Gran complained that her rheumatism was giving her hell, and the dog was fretting.

Suddenly, the pips went. 'I'll write as soon as I can,' Laura called out, but the line had gone dead.

Hanging up the receiver, she wondered why telephone conversations seldom amounted to anything in particular, why they had frittered the time away, saying nothing of importance.

Grace, who had already rung her family, grabbed Laura's arm. 'Let's go outside for a breath of fresh air, shall we?'

'Yes, let's. Where's Ruth, by the way?'

'Writing a letter to her mother!' Grace sighed. 'You know, I really feel sorry for that poor kid. She hasn't anyone close to her except her Ma, and a doddery old aunt, and they're not on the phone. Talk about the Middle Ages!'

Breathing in the fragrance of night-scented stock, Laura thought how good it felt to catch the whisper of a breeze after the clamour indoors; the stuffiness of that basement room where they had been given their half hour briefing by the third officer in charge of the new recruits.

'Let's see where this path leads to,' Grace suggested, ducking her head to avoid the lower branches of the trees. 'Hey, look, there's a lake, and a funny little temple! Well, whaddayou know? Perhaps there's a boat? We could go for a row; trail our fingers in the water. Come on, let's take a gander!'

Laura wasn't too sure about rowing. She preferred to stand still, catching the glimmer of fading sunlight on water, to draw this moment to herself; gaze at the folly perched on its grassy knoll. Grace was right, it did look like a temple, a small, round temple built to the glory of some long dead Roman emperor, with its frieze of musical instruments, cymbals and lyres.

A shiver of excitement fluttered down her spine. Looking at the folly, she felt a sudden urge to run, arms outstretched, to embrace some intangible goal beyond her power of comprehension, as if some untapped source of happiness ran through her veins like wine. As if there were someone, somewhere, waiting to hold her in his arms, as Ronald Colman had held Madeleine Carroll in *The Prisoner of Zenda*.

When the more prosaically minded Flanagan, unable to find a boat, asked her what she had made of the briefing session, Laura forced her mind back to reality. Not that Grace expected an answer to her question, simply to unleash her own impressions. 'I didn't go a bundle on that third officer, did you? And what did you think of all that stuff about upholding the good name of the Women's Royal Naval Service at all times, in or out of uniform? She looked right at me when she said that.' Grace chuckled throatily. 'And what did you think when she said that anyone wanting to opt out of the service during the next fortnight, could hop it with no questions asked? Perhaps she meant me! But I have no intention of opting out, have you? I mean to say, it was hard enough getting into the Wrens, and I wouldn't want to end up in the Land Army or a munitions factory.'

How beautiful the sun looked, shining on the water, Laura thought reflectively. How cool it was here in the garden. Then it occurred to her that this slowly dying sun was the same sun she had watched ascending the sky in the early hours of the morning.

'What were you in civvy street?' Flanagan enquired, as they made their way back to the house.

'A hairdresser.'

'Go on! No kidding? What a lucky break! You can have a go at my hair any time you like! So how come you came to join up as a teleprinter operator?'

'I didn't think I'd be much use in the Land Army or in a munitions factory and . . .' Laura had been about to say because I love the sea so much. Decided not to. She liked Grace Flanagan, but some things were best left unsaid – the way she had felt in the garden for instance, happy yet sad, filled with unknown longings.

That night, Laura felt diffident about undressing in front of the other girls. The red-haired Welsh girl, Blodwen Thomas, drew mocking attention to her modesty. 'What's the matter with you, then? Made different from the rest of us, are you?' Spoken in a thick, Rhondda Vale accent.

'Why don't you shut up and mind your own business?' Flanagan sprang quickly to Laura's defence. Uttering a raucous laugh, Blodwen began stripping off her own clothes, and sprawled naked on her bunk, displaying her pale, plump body with its bush of red pubic hair, as if she were posing for a portrait by Titian.

Ruth looked shocked, Laura turned her head away, as the Welsh girl started talking to her friend, Pat Armstrong, of the 'posh' accent and bleached hair, about men in general, and her fiancé in particular, with whom she had done 'it' four times in one night before he went off to join the Fleet Air Arm.

'Jesus, but he was randy. Cudn't get enough of it, he cudn't. Mind you, I made damn sure 'e bought me an engagement ring first, an' on the understandin' we'd get married on 'is first leave,' Blodwen laughed.

Ruth got into bed and pulled the counterpane about her ears. Laura, who knew only vaguely what 'it' referred to, thought she would rather die than discuss something so private, in public. Mother had warned her often enough that men had no respect for girls who let them take liberties. Not that the nature of the liberties they might wish to take had been clearly formulated.

Mary Prentiss had never discussed the details of procreation with her daughter. It might have been better if she had, if Mum had told her the facts of life simply and straightforwardly, instead of hinting, leaving her to muddle through as best she could; gleaning, she suspected – hoped – inaccurate information from that girl at school, the one who had known about marbles and skipping ropes, who had told her, eagerly, in the playground one day, that men had this bony thing inside their trousers which they used to make women have babies.

Eventually she had discovered, from other girls, that what 'clever-clogs' had told her was basically true, which was why she preferred those shadowy screen heroes of hers. Ronald Colman, for instance, with his kind, quiet eyes, hesitant English accent, and carefully trimmed moustache, and Herbert Marshall with his wooden leg, both of whom seemed incapable of ungentlemanly behaviour.

In the early hours of the morning, desperate to spend a penny, Laura clambered down from her bunk, visited

39

the bathroom, and came back to the cabin to lift the edge of the blackout curtain and gaze at the misty lawns of Armley House spread out like a grey-green carpet beneath a sky already warm with the promise of another scorching hot day.

It was then she heard the faint but unmistakable sound of weeping. Sitting on the edge of Ruth Maple's bunk, she held the girl's hand in hers. 'Don't cry, Ruth,' she whispered, 'remember we're all in the same boat.'

'No, we're not! I'm not brave, like you and Grace. Oh God, whatever shall I do? It's Mother, you see. She relied on me to take care of her.'

'Don't think of that now. Just try to get a little more sleep.'

'You won't leave me?'

'No, I won't leave you. I promise.'

Laura sat beside Ruth, holding her hand, until the girl, comforted by her presence, fell into a light sleep, soon to be shattered by the noisy clamour of the rising bell.

4

' "O Eternal Lord God, who alone spreadest out the heavens, and rulest the raging of the sea . . .".'

Clatter, clatter, rattle, rattle, chink, chink . . .

First Officer Dougal, a fine figure of a woman whose uniform buttons and braid shone like gold in the morning sunlight, took no notice of the racket as a skinny child, who reminded Laura of the Chief of the Die-Hards in John Buchan's *Huntingtower*, emerged from the back door of Armley House, trundling a bogie full of empty milk bottles.

' "Who hast compassed the waters with bounds until day and night come to an end . . .".'

Divisions were held out of doors when the weather was fine. Rattle, rattle, chink, chink . . .

' "Be pleased to receive into thy Almighty, and most gracious protection the person of us thy servants, and the Fleet in which we serve . . .".'

Overcome by the law of gravity, the little lad with the bogie gave up the struggle of trying to hold it back on the curving, downward slope, and clung on to the handles for dear life as it clattered and bounced past the assemblage of officers and ratings gathered together on the lawn for morning prayer. Laura giggled as the child and his bogie, gathering speed, zipped past the astonished onlookers, his spindled legs flying at

41

the rate of knots, his oversize boots striking sparks on the gravel.

'We will now sing the hymn, "Eternal Father, strong to save",' Elizabeth Dougal announced, with amazing aplomb and a strong hint of humour.

Standing in the sunshine, turning the pages of her hymn-book, Laura experienced a sudden, uplifting surge of pride, a feeling of belonging in this women's navy. Possibly the incident of the child, his bogie, and his clattering milk-bottles, had relaxed her. Whatever the reason, she felt ready to tackle her first encounter with a teleprinter keyboard.

'No, Prentiss! Not like that! What are you trying to do, beat the keys into submission?'

Laura ran her fingers distractedly through her hair. Beads of perspiration gathered on her forehead. All she had learned at the secretarial bureau, all the hours of practice she had put in to bring her speed up to the required thirty words per minute seemed a waste of time now, faced with a teleprinter keyboard. The lay-out of the keys was the same, but striking them seemed like hitting a feather-bed after a sprung mattress; dancing a slow foxtrot after a quickstep.

'It is simply a matter of adjusting your rhythm. Don't worry, you'll soon get the hang of it.' Mabel Sedgewick, the officer in charge of the training session, an ex-Post-Office tele-op, a Lancashire lass with no illusions of grandeur, smiled encouragingly. 'Come on now, give it another try. Pretend your fingers are butterflies. Ah, saved by the bell! All right, girls, time for elevenses! Make it snappy! We've a lot of work to get through before dinner time.'

Laura went, with Ruth and Grace, to the canteen where a long queue of girls awaited the doling out of cocoa, and jam and bread. No sooner were they settled at a table than they were called out, one by one, to have their photographs taken.

'Prentiss! This way, please! Quickly! The photographer hasn't got all day.' Chief Allpress smiled her world-weary smile. 'Oh, never mind about your hair!' She added by way of explanation, 'He's only taking pay-book photographs, not publicity stills for J. Arthur Rank.'

Even so, Laura wished the man had given her time to swallow her mouthful of bread and jam before taking the photograph. Then the idea of owning a pay-book caught her imagination as a step in the right direction towards becoming a fully fledged Wren. Civilian clothing seemed out of place somehow. No doubt about it, the Wren uniform cut quite a dash. She loved the penguin neatness of it, and started to worry in case she didn't make the grade. What would happen to her if she couldn't get into the rhythm of teleprinting, if she failed her tests? She was, after all, only here on probation.

Second Officer Sedgewick had warned them that this course, by the nature of its brevity, was necessarily thorough, tough, and demanding. They would have to pass exams in plain language, plus four and five figure code groupings, and learn the rudiments of the complicated teleprinter switchboard, if they expected to emerge with flying colours.

Perhaps the kitting out process at the end of the course was tantamount to dangling a carrot in front of a recalcitrant donkey, to keep the girls aware that they were, as yet, merely on probation, mused Laura. She simply *had* to pass those tests! And if she put a foot wrong, or failed to live up to the high standards expected of her, she might yet find herself in a munitions factory, or, even worse, end up in the cookhouse.

The small market town of Armley struck Laura as the neatest place she had ever seen. The grey stone houses clustered about the central square were uncluttered by gardens and window-boxes; as prim as nuns in grey habits, matching the no-nonsense approach to living of the thrifty Scottish people themselves.

Even Ruth Maple, who had hitherto derived little pleasure from her new surroundings, cheered up at the sight of the stalls with their green canvas awnings. Not that the stallholders had much to sell except unrationed vegetables. The introduction of food rationing had hit hard the butchers' and dairy-produce stalls, but the secondhand clothing merchants appeared to be doing a roaring trade, and so were the 'junk' stalls dealing in brassware, curios, Victorian oil-lamps with cut-glass lustres, chipped decanters, horse-brasses mounted on leather straps, trays of Victorian jewellery – jet mourning rings, diamante-studded side-combs, beads, brooches, silver watch-guards and gold link bracelets.

There were flowers too. At least *they* weren't rationed; bunches of dahlias in flaring, hopeful colours of red and gold – as if the year was telling the time by its blossoms.

This was the Saturday following almost a week of intensive study and preliminary mock exams. There was a feeling of holiday, of release in the air, as if the girls who climbed aboard the transport clutching their passes, had been granted a reprieve from stress. Besides which there was the Saturday night dance to look forward to, a weekly event held in the basement at Armley House, when their cloistered world would be invaded by men, ratings and non-commissioned officers from the naval dockyards at Rosyth; a smattering of Poles and Free French airmen into the bargain, according to Grace Flanagan, who kept her ear to the ground.

'Hey, won't it be great?' she enthused. 'If only I had a decent lipstick. The one I've got is worn down to the rim. Come on, you two. Let's have a look round Woolworths.'

'Just a minute.' Laura's attention had been caught by one of the brooches on the secondhand jewellery stall. 'Isn't that pretty? I wonder what Mizpah means? I wonder who it belonged to?'

'God knows and He won't tell.' Flanagan wasn't interested in Victorian gewgaws. Her mind was on the dance, men, whom she liked in a cheerfully unabashed way, and on buying that lipstick, certain that if lipsticks existed in Armley, she would discover their whereabouts. The word defeat held no place in Grace's vocabulary.

There were shops, too, round the perimeter of the square; grocers, haberdashers, hardware stores, chemists, and two small cafés; dress shops displaying hand-woven tweed suits in autumn colours – muted shades of brown and misty lilac – shoe shops, bakers, and a Scottish branch of the Co-operative Society. Also a tiny cinema whose discreet poster advertised this week's attraction, Robert Young in *Florian*, next week's as Dorothy Lamour and Robert Preston in *Typhoon*.

Grace eventually discovered lipsticks in a chemist's shop down a side street, having first made friends with the assistant whom she had lulled into a false sense of security by purchasing a packet of what she discreetly termed 'ladies' necessaries' before asking the sixty dollar question. She dropped her voice to a confidential whisper, 'Er, I don't suppose you have such a thing as a lipstick?'

The young woman, seemingly mesmerised by her customer's charm, replied, also in a whisper, 'Just a moment. I'll take a peek in the stockroom.'

'Do you think my friends could have some as well?' Grace whispered excitedly when the girl came back with a small box containing a dozen tubes of pre-war Coty lipstick.

'I don't want one,' Maple said primly. 'My mother doesn't approve of my wearing lipstick, or any other makeup!'

'What? How peculiar! But you'd like one, wouldn't you Laura? That "Snowfire" thing of yours is nearly on its last legs, and goodness only knows when we'll be able to buy any more.' Grace turned her brilliant smile on the assistant. 'Thank you ever so much,' she bubbled infectiously, 'you've saved our lives. And they're such lovely colours. Mmm, I don't know which to choose, the pink or the red.'

'Why not have both?' The assistant cast a furtive look over her shoulder to make sure that her boss wasn't listening. 'After all, we can only sell them once.'

*

The basement room was low ceilinged, dimly lit with coloured lights to create a romantic atmosphere. The chief recreations' officer, Violet Hildreth, had piled up the records on a table near the radiogram; waltz, quickstep, waltz, quickstep, Paul Jones, tango, slow foxtrot, quickstep, the Lambeth Walk.

'Must we really suffer the Lambeth Walk?' Dinah Felix demanded in a bored voice, glancing at Hildreth's hastily typed programme.

'Yes, we must! The sailors like it. Besides, it gets people together. So does Boomps-a-Daisy. We're not all budding Ginger Rogers and Fred Astaires, you know!'

'All right, Vi, keep your shirt on!' Having lost that round, Dinah returned to the attack. 'My God, what's that you're putting on the floor?'

'Soapflakes! We've run out of rosin. Now see here, Dinah, if you want to take charge, just say so! It's no picnic arranging these Saturday night flings. Volunteer to take my place! See if I care!'

'Don't be such a bore, Vi! But soapflakes! Ye gods! They'll cake to the soles of our shoes! Imagine trying to tango on soapflakes!'

'I can't think what you are doing here anyway,' Vi retorted, nettled by Dinah's criticism, 'You don't usually grace our Saturday night hops with your presence. I wouldn't have thought a bunch of sailors would be your cup of tea. And would you mind leaving those records alone! I've just put them in order.'

Dinah laughed unpleasantly. 'Don't be so plebeian, Vi darling. Of course I'm not interested in a bunch of sailors.'

'Oh, I get it. You're after one of those Free French officers. Or is he a Pole?'

'A Pole? God forbid! Really! No, if you want to know, he's French. The most delicious, deevine creature you ever laid eyes on. Hand picked! I met him at an officers' mess party last night. The poor sweetie looked like a fish out of water, and so . . .'

'You hooked him? Huh, I thought you were supposed to be engaged.'

'No "supposed" about it, darling! But Giles is in Canada, which is terribly boring of him, don't you think?' Dinah glanced coolly at her diamond engagement ring. 'In any case, I don't imagine that Giles is living a monastic, cloistered existence over there.' The ring flashed fire from the lights of the radiogram.

The room was beginning to fill up now with uniformed and pro-Wrens awaiting the male invasion. The heat was stultifying, but no-one seemed to mind. There was an air of excitement in the stuffy, dimly-lit room, a sweet aura of promise, of forgetfulness of the war, a memory of pre-war times, of other dance-halls in other towns, as the girls drifted together in groups, laughing, chatting, glancing expectantly towards the door.

When the door banged open suddenly, in breezed a contingent of sailors, bringing with them a breath of fresh air, a certain aura of brassy cheerfulness, a swaggering male presence. The effect on the girls was electrifying, as if a collective noun of randy roosters had barged into a hen-run. In the time honoured way, the men stood together sizing up the women, choosing their partners for the first dance. Vi turned up the volume on the radiogram. 'Nice Work if You Can Get

It', blared forth. The Saturday night dance was under way.

Grace and Laura had had a tussle with Ruth upstairs in their cabin. 'I *can't* go down,' she wailed, at the last minute, after Laura had taken the trouble to pin up her lank fair hair in a series of 'sausage' curls stuck through with kirbygrips. 'I can't dance anyway, and I know my mother wouldn't approve. You and Laura go down if you want to. I'll stay here.'

'Like hell you will!' said Grace. 'Now listen to me, Ruth Maple, you're going to that dance if Laura and I have to drag you! It's time you had a bit of fun, and what your ma doesn't know won't hurt her! What do you say, Laura?'

Grace had asked the question at the wrong moment. Laura, too, had begun to wish that she could opt out of going to the dance. Truth to tell, she felt like a trussed chicken in her new brassiere and wished that she had not succumbed to Flanagan's blandishments about using her mascara – a spit-on block of brownish/black Maybelline which had stiffened her lashes into sweeping, artificial crescents, and made her almost afraid to blink in case the stuff came off on her cheeks.

'Well,' Laura said doubtfully, 'I can't dance very well either!'

'Oh, for pity's sake! Not you, too! Anyone would think we are going to a State Ball! It's only a Saturday night hop, for God's sake! Sorry, Lord, I'll go to Confession in the morning! The thing is, it's our duty to join in with the others, to show those sailors a good time. Why, for all we know, they might be lonely and

49

homesick; about to die for their country!' Grace struck a dramatic pose, then giggled.

'Don't be so daft,' Laura said, joining in the laughter. Then her conscience smote her. It wasn't really all that funny. Perhaps some of those sailors *were* lonely and homesick. Possibly most of them would not survive this war. 'Oh very well, then,' she said resignedly.

Linking arms, the three of them, Laura, Ruth and Grace, went marching downstairs, for all the world like the Three Musketeers.

Laura would always remember that night; the heat, the noise, her feeling of inadequacy as she stood there; the beat, beat, beat of the music, the high-pitched laughter of the couples who spun past her; the feeling of loneliness when nobody asked her to dance, the way she and Ruth had gravitated towards a couple of basket chairs pretending not to care that they were wallflowers.

It later seemed that the camera of her mind had snapped and developed impressions with the speed of light; Grace Flanagan dancing in the arms of a young sailor with a laid back collar and a prominent Adam's apple; Dinah Felix lighting a cigarette, glancing at the door as if she were waiting for someone, the expression of amazement on Ruth's face when a sailor asked her to dance with him, her backward look of panic as he led her on to the floor; the way the coloured lights shook slightly to the beat of the music, the continual movement of the dancers; the shuffling of feet punctuated with outbursts of laughter; the way the man entered the room.

The camera of Laura's mind recorded every detail.

The man, dark-haired, wearing the uniform of a captain of the Free French Air Force, hung back a little at first. Then, when the music stopped and couples began drifting to the perimeter of the dance floor, he walked across the room unhurriedly, gracefully, to where Dinah was standing.

He was not very tall or particularly well-built, not even breathtakingly handsome. He simply exuded an indefinable air of magic, as though a spotlight blazed down on him and he walked unselfconsciously in its concentrated beam. Then Dinah stubbed out her cigarette and walked towards him, hands outstretched, smiling, bubbling with self-confidence, the recreations' officer fitted another record on to the turn-table, a quickstep, 'Bei Mir Bist du Schon', the Frenchman's arm slid round Dinah's waist, and the couple spun away together, the cynosure of all eyes, Dinah chattering nineteen to the dozen, in French.

'Showing off, as usual,' Grace commented, 'the silly bitch!'

Then, Flanagan's sailor with the Adam's apple, came back to claim her, and they were off once more, fish-tailing and sashaying, slithering on the soapflakes, and Ruth's nervous romeo with the prominent front teeth and shaving rash popped up again to sweep her into the melée, by which time Laura had begun to wonder what was wrong with her that no-one had asked her to dance. Had her mascara started to run? Did her newly-washed hair look a mess? Were her legs too fat?

'Hi, beautiful! Wanna dance?'

'Oh yes. Thank you.' Relief flooded through her because someone had noticed her at last.

This sailor had blue eyes, fair hair, a cheeky smile, a long, narrow face, like a hatchet with a sharp cutting edge. His hand, pressing into the small of her back, felt sticky with perspiration. Laura hated the feel of his cheek against hers, his hot breath on her face.

Holding herself stiffly, she fell over his feet so often that, with a bit of luck, he would not ask her to dance with him again.

'You should try to relax more, beautiful,' he said, when the ordeal ended, 'a nice looking chick like you. What's with you anyway? Was your mother frightened by a sailor? Like I said, you want to try relaxing. Who knows, you and I might have made beautiful music together!'

Beautiful music! With a creep like that? Marching back to her chair, she wished she had stayed upstairs in the cabin.

'And now, ladies and gentlemen, take your partners for a Paul Jones.'

Dinah had laid claim to her Frenchman, Laura noticed, wondering what to do, whether to stay on for a while longer or go to her cabin and read a book.

Tum-ti-tum-ti-tum. Couples split up to parade round the floor. 'Hey, where do you think you're going?' Grace grabbed Laura's arm and hauled her into the throng. The music changed to a waltz, 'Stay in my Arms, Cinderella . . . ' Laura found herself face to face with the Frenchman. He smiled.

'May I?' His hand was dry and cool in hers, he held her firmly but not too close, guiding her through the maze of dancers with easy, graceful steps, making her feel as if she were floating on air.

'You dance very well, mademoiselle.' He spoke

English with the merest trace of an accent. His hair was dark, eyes gentle. Closing her eyes briefly to the throb of the music, she experienced a kind of magic as the Frenchman led her through the crush of dancers; opened them to catch his gentle, amused smile, and smiled back at him, wishing that this was not a Paul Jones, that she might go on dancing with him all night.

'What is your name, mademoiselle?' he asked, bending his head to catch her reply.

'Laura.'

'Ah, such a pretty name.' He smiled down at her. 'Where are you from?'

'Yorkshire,' she said breathlessly, 'a place called Scarborough. And you?'

'My home is in Normandie.'

'You must miss it very much.'

'Yes, I do. Very much.'

Tum-ti-tum-ti-tum. Laura's shining moment of happiness ended; the music stopped abruptly, the girls joined hands once more, laughing and jostling to form a circle. In that brief moment before they were snatched away from each other, the Frenchman's eyes met hers with an unfathomable expression of sadness, tinged with longing. 'I hope that we will meet again one day,' he said.

Later, in the cabin, 'What on earth happened to you?' Grace Flanagan enquired. 'You simply mizzled after the Paul Jones.'

Laura could not bring herself to tell the truth, that she could not have borne to dance with anyone else after the Frenchman. Seeking refuge in a white lie, she murmured uneasily, 'My bra was killing me.'

'Yeah, well they always dig in a bit when they're new,' Grace commiserated. 'But you missed a treat. That stuck up Felix came a cropper in the tango! One minute she was twirling round, showing off as usual, the next, wham! Down she went! Lord, what a fuss she made about the soapflakes! Of course, she came over all faint and female; said she needed fresh air! I'll bet she did! Bet she couldn't wait to drag that smashing Frenchman of hers out into the garden. By the way, did you notice that she was looking daggers at you when you were dancing with him?'

Laura made no comment. Not that Grace noticed. She was doing her stream of consciousness stuff, the way she had done that evening when they had walked together in the garden and seen the lake and the little folly on its grassy knoll.

The garden . . .

Hunched under the bedclothes, Laura wondered what Dinah and the Frenchman had said to each other beneath the light of the August moon, if they had kissed beneath the trees where the shadows lay deepest; she imagined the witchery of moonlight threading the branches; silver-black shadows on the grass, the heady scent of lavender and roses from the flowerbeds bordering the terrace. Not that it really mattered, she told herself. All this was just a passing phase – this place, this moment of deep unhappiness.

Soon they would all be scattered like chaff upon the winds of heaven, Dinah Felix, Grace, Ruth, herself – the Frenchman. What would it matter, then, what he and Dinah had said to each other beneath the light of that bright, inconstant moon?

5

Events at Armley House had, for Laura, overshadowed the rapidly worsening war news. Acutely aware of her lack of typing experience when it came to the tricky business of mastering those five figure code groupings, she threw herself into her work with a fierce concentration which effectively blanked her mind to what would happen if the Germans invaded England. She dare not think about that.

During those hot days of early September, when the fate of Great Britain hung in the balance, Laura felt that her own fighting spirit was somehow linked to those spindrift vapour trails high above the quiet fields and meadows of south-east England. Shoring up her courage for the final exam, she sat quietly at the teleprinter keyboard, squared her shoulders and concentrated on the tests confronting her.

Miraculously she passed the exam with flying colours.

But being young and human, her 'Agincourt' altruism received a severe setback when she tried on her uniform.

She had queued up excitedly with the rest of the pro-Wrens to receive her navy skirt and jacket, shirts, collars, stockings, shoes, underclothing, mackintosh, hat and greatcoat – oh, no, not another coat – only to discover that they hung on her like flags at half mast.

Bunching up the spare material of her skirt, she came to the conclusion that her particular uniform must have been run up in a factory specializing in the manufacture of barrage balloons.

'Just look at me! What shall I do?' she wailed despairingly to Grace Flanagan.

'Take it back to stores and ask for a smaller size. You've lost a bit of weight, that's all. Only whatever you do, don't trade in that hat! Talk about an Ascot model! How come mine has a brim only half the width of yours?'

'Do you really think I've lost weight?' Laura asked hopefully.

'Haven't we all? No wonder, when you come to think about it. I've never run about, or sweated so much in all my life as I've done since I joined this outfit! Talk about extracting their pound of flesh! They've extracted a good half stone of yours, by the look of it!'

'Really? I hadn't noticed.' Laura's eyes shone.

'Hey, get a load of me in this collar and tie,' Grace giggled. 'A donkey looking over a whitewashed wall isn't in it! God but this collar's stiff. I feel as if I've been guillotined. What about you, Katie? How are you coping?' Flanagan turned her attention to the 'bit of a rough diamond' from Liverpool, Katie Boot, a girl with closely cropped hair and a mannish figure.

'I see no reason for complaint,' Katie said sharply. 'After all, this isn't a fashion parade. I came here to do a job of work. Whether my uniform fits me properly or not doesn't matter a damn, as far as I can see.'

'Ah, you're wrong there, mavourneen,' Grace

retorted mischievously. 'What if your bloomers fell down during pay-parade?'

'Don't be ridiculous!' But even the 'rough diamond' was not impervious to Grace's infectious gaiety and charm, although she regarded the two other inmates of the cabin as being totally expendable to the war effort; Blodwen Thomas and her vapid blonde side-kick, Pat Armstrong, whom she treated with utter disdain.

'I wonder where we'll be posted to from here?' Grace said reflectively, easing her collar. 'Strange, isn't it, to think that the day after tomorrow we might never see each other again?'

'I've put in a request for the Outer Hebrides,' Katie said proudly in her thick Liverpudlian accent.

'Oh blimey!' Flanagan shuddered her distaste at the thought of being stuck away among all that nothing-ness of sheep and heather. 'I don't think I could stand it if they sent me there. I want to go somewhere lively, have a good time!' She added, defiantly, 'That's why I joined up in the first place, because I was fed up with keeping an eye on the kids and acting as a referee when my parents started throwing things at each other. To be honest, I can't take this war at all seriously, so now you know!'

The lists of postings were tacked up next morning on the notice-board and the girls – the long-standing Wrens and their newly sworn-in brethren – jostled excitedly to find out who was being sent where.

Suddenly, 'I've got it! I've actually got it at last!' Dinah Felix cried ecstatically. 'Ringley, here I come!'

At the same moment, Katie Boot grunted her

satisfaction that her request for the Outer Hebrides had been granted, while Pat Armstrong emitted a wail of anguish and collapsed, weeping, against Blodwen Thomas's shoulder. 'I won't go!' she sobbed. 'I simply won't go to that God-forsaken place!' She too, had been posted to the Outer Hebrides.

Selfish to the core, Blodwen could not have cared less about Pat Armstrong. 'Well, there's funny, isn't it? I'm posted to Ringley, too,' she said in her sing-song Welsh accent, shoving Pat aside. 'But where the hell is it, that's what I want to know?' She stuck out her chin belligerently, 'If it's poked away at the back of beyond . . .'

'Don't be such a sublime idiot, Thomas,' Felix retorted. 'Ringley's the plum posting of all, on the south-east coast, adjoining an Air Force Rescue station. Need I say more? I gather that the men there are absolutely out of this world, and there are literally hundreds more of them at the nearby army and naval bases.'

Laura frowned. What kind of a girl was Dinah Felix to wear one man's engagement ring and yet be so concerned with adding more scalps to her belt?

Tired after the emotional upheaval of the past fortnight, she turned away from the notice-board, feeling that the strong thread of purpose she had held so firmly during the final exams had disintegrated, when Flanagan gave a resounding whoop of joy.

'Wow! What a break!' she chortled. 'We're not going to be split up after all – the three of us! You, I, and Ruth are posted to Ringley too!' Catching Laura by the sleeve, she swung into a kind of war-dance. 'Where *is* Ruth, by the way? Oh, there she is! Why, whatever's the matter with her? Ruth!'

The girl's eyes were swimming with tears. 'I thought you'd be thrilled to bits that we're staying together,' Grace said in that blunt yet gentle way of hers, putting her arm round Ruth's shoulders. 'What's wrong, mavourneen? Don't you want us to be together?'

'It isn't that.' Ruth fiddled in her shoulder-bag for a handkerchief, 'I'll be further away from Mum than ever. Oh, it's no use, I'll have to tell them I can't go.' Tears streamed down her cheeks. 'I mean, Third Officer Dennis said we could opt out if we wanted to. And I want to! I *must*. Don't you see? I *have* to go home . . .'

Grace and Laura exchanged glances. 'Yeah, well old thing,' Grace said compassionately, 'but it's too late for that, I'm afraid. There's nothing any of us can do now we've been sworn in.'

Ruth sobbed. Flanagan tried another tack. 'In any case, you *are* going home. They're giving us a forty-eight-hour leave. Just think how proud your ma will be when she sees you in uniform!'

'That's just it,' Ruth wiped away her tears, 'Mother's going blind. All she has is partial sight in one eye. That's why she relied on me to take care of her. But she's so brave. When she knew I would have to join up, she did nothing to prevent me.' Ruth emitted a shuddering sigh of despair. 'She said she'd get Aunt Ada to keep an eye on her. Keep an eye on her! That's funny, isn't it?'

Understanding her bitterness, Laura said quietly, 'I know how you feel. I didn't want to join up either, but we're in this war together, and it's up to us to make the best of a bad job.' Her words sounded lame, but Laura felt she was speaking the truth, albeit a simplified version of the truth.

She wanted desperately, at that moment, to hear the sea washing up on the shore, the seagulls crying, to feel the wind in her hair, the rain on her face, but it wasn't windy and it wasn't raining. It was just hot, boringly, monotonously hot.

And then she remembered what Grace had said about a forty-eight-hour leave, and her heart lifted. Home. She was going home. A feeling of peace washed over her.

Mary Prentiss glanced anxiously at the clock. Another half hour and Laura would be here. She felt suddenly nervous as she bustled to get ready for the station, although she couldn't for the life of her think why.

Then, in a rare moment of introspection, as she pinned on her hat and arranged her scarf, she knew that her nervousness had to do with her failure as a mother, in never knowing how to cope with a growing girl fast approaching womanhood, her inability to answer the questions Laura had asked at the time of her first period.

The girl had been shocked, horrified, on her twelfth birthday, to find that her knickers, clean on that morning, were soaked in blood. Mary knew that she should have told Laura the facts of life at that crucial time. But there were things too difficult to put into words. Never had her own mother discussed matters sexual with herself and her two younger sisters, Marjorie and Lally, persisting in the Victorian attitude that they would find out soon enough what sex was all about; what men expected of their wives once their wedding rings were safely on their fingers.

Patting her hair into place beneath her brown felt hat-brim, Mary thought, in defence of her mother dead these many years, how hard it must have been for her to bring up her family after the death of their father, how relieved she must have felt when Madge and Lally had eventually married decent, hard-working husbands – Madge a LNER engine-driver, Lally a burly farmer with a house and fifty acres of land two miles south of Devizes. Then, after her two younger sisters were married, she had been left alone to care for their ailing mother and the sprawling Victorian boarding-house at Earl's Court.

Gazing at her mirrored reflection Mary remembered the trauma of her mother's illness, the sick-room where she had lain for three months, riddled with cancer; the overwhelming tiredness she had experienced with a terminally ill woman to look after and a big house to run with no help apart from a daily woman who arrived at seven to swill the front steps, dust the downstairs rooms, and do the breakfast washing-up.

Just after the Great War, that was, in the jangling aftermath of the trenches, when it almost broke one's heart to see mutilated ex-servicemen begging from door to door. Thankfully, most of her lodgers had been elderly folk, not too demanding in the matter of food, and sympathetic about her mother's illness, and Madge had come in once a week from her home in Walthamstow to sit with Mother when she, Mary, went out to do the weekend shopping. Then, one day, the doorbell rang, and there was a young man on the doorstep wanting to know if she had a single room to let.

'You'd better come in,' she'd said, too weary to care that her hair was untidy, and she wore an old apron about her waist – the daily help having sent word that she was poorly and could not come in that morning. 'You'll have to excuse my appearance.' And that had been the start of it. The young man's name was William Prentiss.

She scarcely remembered what she had said to him after that, simply that she had a room to let on the top floor, and would he care to look at it? She would not have blamed him if he had turned tail and hurried away, she looked such a wreck. That he had not done so redounded to his credit. Indeed, he had betrayed a compassionate warmth and sympathy when she had sketched in, briefly, the nature of her problems; that she had a seriously ill woman on her hands, practically no help in the house and, even though the war was over, food was still not easily obtainable.

Then she had thought to ask him the nature of his employment, and learned that since his repatriation from the Army, he had been training as a barber at a nearby government centre, that, when his training was complete, he hoped to return to his native Yorkshire to open his own business.

A fortnight later, her mother had died as stoically as she had lived, a shrivelled up skeleton weighing less than five stones, by which time Will had become quietly indispensable in the house, helping with the washing-up, bringing in coal from the yard, cleaning out grates, laying the fires before setting off for the training centre, taking the heavier burdens from her shoulders, seeing that the doors were securely locked at night. All these things Mary had noticed and appreciated. And, in the early hours of the morning, just after her mother had passed away, it was Will who had stayed with her, keeping the fire in the kitchen stoked up, making her a pot of hot, strong tea when the ordeal was over, shoring up her courage with his undemanding sympathy.

After the funeral, Madge and Lally and their husbands had sat together in the front parlour, discussing the future. Their mother, Evelyn Jackson, had long since told her daughters what she wished done about her belongings after her death. Nothing had been set down on paper, but they knew, for instance, that the silverware – such as it was – the best china tea-set, and the roll-top desk in the back parlour, were meant for Madge; the linen sheets, the tallboy in which they had lain for many a long year smothered in mothballs, and the massive mahogany sideboard in this room – which seemed grossly to dwarf the rest of the furniture – were Lally's. The rest of the furniture, plus Mrs Jackson's life-insurance policy, amounting to £150, Mary's. The house itself was rented – a mere repository for the mass of shabby, valueless furniture it contained, Mary had thought bitterly: a means of keeping body and soul together as long as she continued to take in boarders to pay the rent.

Even so, she jibbed at the idea put forward by her sisters, backed by their husbands' approval, that she should give up the house and divide her time equally between them, spending six months of the year with Madge and Herbert in Walthamstow, the rest of the year with Lally and Bob in the West Country. 'What would be the point of that?' she had asked wearily.

'But Mary, love,' Madge said tearfully, 'you can't stay on here alone, slaving your life away.'

'Why not? It's what I'm used to.'

Her bitterness had had to do with Madge's obvious reluctance to share the burden of their mother's illness, despite the fact that she lived relatively near.

As for Lally and Bob's offer. What on earth would she do on a farm? Milk the cows? Feed the hens? 'No,' she said, 'I'm staying put!' She'd hated the thought of being passed, like a parcel, from one sister to the other, of losing her independence.

She had known that Will's training was nearly over. He had mentioned that his mother had been on the look out for a lock-up shop in Scarborough, and told her, enthusiastically, that he was looking forward to starting his own business; had shown her a sundries-man's journal containing a picture of the kind of barber's chair he wanted, which he would buy with his War Gratuity: had experienced a feeling of despair that he would soon be leaving.

She had come to rely on his sympathy and help, a feeling she had kept to herself so successfully that Will had almost decided not to ask her to marry him after all, seeing her as she wished to be seen, a strong-minded, independent woman with a no-nonsense attitude to life, who seemed to forget that he had glimpsed a softer side to her nature during her mother's illness, and after her death, when she had covered her face with her hands, and wept, and he had held her tenderly in his arms and felt her tears wet against his cheek.

It unnerved Will afterwards to think how close he had come to not making his proposal of marriage that day he came downstairs, for the last time, to hand over the key to his room. Mary had seemed so stiff and defensive then, standing there in the best parlour, asking him what time he would arrive home. He had said miserably, 'I wish you were coming with me, Mary. I can't imagine what my life will be like without you.'

Words had come tumbling out once the ice was broken. Standing there, hat in hand, his suitcase at his feet, Will confessed how much he loved her. 'I know it's asking a great deal of you to give up your home,' he said, 'but I think I could make you happy.'

'Happy?' Mary had almost forgotten what happiness was. But marriage? The old shibboleths remained.

'I know you'll need time to think things over,' Will said, conscious of the time, that he must hurry to catch the eleven o'clock train from King's Cross, disappointed by Mary's lack of enthusiasm at his proposal. His heart leapt when she said calmly, 'No, I don't need time. Not to think things over, at any rate. Only time to sell up here. Then I will marry you, if you want me.'

'Want you? Oh, Mary!'

Unable to return his kisses, she had stood there in the circle of his arms, a prim little woman in mourning, coolly considering that marriage appeared to be the only way out of her dilemma. She liked and trusted Will Prentiss. The word love had no place in her vocabulary. If he noticed her lack of response, he appeared not to mind as he showered her cheeks with kisses, and nuzzled his face against her hair, making allowance for her modesty.

*

Staring into the mirror, Mary wondered how she could have been so stupid as to imagine that a registry-office wedding would absolve her from the intimacies of the marriage-bed.

The simple truth was, she had not considered herself properly married, with none of her family present to wish her well. Both her sisters were pregnant at the time, too cumbersome to travel. But her husband had held no such inhibitions as he made love to her. Ever since that wedding night, Mary had lived with the humiliation of his powerful invasion of her body. Will would never realize what it had cost her – a sexually frigid woman – to succumb to his lovemaking.

Things were different now. Time had blunted the edge of Will's ardour. After Laura was born, marvelling in the perfection of his daughter, he had seemed satisfied with less frequent expressions of physical desire. Now they seldom made love at all, to Mary's intense relief. But it would be grossly unfair and untrue for anyone to say that she was not devoted to Will.

By his own admission, she had made him a loyal wife who had stood by him throughout the years, helping him to realize his ambition to give up barbering and become a ladies' hairdresser; taking his mother to live with them when the old woman became too crippled with rheumatism to fend for herself.

Mary was devoted to Laura, too. She simply seemed incapable of expressing that devotion. And this was the cross she had to bear.

Will Prentiss could scarcely believe that he would be seeing his little girl again, so soon. His heart surged with relief. He whistled as he put on a clean starched collar in front of the bathroom mirror. It was then he noticed, with a feeling of shock, how old and tired he looked. Christ, he thought, I'm an old man! But when had the metamorphosis from youth to age taken place? On which day had the first of those silver threads appeared at his temples? When had his neck begun to thicken so that a size fifteen collar no longer fitted him as snugly as it used to? Exactly when had his knuckles become slightly swollen, his hands less dextrous than before? Where had he been, what had he been doing whilst all these alarming physical changes were taking place? Watching Laurel and Hardy films at the Aberdeen Walk cinema? Feeding the ducks on Peasholm Park lake? Teaching Laura the art of cutting and pin-curling? Doing crossword-puzzles? Playing dominoes with his pals at the Old Bar Hotel? Worrying about his mother's increasing age and infirmity? Regretting his wife's lack of enthusiasm in bed?

He had so wanted to make Mary happy; now his life seemed overshadowed with failure. The young man who wanted, expected, so much of life, had achieved practically nothing after all, except his daughter, the one bright star of his existence.

Carefully knotting his tie, Will Prentiss remembered how Laura had come to him so confidingly that rainy day, last spring, to tell him that she wanted to join the Women's Royal Naval Service. He had wondered what was coming at first, by her serious expression, her air of timidity, that way she had of standing on first one foot then the other when she had something important to say, or had done something wrong – forgetting to light the Equator boiler, for instance, or wanting to borrow a shilling from her wages to see Errol Flynn in *Captain Blood* at the Odeon Cinema, a film she had already seen three times. He had scarcely been prepared for her jolting revelation that she wished to join up. 'You see, Dad,' she said, 'I'm bound to be called up sooner or later. If I volunteered, I might stand a chance of getting into the Wrens. But I won't do it unless it's all right with you. I couldn't bear to hurt you; to leave you in the lurch.'

'Don't worry about that,' he said, 'go ahead and do what you think best. I'll back you all the way.'

How strange, he thought, shrugging on his jacket, that seldom, throughout the years, had they admitted how much they meant to each other. Even their birthday cards had been funny ones, lacking in sentimentality. Laughter, and trust, had been the keynote of their relationship. He recalled how they used to set off to the cinema together to revel in the antics of Laurel and Hardy when Laura was just a little girl. And yet he had discerned, even then, a deeper side to her nature, a sensitivity, a kind of tenderness which had blossomed, as she grew older, into a passionate awareness of beauty, a kind of innocence laced with strength. It was that innocence he had tried so hard to protect from the harsher realities of life.

But he had known, that wet spring day when she put forward her idea of volunteering for service, that he could no longer stand as her buttress against the world, that the time had come for his girl to stand on her own feet.

Now he was filled with a sense of joy that she was coming home. The days without her had seemed empty, bereft of happiness.

Grandma Prentiss could not help wishing that her son had married a different type of woman. Mary had called up the stairs twice already that they'd be late for the station if she didn't hurry. As if a woman of her age, crippled with rheumatism into the bargain, could be expected to get ready so quickly. Why, she could scarcely get her shoes on after wearing carpet slippers all day long. Nor could she see to find her glasses without her glasses.

Oh, *damnation*! 'All right, all right,' she snapped. 'I'm coming as fast as I can!'

Whatever had possessed her son to marry a bossy, stuck up woman like Mary, she would never know, Gran thought, jamming her dentures into her mouth. She had known that he had chosen the wrong girl from the moment she set eyes on her – his Mary – with her prim, butter wouldn't melt in her mouth expression and her cool, dismissive handshake. But there was Will, fairly bubbling over with joy on the station platform, making a far greater fuss of his fiancée than his own mother.

Heartless, that's what she is. Frigid! A prude! Gran had thought at the time. Not that she had dared voice her opinion in her son's hearing; the poor boy was so obviously in love with the girl.

Even so, time had proved her right, she thought with grim satisfaction. Not that Mary hadn't done her duty when it came to taking her to live with them when she couldn't manage on her own any longer. But she could never forgive her daughter-in-law for the condescending way in which she often treated poor Will, and not telling Laura the facts of life when the child came crying to her on her twelfth birthday, believing that she was to blame for the state of her knickers.

She and Mary had engaged in a battle royal that day, Gran remembered, trying to find her glasses. 'You mean you're not going to tell her why she's bleeding?' she'd asked disbelievingly, after Mary had sent the child away weeping. 'Well, if you won't, *I* will!'

She had never forgotten Mary's reply. 'I'm not filling my girl's head with all that sex nonsense! And if you dare to interfere, I'm warning you, you'll leave this house! Is that clear?'

'Very clear! But if you call yourself a good mother, I don't! It's wrong, in my opinion, to let a girl find out about sex in the school playground. But perhaps that's the way *you* found out about it? The trouble with you, Mary, is you're blind and blinkered, always were and always will be! Now, turn me out if you want to, I shan't care! But I'll make damned certain that Will knows the reason why!'

Mary's voice floated up the staircase once more, 'Grandma, Will and I are leaving now. If you're not ready, we'll go to the station without you.'

'I'm ready! I'm coming!' Gran forced on her left shoe, winced as leather met bunion, and hobbled painfully downstairs.

Meanwhile, Laura was coming home.

6

She had thought that this unexpected leave would ease her restlessness, and yet it seemed to Laura, as she stood in the corridor watching familiar landmarks slip past, that a sea-change had come over her during the past fortnight. The last mile of the journey had always held the power to enchant her. Now she felt strange in her brand-new uniform, collar and tie, thick black stockings, and broad brimmed hat.

The brilliant September day, washed over with a tremulous heat-haze, made the familiar countryside shimmer with the fading blue and gold of autumn. The trees on Oliver's Mount betrayed the first hint of autumn in the quietly changing colours of the leaves. Crimson-berried rowans, clustered thickly on the slopes, echoed the scarlet dahlias in the Seamer station-master's garden, the hips and haws growing in profusion alongside the track. She noticed that the bracken on the Mount was delicately changing from summer green to autumn pink. Nervousness began to chew at her as the train slid past the high railings and houses of the Westwood embankment, into the station, and jerked to a halt near the iron buffers.

She knew her family would be at the station to meet her, and wondered if they would notice the change in her; dreaded the critical looks and quickly-fired questions. Grandma, in particular, would never rest until she had extracted every detail of the past two weeks. But there were certain aspects of her time at Armley House which she could not divulge to anyone except, possibly, her father, who would be the last person to question her at all.

Suddenly, 'There she is!' Gran cried excitedly as Laura stepped down from the train with her assortment of luggage, and walked slowly towards the barrier, pausing to pull herself together, pretending to search through her shoulder-bag to find her travel-warrant, although she knew perfectly well where she had put it.

It was Nell who eased Laura's nervousness as she bunched forward on her lead, barking an hysterical welcome, thrusting her nose through the railings to lick her hands in a frenzy of delight.

'Now, tell us all about it,' Mum said over the tea-cum-supper table, incapable of understanding her daughter's delicately-balanced metamorphosis from pupa to chrysalis, matter-of-factly curious about the kind of food she had eaten – which must have been insufficient by the look of her – and why she hadn't written more often.

'I'm sorry,' Laura said, feeling guilty. 'I didn't have much spare time, we were kept on the go from morning to night.'

'Don't harass the girl, Mary,' Will said mildly, 'I expect she's tired after her long journey.'

'Harass? I wasn't aware that a few questions . . .' Mary frowned, not finishing the sentence, resentful of her husband's interruption; serving the sausages –

breadcrumbs in battledress – mashed potatoes and carrots, with a martyred air.

Oh God, Laura thought, please don't let there be an atmosphere, with Mum in one of her misunderstood moods, Dad trying to pour oil on troubled water, and Gran itching to have her say, making things worse not better. She'd already had a lot to say about the sausages which, she declared, she would not enjoy since they were bacon disguised as something even more diabolical.

'I'm sorry,' Laura said desperately, catching her father's look of sympathy, 'such a lot has happened I scarcely know where to begin.'

'Begin at the beginning, and go on from there,' Gran said, avidly mixing up the mashed potatoes and carrots on her plate with a smattering of gravy, and poking the sausages to one side. So Laura told them about the journey to Waverley, leaving out the acne-faced soldier's remark about her figure – she could just imagine her mother's reaction to *that* piece of information. Thinking about it afterwards, she realized that she had left out all the other events, too, which had impressed her most deeply. The way she had felt in the garden of Armley House; Blodwen Thomas's pubic hair; dancing with the Frenchman. Mum, she knew, would understand none of these things.

'And where are they sending you next?' Gran asked, over apple fritters and custard.

When Laura told them, Mary uttered a shrill cry of protest. Her imagination ran riot. Every news bulletin and cinema newsreel was focused on events in the south east of England where the Battle of Britain was being fought; on the threat of invasion, dog-fights over

73

the English Channel, German planes crossing the coast to bomb military targets.

Will knew what his wife was thinking, that he should not have encouraged Laura to join up, and perhaps she was right. If only Mary and his mother would give the girl time to settle down before subjecting her to a barrage of questions.

When the matter of her posting had been thoroughly gone into, and Mary had expressed her horror of young girls being sent into what she dramatically termed 'the firing line', Laura changed the subject, conjuring up memories of the day she went to the naval dockyards at Rosyth for fire fighting instruction. Memories of that day remained vividly accurate. It had been such fun scrambling aboard the transport with the other pro-Wrens; an unexpected respite from the rigours of the teleprinter keyboard – especially when Grace Flanagan had produced a mouth-organ and struck up a lively chorus of 'Oh, Johnny'.

Soon they were all singing the words, half hysterical with laughter, wiping tears of mirth from their eyes, in love with the world and everything in it. How they had giggled when a group of sailors, watching them dismount, had greeted them with a series of wolf-whistles and cries of, 'Nice legs, sister!' 'Does your mother know you're out?' and, 'What are you doing tonight, sweetheart?' It had been innocent fun, but Mary Prentiss did not see it in that light.

Primming up her mouth, she seemed about to launch into a bitter attack on the men responsible for embarrassing young girls in such a way. Not that Laura noticed. She might have stopped had she done so. Instead, hearing her father's and grandmother's laughter, she plunged into a graphic account of fire-drill. How, after a lecture on incendiary bombs, and the use of stirrup pumps and sandbags, they had been taken out to a yard and given a practical demonstration.

Mary got up from the table, her face flushed with anger. 'You mean to say that you were actually expected to tackle live incendiaries? No, Will! It's no use trying to calm me down! I suppose you don't care tuppence that Laura might have been seriously injured? Well, if you don't, *I* do!'

'It wasn't like that at all.' Laura wished she had never mentioned the episode. 'There wasn't any real danger. In any case, it was part of our training.'

Flattened by her mother's overprotectiveness, she knew Gran had been right when she said it was time she left home. And yet she loved Mum, had always loved her. If she only knew how to express that love. But displays of affection had so often been wasted on her mother. Knowing it was useless to continue, Laura began stacking the plates. 'I'll help with the washing-up,' she said.

'There's no need. I can manage perfectly well,' Mary snapped. 'Besides, you might get your skirt wet.'

'Oh, for heaven's sake, Mum! I'll wear a pinafore!'

As they went into the kitchen, 'No need to bite my head off! I don't know what's come over you, Laura. If this is what your Wren training has done for you,' her mother said.

'I'm sorry, I didn't mean to upset you. I thought you might be glad of my help. You look a bit tired.'

'Tired?' Mary said bitterly, 'I *am* tired with one thing and another. This food rationing doesn't make life any easier, and Gran's so faddy, won't eat this, doesn't like that! And your father isn't well.'

Laura's heart skipped a beat. 'Dad? Why, what's wrong with him?'

'Business worries mainly, if you must know. Would you believe it, the Eugene traveller called yesterday. Not to bring the last order your father gave him. Oh no, far from it! Quite cocky he was, when he told us that his firm is cutting orders to the bone. I never did like that man! Just fancy, after all the money your father has spent with them in the past! Not only that, three perms cancelled last week. Said they were frightened of sitting under the machine for fear of an air-raid, the silly old things! And well, perhaps I shouldn't say this, but it's no use beating about the bush. A number of the younger clients cancelled when they knew you wouldn't be here to attend to them. The fact is, the business is going downhill fast, and I'm worried sick about it!'

'Oh Mum! I had no idea! Would it help if I sent you something from my pay packet once a fortnight?'

'Don't be silly! As if we'd take your money!'

Music blared from the living-room. Gran had switched on the wireless to listen to her favourite programme, *Ack-Ack, Beer-Beer*.

Feeling as if the weight of the world had settled on her shoulders, Laura put away the dishes and went through to the other room. Gran was sitting with her ears glued to the set. Dad looked up from the evening paper and smiled. 'There's a good film on at the Capitol,' he said. 'Bette Davis and Miriam Hopkins in *The Old Maid*. What about it? Shall we go?'

'You and Laura can go if you want to,' Mary said

off-handedly, 'You know I'm not all that struck on Bette Davis. Besides, I have some mending to do.'

Sitting with her father in the darkened cinema, Laura felt as if nothing had changed much after all, as though she were back again in the safety and security of her old world, with countless days and nights of happiness to look forward to, until she noticed the preponderance of uniformed figures in the audience.

Walking home, she remembered the way things used to be before the war, when there was no need to dodge lamp-posts or carry a torch: remembered that, when the moon was full, she had danced in the arms of the Frenchman, and wondered where he was now, if he were alive or dead. Tired after her long day, wanting to be alone, Laura said good night, and went upstairs to her room.

Her mattress felt as soft as goosefeathers after the hard bunk at Armley House, she thought, as she lay down to sleep, but sleep would not come. Tossing restlessly she wondered if she had fallen in love with the Frenchman, memories of whom tormented her. Well, if this was love, she'd be better off without it. How could she begin a new life with this detritus of memories clinging about her?

Next morning she took Nell for a walk, deriving pleasure from the wash of the sea on the rocks beneath the concrete promenade, the shimmering expanse of Scarborough's North Bay crowned with a solid phalanx of hotels and boarding-houses.

Visitors, once the life-blood of the town, had

vanished like autumn leaves when war came. Now, most of the hotels and boarding-houses had been requisitioned by the Army and the Air Force as billets and training-centres. It was the small boarding-house keepers, people like Mum, who had taken in summer visitors as a means of paying the rates and providing warm winter clothing for their families, who had suffered most.

Resting her hands on the railings, watching a fishing coble butting towards the open sea, Laura thought how insensitive she had been not to realize how deeply the loss of those summer visitors would affect the family income. No wonder Mum was worried. Dad too. And wasn't she being insensitive standing here day-dreaming when she might be doing something positive to help her father?

Will Prentiss's relief was evident. A mere fortnight had passed since Laura last stood beside him in her white overall, handing him the permanent wave clips and sachets, helping him with a client who, thankfully, had not cancelled. His hands, which had seemed less dextrous during her absence, were recharged with energy as he wound the client's hair on the long metal rods.

Now, the Saloon, which had seemed so depressing without her, appeared bright and shining once more, as it had done when she first left school and came into the business as his apprentice. Filled with that old feeling of rapport – almost as if they were a mind-reading act – Laura knew exactly what to hand him next, crepe hair, cotton wool, and the linen threads on which the curlers were hung, without being asked.

Glancing at his face in the mirror, Laura realized, with a sudden shock, that Dad was no longer a young man. Strange that one never noticed the day-to-day changes in a person one loved. Now, returning after a short absence, she noticed things she had never really looked at before; the scattering of grey hairs at his temples, the tired lines under his eyes, the forward stoop of his shoulders, as though a photograph, once sharply in focus, had suddenly become blurred with the tears of the beholder.

Later, when the perm was cooling off after the baking process, Laura went through to the kitchen where Dad had put the kettle on for a cup of tea.

Mum had gone out shopping. Gran was upstairs in her room, Nell asleep in her box under the kitchen table.

'How are things really?' he asked wistfully.

'The exams were harder than I expected,' she said, 'and there were so many other things to remember. Daft things, really. Calling the bedrooms cabins, for instance, and making up our bunks with the anchors on the covers pointing down, not up. That kind of thing drives me mad. As if they made any real difference to the war effort! The kettle's boiling!'

'So it is.'

Mum came in at that moment, tired out with queueing up for fish, vegetables and groceries. Dumping her shopping bag on the table she complained, 'This thing weighs a ton. I've lumped it all the way from Newborough!' Then Gran came downstairs, and hobbled into the kitchen saying that her rheumatism was killing her, and she had run out of wintergreen lotion.

'If you'd told me you were going out, Mary,' she snapped, 'I'd have asked you to bring me a bottle.'

'I'll go,' Laura offered, 'and take Nell for a run at the same time.'

The purchase of a bottle of wintergreen had provided a chance of escape. Walking to the chemist's, Laura realized that her joy in homecoming had been nullified by the constant bickering of her mother and grandma. Funny, she had never taken much notice before, living in a cloud cuckoo land of dreams, acting out the role of a screen heroine as she had walked along the seashore imagining she was on her way to keep a tryst with Ronald Colman or Errol Flynn; lifting her face to the wind, loving the feel of the sand beneath her shoes.

Now that the war had opened her eyes to reality, she felt stranded, unsure of herself, a misfit.

Oh God, she thought, a whole day to live through before bedtime.

The sound was unmistakable. 'Moaning Minnie', Gran called the air-raid siren.

Stumbling out of bed, Laura swished together the bedroom curtains, switched on a torch, and felt in the wardrobe for an old pair of slacks she used to wear on walks along the beach. Adding a thick knit jumper, she heard her mother and Gran on their way downstairs to the cupboard under the stairs, the slam of the back door as Dad hurried across the lane to the wardens' post.

Recalling the 'phoney' war of last year, taking shelter seemed an unnecessary precaution, but Mum would insist on sitting in the cupboard until the all-clear sounded.

'Oh, there you are!' Mary ducked back into the cupboard as Laura came down. 'Your father's gone over to the Post.'

'Yes, I know. I heard him go out.' Laura squatted on a stool next to her grandma, wondering why Mum had felt it necessary to light a candle instead of the electric lamp. They must look like the Witches of Endor, sitting there with the candle casting weird shadows on their faces, she thought.

Suddenly Gran said fiercely, 'I'm sure I don't know why Will volunteered to rush out in the middle of an air-raid. A man of his age! Silliness, I call it, when he should be here looking after us. I tell you straight, Mary, if he takes that fire-watching job, I shall never know another minute's peace of mind!'

'What do you mean, Gran? What fire-watching job? Where?'

'*Gran!*' Mary's voice trembled with anger. 'Will distinctly asked you not to . . .'

'Oh, all right. So I've put my foot in it again. But Laura has a right to know.'

'I wish you'd tell me what you are talking about!' Laura said, mystified.

'Very well, Laura, since your grandmother has already mentioned it, I might as well tell you. Your father has been offered a paid fire-watcher's job at Barry and Jackson's,' Mary said stiffly.

Laura knew the shop her mother meant, the draper's establishment in Westborough where all those puffed-sleeved dresses of her youth had come from.

'The manager wants someone to sleep on the

premises, and he has asked your father if he'd be willing.'

Horrified, Laura gasped, 'You mean he'd be on duty all night, and working all day? But that's impossible! He'd never get a wink of sleep.'

'Don't be ridiculous,' Mary said, 'of course he'd be able to sleep, unless an incident occurred. There's a perfectly good bed-chair over there . . .'

'A *bed-chair*!' Anger rose up in Laura. 'He can't do it! I won't let him.' How could her mother even contemplate such a thing?

'No need to raise your voice, Laura! In any case, it's not your decision to make. It's up to your father to decide. Besides, we could do with the extra money.'

'*Money*,' Laura said disgustedly, 'Mum, how could you? You said yourself that Dad hasn't been well lately. How do you think he'd be, never getting a proper night's sleep?'

'Don't blame me,' Mary snapped, 'and don't be so high-handed about money! No-one can manage without it!' She broke off suddenly, holding her head in a listening attitude as she heard a queer, droning noise overhead, the unmistakable sound of enemy planes by the curious beat of their engines. A sound which she associated with German, not British aircraft. 'Listen,' she said breathlessly. '*Listen!*'

'Don't be so melodramatic, Mary . . .'

'*Hush!*'

The silence was broken suddenly by a series of explosions. The ground rocked beneath their feet. Gran gave vent to a piercing cry of terror as the candle guttered and went out.

'Oh my God!' Mary cried hysterically. Then, as

Laura squeezed past her in the darkness, 'Laura! Where are you going? Come back! You mustn't go outside!' But Laura was already feeling her way to the front door, fumbling for the doorknob. 'You don't understand, Mother,' she said, shrugging off Mary's restraining hand, 'I *have* to go. I'm not a civilian now! Not any longer!'

The crescent garden and the houses opposite were bathed in the lurid glare of burning incendiaries. The scene resembled Dante's *Inferno*. The noise of the hissing, cracking and spluttering snout-nosed grey cylinders which had landed in the road, on the grass, and in the basement areas of the houses across the way, was frightening.

Columns of black smoke were billowing up against the night sky. Sparks showering like the golden rain of a fireworks' display. Windows had been shattered by the explosions. Splintered glass had gouged holes in front gardens, and littered the roadway. Above all rose the choking smell of burning wood, of blistering paintwork.

Now other people were beginning to emerge from the houses: women dressed in slacks and sweaters, one or two wearing raincoats flung on over their dressing-gowns. Men, too, most of whom were elderly, bleary-eyed from loss of sleep: members of the local defence volunteers, horrified by the suddenness and scope of the emergency. People who had become too complacent during the 'phoney war' to keep filled the buckets of water for the stirrup-pumps, or remove the growth of moss from the piles of sandbags stacked around the perimeter of the central garden.

Aware of her former neighbours as mere shadows,

as unidentifiable figures moving helplessly about the central area of the conflagration, angered by the lack of water, and remembering her fire-fighting drill at the Rosyth dockyards, Laura took command of the situation.

Throwing herself flat to the ground, shouting to the man, apparently in charge of the volunteers, not to bother about the stirrup-pumps, just to go for the sand-bags, she inched her way forward on her stomach, throwing one sandbag after another on to the spurting incendiaries until the all-clear sounded, until the smoke began to clear, and the moon and stars were visible once more.

Laura rolled over on her back then, exhausted but strangely exhilarated, uncaring that her hands were blistered, that her slacks and jumper were ruined past redemption, and her hair was hanging in rats' tails about her smoke-blackened face.

Heart in mouth, Mary Prentiss had watched, from an upstairs window, the part her daughter had played in quenching those flaming incendiary bombs.

Now, so proud of Laura that words failed her, she said harshly, in that demoralizing way of hers, when her girl came limping home, 'What a sight you look! You're as black as a chimney-sweep! You'd best have a bath, then go back to bed.'

Mary wanted to hold Laura in her arms at that moment and tell her how much she loved her. But old habits died hard. Words of love froze on her tongue as they had so often before. All she could utter, by way of recompense was, 'When you've had your bath, I'll bring you a cup of tea.'

'Thanks, Mum.'

Putting the kettle on to boil, Mary thought that when she took the tea up to Laura's room, she would sit on the edge of the bed and tell her how much she loved her, had always loved her.

But nothing in Mary Prentiss's life had ever happened as she hoped it might. When she went upstairs, later, with the tea, Laura was fast asleep. Mary's moment of truth, her time of confession and reconciliation was over and done with before it had even begun.

Part Two

7

Dragging his hands wearily across his face, Rob Peters felt as though his features had been carved into a mask by the salt spray flung back relentlessly from the bows of the rescue launch.

They had been out almost two hours now, in rapidly worsening weather conditions, searching for a *Blenheim* bomber somewhere out there in that heaving waste of water, steadily decreasing the area of the search to pinpoint the wreckage – if there were any – praying to God that the crew had had time to inflate their life-raft before the plane hit the full force of the onrushing sea.

The mayday call had come when the *Blenheim*, hit by enemy anti-aircraft fire, had begun losing height, which meant that it had gone down near the French coast. Now it might be anywhere. The shattered aircraft could have come down miles away from its last known bearing, and if the crew had been injured, the chances were that they then might not have been able to launch the dinghy.

'Well, Tim, how does it look to you?'

'Not too good, Skipper. I suppose you know we're over a bloody Jerry minefield?'

'The thought had occurred.' Peters smiled grimly at his coxswain, Tim Merrydew. 'But to hell with the mines! What I'd like to see right now is a dinghy with the crew of that *Blenheim* safely aboard.'

Screwing up his eyes against the curious light of the watery sun between gathering storm clouds, wishing like hell that the good weather of the past few weeks had not chosen to turn bad at this particular moment, Peters felt the first drops of rain on his face. Scanning the surface of the sea, he knew that his own craft, perilously near the French coast, was well within range of the German shore batteries; that Jerry would not hesitate to open fire if they were spotted.

Then, suddenly alert and watchful, recharged with renewed hope, 'I think we've got them, Tim,' he shouted exultantly. 'Look! Over there!'

Merrydew grinned. 'OK Skipper!' Quickly he gave the order, 'Ease back the throttle. Lower nets on the portside.'

The crew went swiftly into action, men trained to do their jobs with skill and determination, inordinately proud of the team to which they belonged, of their skipper, and their favourite lady, *Rosie*, with her yellow painted decks and sweetly tuned Sea-Lion engines.

The sea, scurried by a sudden downpour, heaved sullenly against the sides of the launch as the scramble nets descended and the crew of the *Blenheim* were helped aboard. The men, shivering, exhausted, grim-faced, shocked by the loss of their aircraft, were taken below decks to receive medical attention. The young rear-gunner, no more than 19 by the look of him, was bleeding badly from a head-wound.

Aware of the German shore-batteries to starboard and the minefield beneath the rain lanced water, when the scramble nets had been lifted, Peters gave the terse order, 'Now let's get the hell out of here!'

Rosie's turret Brownings, he knew, would give a good account of themselves if necessary, but now he wanted his men, the injured rear-gunner and the rest of the *Blenheim* crew back to base as quickly as possible. The wireless operator had already sent a signal requesting a stand-by ambulance. It would be good, Rob thought, after making his report, to peel off his salt-caked slacks and sweater, bathe, have a meal, and go off duty for a much needed rest. God, but he needed a shave.

Peering through the rain for the first welcoming glimpse of the White Cliffs, he suddenly remembered Caroline, experiencing a dull ache of regret that she was no longer a part of his life except in that storeroom of fleeting, often unlinked, impressions of the past that one calls memory. But memory played cruel tricks at times. Occasionally would come moments of blind panic when he could not clearly recall her face. Then he would look at her photograph and feel an assuagement of fear as he remembered her smile, the softness of her hair, the touch of her hand on his. He would feel comforted, then, warmed by the memory of happier days.

Coming into port, he saw the flash of the Aldis lamp from the harbour and called to Sparks to flash back their personal identification signal. Then *Rosie*'s 400 horse-power engines were throttled back at his command, and she dawdled into harbour against the heavy sea-swell.

The town of Ringley, midway between Dover and

Hastings, had been, pre-war, nothing more than a quiet seaside resort catering for small numbers of visitors who preferred its picturesqueness to the more blatant attractions of Bournemouth, Brighton and Southend.

It came as a shock to the inhabitants that the War Ministry had earmarked their town as a naval, army and air-force base. First an aerodrome had been built on the rolling land to the west – once the province of the local golf-club. Soon the landscape had been scarred by an unsightly outcrop of hangars and nissen huts, to the disgust of a body of townspeople who had witnessed, with a growing sense of alarm, the despoilation of the harbour as dredgers moved in to deepen the channel, and gangs of workmen began lengthening and widening the fish-pier in readiness for the naval signals' station.

There had been an uproar in the council chamber when a public meeting was called to discuss what the former president of the now defunct Golf Club referred to as 'the rape of our fair town'. Then other incensed members of the community had voiced their fears that the town's architectural gems – the ancient Lord Nelson hostelry in the High Street, the row of timbered sixteenth-century cottages in Stocking Lane, and the parade of fine early Victorian houses on Marine Parade – might be bulldozed and swept away by the War Ministry which had already reduced to rubble the old Bethel chapel on the quayside.

The pity was, thundered the former president of the Golf Club, the threadveins on his cheeks purple with rage, that the War Ministry had not seen fit to bulldoze a few of the eyesores perpetrated by the council in an attempt to attract more visitors to the town. He referred specifically to the two cheap-jack cinemas, the Olympia Dance Hall, the modernistic pubs, cafés and ice-cream parlours which had been inflicted upon Ringley at the expense of the ratepayers.

Councillor Pigg, currently the mayor of Ringley, had then reminded his incensed opponent that neither he nor his fellow councillors were responsible for decisions taken after the First World War; that the so-called 'eyesores' *had* brought prosperity to the town, prior to the present conflict. 'Furthermore,' he said pompously, 'I predict a new era of prosperity for Ringley when the troops move in. And you have my personal assurance that the Lord Nelson, the cottages in Stocking Lane, and the houses on Marine Parade, will suffer no harm.'

Even so, dismay had run rife among the older inhabitants of Ringley when the troops moved in to clutter up their town: when aircraft roared overhead day and night, and uniformed figures invaded the hitherto quiet bar-parlour of the Lord Nelson inn.

Curiously, it was the older fishermen, those veterans of the First World War, who least resented sharing their harbour with the men of the Air Sea Rescue Service, with whom they shared an intense love and fear of the sea, a deep understanding of this, the most fickle of all mistresses.

Laura, Grace, Ruth Maple, and Dinah Felix, travelled to Ringley on the ten-fifteen train from York, and found themselves crowded into a compartment with half a dozen sailors who took it in turns to rush out on to the platform to buy cups of tea whenever the train stopped, which it did with monotonous regularity.

Dinah, who had been escorted to the train by her wealthy industrialist father, Sir Wilfred Felix, and obviously regarded the brash young sailors as her social inferiors, sat stonily in a window seat facing the engine, smoking cigarettes which she fitted with careless elegance into an expensive, monogrammed holder.

Minutes before the train departed, her father's chauffeur handed her a carrier bag containing delicately cut smoked salmon sandwiches which she ate, at midday, accompanied by a flask of steaming hot coffee sipped from a blue and white china cup, while the less fastidious Grace Flanagan bit into a station-buffet pork pie.

'Really, must you?' Dinah wrinkled her nose in disgust when Flanagan giggled and commented that her pie tasted as if it had been made from decayed enemy corpses.

'Sorry, duchess,' Grace retorted, not one whit abashed, 'am I putting you off your caviar butties?'

In skittish mood after an unsatisfactory forty-eight-hour leave, Grace flirted outrageously with the sailors; wise-cracking to blunt the memory of the flaming row which had broken out when her father came home drunk on Saturday night. Incensed by his wife's scorn, unable to withstand her criticism of his behaviour, Michael Flanagan's initial smiling foolishness had finally erupted into violence when, goaded beyond endurance, he struck Mrs Flanagan full in the face, splitting her lip with the force of the blow.

The children, disturbed by the row, had crowded downstairs to find their mother huddled on the hearthrug with blood pouring down her chin. It had taken her an hour to settle them down again.

Later, when Grace had ventured downstairs, her mother was in the scullery, holding a wet cloth to her swollen mouth and Grace had seen, with horror, that Mum's two front teeth were missing. Meanwhile, Michael Flanagan had sunk snoring into his chair by the kitchen fire.

And yes, Grace thought bitterly, tomorrow he would go to confession, the priest would impose a penance – possibly a decade of the rosary – and her father's conscience would be as clear as a whistle until the next time he came home drunk.

Little wonder she thought dully, behind her façade of flirtatious smiles, that she was no longer a devout Catholic.

Suddenly her conscience smote her. Come to think of it, Ruth and Laura seemed very quiet and withdrawn, as if they had not enjoyed their leave much either.

'You OK?' she asked Laura.

Laura smiled. 'I'm a bit tired, that's all.'

'Been whooping it up, have you?'

'Not exactly. We had a bad air raid last night. The worst so far. I helped put out a few incendiaries.'

'Blimey! No wonder you look frazzled! Much damage?'

'Well, you know how it is with incendiaries.'

'You weren't burned, or anything?'

'The front of my hair got a big singed.'

'Bloody hell!' Grace said fervently. Then, turning her attention to Ruth, 'What about you, mavourneen? Did you enjoy your leave?'

Ruth felt for her handkerchief. 'No, as a matter of fact, I didn't! I wish I'd never gone home at all,' she sniffed, dabbing her eyes. 'I knew the minute I opened the door that Mother and Aunt Ada were getting on each other's nerves! They did nothing but snap at each other all the time I was there.'

'Oh Lord,' Grace muttered inadequately, wishing that Ruth would stop crying and get on with her own life for a change. After all, why should the young shoulder the burdens of an older generation?

As for Dinah Felix, she thought bitterly, as the train jerked to a halt at Grantham, or Peterborough – though one could never be sure where one was any more since that bloody government order to remove all signposts had come into force last May – what Felix needed was a good boot up the arse for being so snobbish and anti-social.

The journey to Ringley had been a nightmare for Laura, worrying about her father taking on that fire-watching job. Her first glimpse of HMS Ringley, seen through a rain-scurried dusk, did nothing to restore her flagging morale. A far different cry from Armley House this stark signals' station, surrounded with electrified wire fencing and 'Keep Out' warnings splashed in red paint.

Crowded into a RN transport with a dozen or more Wrens, the town, seen dimly through steadily falling rain, made an unfavourable impression on Laura as the vehicle veered through narrow streets flanked with stone faced villas and boarded-up shops.

Blackout regulations had robbed even lovely places like Scarborough of their former brilliance when night came. But this town was both prim and ugly. She doubted if even the fairy lights, which must once have glimmered among the trees in the municipal park they had just passed, would have added much lustre to a dump like this.

Even the rain, which she had longed for to break the monotony of that seemingly endless heatwave, beating down on unfamiliar streets failed to compensate for her feeling of imprisonment when the transport stopped at the guard-house and a dour sentry demanded to see their identity cards.

The Wren quarters, adjacent to the signals' station, had already been blacked out. Harsh neon lights glared down from low ceilings. The cabin Laura would share with Grace, Ruth, Dinah and three other girls had green painted walls posted with long lists of regulations, bare scrubbed floorboards, and narrow lockers between the bunks.

Shivering with cold and nervous tension, Laura elected to sleep in the bunk above Ruth's. She stowed away her belongings and went down to the refectory where the air was permeated with the sour smell of boiled cabbage.

Tucking hungrily into an indifferent lamb stew, Flanagan declared she was so famished that she could eat a horse, while Laura, put off by the grease congealing on a cold plate, and the overboiled cabbage sinking wetly in a sea of thin gravy, merely poked at the food.

When the first course was followed by a stodgy suet pudding and lumpy custard, even Grace pulled a face. 'Blimey, this isn't much cop', she muttered. 'Huh, just take a look at Miss High and Mighty over yonder' –

she meant Dinah Felix – 'bet she wishes she'd never been given her bloody posting to Ringley after all.' She added, with unaccustomed venom, 'But I suppose "Daddy" will send her nice little food parcels; quails' breasts in aspic, Fortnum and Mason's caviar, and all that stuff.'

Disturbed by Grace's edge of ill-humour, Laura wondered about the sea-change in her usually sunny personality. Not that she had time to reflect on the matter. Supper over, the new contingent of Wrens were ordered to go, as quickly as possible, to the lecture-room.

'Oh God! Not another bloody lecture!' Flanagan muttered. 'Now what, I wonder?'

Second Officer Bradley, a middle-aged woman with an equine face, came quickly to the point. The point being discipline. 'I will tolerate no shirking,' she said coldly. 'You will be expected to obey orders without question, and remember that the weight of responsibility for the successful running of this station rests firmly on your shoulders.'

'The old cow!' Flanagan muttered, as Bradley went on to remind them that the wearing of jewellery, apart from wedding and engagement rings, was strictly taboo.

'Neither will you wear nail varnish, perfume, heavy makeup, nor keep photographs in your pay-books. Is that understood? Now, if you will proceed to the regulating office, you will be given your watch numbers and told when to report for duty. Any questions?'

Grace put her hand up. 'Please, ma'am, what is meant by watch numbers?'

'A sensible question.' The officer launched into a long-winded account of the naval watch system – so many hours on duty, so many off – harking back to Nelson and the Battle of Trafalgar, which she pronounced *Trah*falgar.

'Why the hell didn't I keep my mouth shut?' Flanagan grumbled when they filed out of the lecture room.

'What's the matter with you, Grace?' Laura asked concernedly.

'I had a rotten leave, that's all. Oh, take no notice, I'll get over it. My ma and pa had a dust-up, and I feel so bloody helpless. Remember I told you I joined up to have a good time. Well, that's what I intend doing! What say? Let's live it up a bit, shall we?'

'It all depends on what you mean by "living it up",' Laura said doubtfully.

'What do you think I mean? What's wrong with going dancing once in a while, to the cinema, or the *Lord Nelson*? God, I'd give my right arm for a good night out!'

'I've never been inside a pub.'

'So what? We needn't get reeling drunk, just – merry. And we'd be meeting new people.' She meant men.

Too tired to argue, Laura remembered that she had promised to ring home to tell her family she'd arrived safely at Ringley.

After they had been allocated their watch numbers, she went along to the telephone box in the hall.

Standing there, awaiting her connection, she saw a poster pinned up near the coin box. '*Your* Courage, *Your* Cheerfulness, *Your* Resolution will bring us Victory'. How ludicrous, she thought, hearing the rain beating against the blacked out windows of this depressing new place she had come to.

She had never felt less courageous, cheerful, or resolute in all her life.

The teleprinter room, low-ceilinged, fuggy with cigarette smoke, noisy and busy with the constant coming and going of sailors from the W/T section across the corridor, seemed to Laura a bewildering vortex of chatter and confusion as she tapped her way through the sheaf of four-letter signals propped up in front of her.

Eyes smarting from fatigue and cigarette smoke, she wondered if she should have gone into the Land Army after all, where all she would have had to wrestle with were turnips, potatoes and cows. To add fuel to her distress, the girls of No. 4 watch were required to attend squad drill this afternoon on the parade-ground to the rear of the station. The thought filled her with dismay. Being forced to march, to keep in step with the rest, under the watchful eye of a Marine colour sergeant, was something she could do without. And no matter how diligently she practiced the naval salute in front of the washroom mirror, she could not get the hang of keeping her right hand in stiff line with her elbow, nor avoid knocking her hat askew.

At dinner, Laura was reminded of Gran as she poked a couple of sausages to the side of her plate. Not because she disliked sausages, she simply wasn't hungry.

'If you are not going to eat those bangers,' Grace suggested greedily, 'I wouldn't mind having them.'

Dinah Felix, sitting opposite, treated Flanagan to

a frosty stare of disapproval. 'Well, *really*!' she sniffed.

'OK. So I know that shovelling food from plate to plate isn't done in the best circles,' Grace said hostilely, 'but *I'm* bloody hungry! Besides, *I* haven't a rich father, or a chauffeur to hand me smoked salmon sandwiches at the drop of a hat! So why don't you mind your own business, Leading Wren Felix? But then, *I'm* not engaged to be married and playing around at the same time with good looking Free French officers! I call that very common indeed!'

'Don't, Grace! Please don't!' Laura felt she could not bear the enmity which had sprung up between Flanagan and Dinah Felix. Having succeeded in pushing thoughts of the Frenchman to the back of her mind, Grace's words had reminded her once more of his face, his hair, his smile, his gentleness and charisma.

Later, in the cabin, nursing a couple of blistered heels after her first experience of squad drill, Laura wondered if she had painted too romantic a picture of the Women's Royal Naval Service, based on newsreels she had seen of trim uniformed girls taking their place alongside the men of the Royal Navy, as the commentator put it. Now she thought that there was nothing in the least romantic about marching round and round a rock-hard parade ground until the blood from her blisters began trickling into her shoes.

At that moment, she hated the Women's Royal Naval Service, and especially this place with its strip lighting and close, fuggy atmosphere; the curtness of the junior officers, the indifferent food, and the weight of responsibility she felt typing those four- and five-letter signals, knowing how important they were.

She had been assigned a teleprinter near a window

overlooking the harbour, so at least she could lift her eyes occasionally from her work to seek spiritual refreshment from the far-flung horizon, and catch glimpses of the men of the cheek-by-jowl RAF Air Sea Rescue Service busy about the task of preparing their launches for duty, swabbing the decks before heading for the harbour mouth.

Flanagan burst into the cabin at that moment, groaning because she, too, had blistered heels. 'Oh God,' she lamented, flopping down on the edge of her bunk and pulling off her shoes to ease the pain. 'I'm sick and tired of this for a lark! What say you and I get out of this dump for a couple of hours after supper? There's a good film on at the Plaza. Anton Walbrook and Diana Wynyard in *Gaslight*.'

'Fine,' Laura sighed, 'but what about Ruth? We can't very well leave her behind.'

'Oh Ruth!' Grace objected. 'No use asking *her* to come with us, she'd only refuse. God, I could give that girl a good shake-up. She's so determined to be miserable, she gives me the heebie-jeebies!'

'Even so, she might like to come with us. Besides, I wouldn't enjoy the film very much knowing that we hadn't even asked her.'

'Yeah, I suppose you're right. Neither would I,' Grace admitted, inspecting her blisters. 'So ask her to come with us if you want to, but don't be surprised if she refuses. Honestly, she's a dead loss!'

Surprisingly, Ruth accepted the invitation.

The three of them emerged from the Plaza into the blacked-out streets with no clear idea where they were heading. It was simply a matter of walking downhill in the general direction of the harbour.

The night was dark and windy. A drizzle of rain blew into their faces as they stepped warily into the blackness, feeling for the kerb edges with their feet; keeping on the qui vive to avoid lamp-posts and other vague shapes which loomed suddenly out of the darkness.

'I can stand everything about this war except this bloody awful blackout,' Flanagan complained, tripping over an uneven paving stone. 'God, what wouldn't I give for a bit of warmth and comfort! I mean to say, that film we've just seen wasn't exactly a ball of fun, was it? Truth to tell, I came over jittery watching Anton Walbrook creeping about in the fog, driving his wife dotty into the bargain! I wish now we'd gone to the Roxy to see *Irene*!'

Laura, who had enjoyed the film, and Ruth, who was clinging to her arm like a limpet, bumped suddenly into Grace from behind as she stopped walking and stood still on the pavement, listening to the sound of laughter from the *Lord Nelson*.

'Come on, girls,' Flanagan said, taking the lead as usual, 'lets go in for a quick drink, shall we?'

The crew of *Rosie* – Coxswain Tim Merrydew, Gavin Truefitt, the medical orderly, and Jimmy McGregor 'Sparks' – were sitting together at their usual table discussing the merits of the slow, summer game of cricket as opposed to the faster, winter cut and thrust of Rugby, when the door opened and the three girls came in from the darkness.

Not that the *Lord Nelson*'s bar-parlour was brilliantly lit. The management had created a cosy atmosphere dependent upon understated lighting, an atmosphere which Flight Lieutenant Peters, standing alone at the bar, thought of as *gemutlich* – the German word for shine and comfort, which he had learned before the war on blissful summer holidays spent touring the Rheinland from Koblenz to Heidleburg, stopping at the various youth hostels along the way, never dreaming that there would soon be a Second World War.

As a matter of course, every full-blooded male took notice of girls who came in from the blackout to wend their way between the tables to the bar.

The three entering now received the usual accolade of wolf-whistles. Not that the girl in charge of the trio, a chunky lass with a fringe seemed whistle-worthy to Rob, leaning against the counter, drinking his half-pint of ale. Nor did the second girl with lank fair hair, watery eyes, and a pinched nose, who followed in her wake. But the third girl! Rob's heart beat faster as he looked at her. Caroline, he thought. *Caroline!*

The likeness was remarkable, almost uncanny. Here was Caroline, resurrected from the sleep of death, come back to life to haunt him with her beauty, soft fair hair, peach-bloom cheeks, dark-lashed eyes and tender young mouth. So acute, so real was the likeness, that Rob could not take his eyes off Laura, the way she moved and smiled . . .

The suppressed emotion of the past few months rose up to unnerve him, the shocking suddenness of Caroline's death, the pain and loneliness he had endured which he kept hidden behind a carefully erected barrier of efficiency, of total dedication to his job. Now he felt his hands shaking, and thought for one terrifying moment that he was about to weep. Abruptly he turned away, leaving his drink on the bar, and pushed past the tables to a passageway leading to the cloakrooms.

The door at the end of the passage opened into the walled yard of the *Lord Nelson*. Parting the blackout curtains, he stepped outside and stood there among the stacked crates of empties, gulping in deep breaths of air, glad of the wind and the rain on his upturned face, berating himself for a fool to have been caught off-guard. He had believed, for one heart-stopping moment, that Caroline had walked into the bar.

Meanwhile, Grace had recklessly ordered three large gin and tonics. 'Oh, I can't possibly drink this,' Ruth demurred when the drink was thrust into her hand. 'I've never had anything stronger than sherry before!'

'High time you did, then! Go on, get it down you. It'll do you good. Cheers!' The unrepentant Grace lifted her own glass. 'You too, Laura! Oh, for heaven's sake! Don't tell me *you're* going to come over all puritanical as well? For God's sake, girls, relax, enjoy yourselves.'

Delving into her shoulder-bag for a cigarette, she twinkled flirtatiously at the young sailor who offered her a light.

Knowing Grace as well as she did and worried about the time, Laura moved forward to look at the clock above the bar. Unable to see it from where she was standing, hemmed in by the crush of servicemen and women leaning on the counter, she moved forward. At the same moment, Rob Peters returned to finish his drink.

The collision was inevitable. Laura's glass tilted

suddenly and she uttered a cry as half its contents spilled down the front of her uniform.

Oh Lord, she thought, an officer. 'I'm sorry, sir,' she apologized, 'I was trying to look at the clock. We have to be back at base by ten-thirty.'

'You'd better get a move on then,' Rob said brusquely, 'unless you consider it amusing to report late for duty!'

'No, not at all, sir.'

Oh Christ, he thought bleakly as the three girls hurried away. Why was I so bloody rude to her? But he knew why. Because she had reminded him of Caroline. In his overwrought emotional state, he had wished to punish her for not being Caroline. He also knew that somehow, somewhere, he would meet that girl again.

8

Meggie hunched her shoulders over the letter she was writing.

It was getting late, and her bedroom felt cold. Or perhaps the chilly feeling came from the bleakness of her heart. Never a great hand at letter writing, she had torn up several sheets of paper already, wanting to explain things properly.

'Dear Laura,' she wrote at last, then sat nibbling her pen, wondering how to continue. 'It seems ages since I saw you, and I miss you very much, especially our visits to the pictures . . .' Here, inspiration ran out. Oh why couldn't she frame her thoughts? Laura wrote such lovely letters. Shivering, Meggie tucked her woollen dressing gown closer about her knees, and tried again.

'The trouble is, Fred Briggs – I don't know if you remember him, his father owns the farm next to ours – has started asking me out . . .' Oh God, how lame that sounded. Tears filled Meggie's eyes, blurring the words she had written. Then, desperately, she started writing once more; spilling her thoughts on to the paper haphazardly, as they occurred to her, hoping that Laura would be able to make sense of them. Conjuring up images of Fred guiding her firmly to the back row of the cinema, placing one arm about her shoulders, and, when they were settled, gradually allowing his free hand to slide up her skirt as far as her knicker elastic, she wrote, 'When I told him to stop, he just laughed and said I wouldn't be so prissy after we were married. When I asked him what he meant, he said it was an understood thing, now that we're courting . . .'

Tears ran down Meggie's cheeks, recalling her humiliation when Fred told her he'd already had a word with her father about their getting married one day: 'Married?' I said, pushing his hand away. 'Why, I wouldn't marry you, Fred Briggs, if you were the last man on earth!'

How could her father have done such a thing? Giving his consent to a courtship without telling her, as if she were some kind of servant girl living in the Middle Ages? A relic of the feudal system, without a soul to call her own: 'Oh, I expect Dad didn't realize . . . You know how easy going he is. Ma, too! I guess they thought how lucky I was to get any man at all to take an interest in me. Well, I'm no oil-painting, am I? But Laura, I really can't bear it. I hate Fred Briggs, and those big red hands of his . . .'

Pushing her fingers through her hair, re-reading the letter, Meggie thought how ridiculous it sounded, set down in black and white. But Laura, above all people, would understand how she felt.

She ended the letter: 'I know Dad needs me here on the farm. He said only yesterday that I was doing work of national importance. But he doesn't know how I feel about Fred Briggs, which is why I've made up my mind to join the Forces. The WAAF for preference. I went down to the labour exchange in Devizes, yesterday, to fill in the forms. Well, Laura, that's all my news for the time being. Please write to me soon. I could do with a bit of moral support. Your ever loving cousin, Meggie.'

Dinah Felix's spirits lifted as she walked into the officers' mess at RAF Headquarters, Swanley-by-Ringley.

This was the kind of atmosphere she was used to, where drinks flowed freely, and men in well-tailored uniforms knew how to treat a woman. Men who turned their heads approvingly as she and her new boon companion, Leading Wren Castleford, a willowy blonde with a peaches-and-cream compexion, entered the room.

Immediately, a tall imposing figure, wearing the uniform of a wing commander, hurried forward to greet them. 'Welcome, mi dears. I'm Ralph Stacey. How delightful that you could come.' He beamed down on them from a great height as Dinah introduced first Maisie Castleford, then herself, to the benevolent giant.

'Felix? That name rings a bell!' The wing commander tugged thoughtfully at his handlebar moustache. 'You're not Sir Wilfred's daughter, by any chance? You are? Well, 'pon my soul! Know him well! We were at Cambridge together, don't you know?'

'Really? How amazing!' Dinah widened her eyes, aware of the impact she was making on a group of men standing near the bar. In her element as the centre of attraction, shrewdly sizing up the other women present, she knew that none of them – not even Maisie Castleford, lovely but lacking in personality – could hold a candle to her.

Completely disinterested in the wing commander's waffle. Dinah appeared to hang on his every word, uttering the occasional, 'Really?' 'How frightfully interesting.' 'Do tell me more.'

Stacey, she thought, was probably a doting grandfather. A pet, but terribly boring. Most of her father's university chums were. As though she cared two hoots that they had once played cricket together. She breathed a sigh of relief when, rallying to his duties as host, he began a round of introductions to the men at the bar.

One man in particular had caught her attention. A dark-haired squadron leader, extremely good looking, with a charming smile, and curiously attractive eyes.

'Squadron Leader Jackson,' Dinah acknowledged their introduction with a butterfly touch of her fingers, the slightest inclination of her head. At that moment, Wing Commander Stacey, required to welcome a further influx of guests, made his apologies.

'You will excuse me? Duty calls. Neville, old chap, I leave these gals in your capable hands.'

'First things first,' Jackson said easily. 'What will you have to drink? I'd love to offer you champagne.' He smiled at Dinah. 'Unless I miss my guess, you are champagne ladies, inured to the best in life. But, as things stand, I guess you'll have to make do with gin, port, or whisky.'

'Very sure of yourself, aren't you?' Dinah glanced at him teasingly. 'What if I told you that I never drink anything but beer?'

'I wouldn't believe you!' Jackson's eyes sparkled with fun. 'I'll go further. I'd wager a month's salary that you have never even tasted beer. A girl like you would never ruin her palate with such foul tasting stuff.' Closing his eyes, his face assumed a trance-like expression. Clapping a hand to his forehead, he said, in a high, womanish voice: 'I see it all, dearie! Wine's your favourite tipple, ain't it? I can see you now, sitting on the Cote d'Azur, palm trees waving in the breeze, supping Pouilly-Fuissé – or could it be St Emilion?'

'Fool!' Dinah burst out laughing. 'All right, you win your bet. I can't stand the smell of beer, let alone the taste.'

The familiar chemistry had begun to work, a feeling Dinah knew well, compounded of excitement, awareness and her power to attract. She knew that Squadron Leader Jackson found her desirable. The signs were unmistakable.

They had eyes only for each other, knowing that this was the beginning of an affair, made more exciting, more urgent by the underlying tension of making every moment count. Dinah knew that she wanted this man as much as he wanted her, scarcely remembering that she had wanted Giles just as intensely at their first meeting. And what Dinah wanted, Dinah intended to have.

Spoilt from the cradle, the only child of indulgent parents, she had grown up in a hot-house atmosphere of wealth, parties, and pretty clothes, skimming the surface of life like a dragonfly.

She had met Giles Pritchard at Bryherton Hall, home of her mother's cousin, Iris Charlton, just prior to the outbreak of war. The Charltons' daughter, Felicity, had become engaged to marry the heir to a pharmaceutical fortune. A weekend house-party and dance was being held in their honour.

Felicity had been showing her engagement ring, a flawlessly cut emerald, to an admiring group of people, when a tall, fair man, wearing the uniform of a group captain, entered the room.

Hurrying forward to meet the new arrival, 'My dear Giles,' Iris Charlton enthused, 'I'm so glad you could come after all. But why the uniform? Oh God, don't tell me that war is as close as all that?'

Later, dancing with Giles, Dinah discovered that he would spend the night at Bryherton Hall before travelling to London next day to join his squadron.

'No need to look so worried,' he said lightly, 'This could be a repetition of last year's Munich crisis.'

'Do you really think so?'

'No, actually I don't,' he admitted. 'I think it's for real this time.'

'Which means that I might never see you again?' Dinah said, looking into his eyes.

'Would that matter to you?'

'Well, yes. I rather think that it might!'

Dinah had spoken the truth as she saw it at the time; had known by the strange clamouring of her heart that she wanted him physically; to spend the night with him; knew that he felt the same by the tightening of his arm about her waist; the way he held her, his strange, quizzical expression of longing as he looked down at her.

But there was more to it than that. Dinah had discovered, by dint of clever questioning, that Sir Giles Pritchard was extremely wealthy; educated at Eton and Oxford, a stockbroker, owner of a stud farm in Berkshire, and unmarried. Quite a catch! Even so, none of these things would have mattered to her, not even his title, Dinah had reasoned with herself, if he had been squat, balding, fat and ugly, in which case she would not have wanted him to make love to her; would never have danced so closely in his arms; would never have allowed him into her room when the dance was over and the house lay still and quiet in the early hours of the morning.

She had been waiting for him, wearing a white satin negligee tied about her slim waist with a gold tasselled cord. In a fever of anticipation, she had brushed her shoulder-length hair until it stood, in a nimbus about the bright triangle of her face; had experimented with the lighting until she got it just right. The overhead lights, she decided, were too harsh, too revealing. At last she had settled on the red-shaded bedside lamp, and its matching dressing-table companion.

And all the time, sitting on the dressing stool making certain that her makeup was perfect, delicately applying her favourite French perfume to her throat and wrists, the pulse spots that men loved to kiss – her eyes kept straying to the enamelled clock on the mantelpiece, measuring the minutes, the seconds, wondering if she had made a mistake. Had she perhaps misjudged the situation, made a fool of herself in thinking that he would come to her, that he wanted her as much as she wanted him? And yet she had been so sure of her impact, certain that he understood the silent signals that had passed between them.

Heart in mouth, she heard a light tap at the door. Jumping up, she hurried to let him in. 'You knew I'd come?' he said gruffly. 'You were expecting me?'

'I – I hoped that you might,' she replied lightly, sure of herself once more, 'to say good night to me, or goodbye. After all, we may never see each other again, after tonight!'

Closing the door, he said, 'Tell me, Dinah. Do you believe in love at first sight?'

'I didn't before, but I do now,' she said breathlessly. 'Oh, Giles, I do now!'

Sitting alone in the common-room, pretending to read a book, Ruth Maple knew that no-one except Grace Flanagan, or Laura Prentiss, would bother to interrupt her.

She also knew that the other girls, chatting and laughing together, considered her a dead loss; stuffy, boring and uninteresting. Well, they were right, she thought bitterly. She was all those things, and as plain as a pikestaff into the bargain.

Take her hair for example. Her Methodist mother had considered visits to a professional hairdresser a waste of money when she could just as easily trim her daughter's hair herself. As for makeup! Her mother had thrown up her hands in horror the day she discovered a tube of Tangee lipstick in Ruth's handbag.

'If the good Lord had meant you to have redder lips, my girl, He'd have given them to you,' she'd said sanctimoniously. With that she had marched out into the yard and thrown the offending item into the dustbin.

Tears had gathered in Ruth's eyes at the injustice: the loss, not only of her precious lipstick, but the invasion of her privacy. 'You had no right to search through my handbag, Mother,' she'd cried hysterically.

'No right? I'm your mother, and don't you forget it,

young lady! Goodness knows what your poor father would have said if he were alive. Oh dear, now my eyes have started irritating again! Just go to the bathroom cupboard and fetch me those drops the doctor prescribed for me, there's a good girl.'

'Yes, Mother.' Guilt had gnawed into Ruth as she lay down to sleep that night; had continued to gnaw at her ever since, as if her mother's deteriorating eyesight had something to do with the Tangee lipstick. As if the innocent purchase of a lipstick were a kind of judgement on her vanity.

Knowing her call-up was imminent, dreading telling her mother that she had thought it out carefully and decided to volunteer for the Wrens, Ruth had scarcely known how to broach the subject, until Mrs Maple demanded to know what was on her mind; why she was drooping about the house like a dying duck in a thunderstorm!

When Ruth blurted out her intention, Mrs Maple leaned back in her chair, a skinny hand clasped to her bosom. 'My smelling salts,' she murmured faintly. 'Oh, to think that it has come to this! My only child wanting to leave me! What would your poor father have said?'

'It isn't a matter of wanting to leave you, Mother,' Ruth said tearfully. 'You know I haven't any choice in the matter. Not unless I volunteer for service, and I'd rather do that than be pushed into the ATS or the WAAF.'

'I suppose it never occurred to you to seek – whatever they call it – on compassionate grounds? But no, it wouldn't have! Selfish to the core, that's what you are, my girl!' Mrs Maple held the smelling salts to her quivering nostrils.

'I don't think I'd stand an earthly chance of prefer-
ment,' Ruth said miserably. 'I mean, it isn't as if you
are crippled or bedfast . . .'

'What a callous thing to say! Not crippled or bedfast!
But I might well be, left alone to fend for myself.'

'You could ask Aunt Ada to come and live with you.
You know she hates living on her own.'

'Huh, I see that you have worked everything out
very carefully to fit in with your own selfish desires.'

'Please, Mother, don't say that. It isn't my fault
there's a war on.'

'Ah, well, I suppose I must manage somehow. But
I daresay you won't ever spare a thought for your poor,
ailing mother, when you are far away from home.'

Now the thought of her own selfishness and her
'poor, ailing mother' clung to Ruth tenaciously, adding
daily to her burden of guilt.

9

It happened with soul-shattering suddenness. Sitting at her teleprinter, watching with half an eye as one of the Air Sea Rescue launches put out to sea, following the creamy wake of its progress as it skimmed towards the marker buoys bobbing in the channel, Laura thought how wonderful that skimming sensation must be, almost like flying.

Seconds later came the dull crump of the explosion. A fountain of spray jetted skyward, the sea was littered with wreckage. The launch and its crew had been wiped from the face of the earth as if they had never existed.

The shock of the incident taught Laura her bitterest lesson so far; awareness of the transient nature of life in wartime; that only the here and now mattered a damn; that this hour, this one brief moment in time were all one might ever have. She saw the future as a formless blur and felt suddenly afraid. Then came a deep desire to love and be loved before it was too late.

Lying awake in her bunk, staring into the darkness, she thought about the Frenchman: imagined kneeling at his feet; the warm touch of his hand on her hair; spilling out her secret hopes and fears; giving all she had to give of youth, love and passion while there was still time, knowing that all she had done so far was dream her way through life, conjuring shadows without substance.

The only 'lovers' she had ever known were larger than life images flickering upon a cinema screen. Real passion was something of which she knew nothing: a second-rate emotion bought for the price of an admission ticket to the pictures, where one sat in a state of euphoria living in a dreamworld of manufactured emotion. Where, at the end of the show, the film was put back into metal containers, and the projectionist went home to bed.

Tormented by memories of the Frenchman, she plucked up courage to ask Dinah Felix his name.

'Oh, you mean Pierre Lefevre?' Dinah said carelessly, her memory of an old flame quenched by the new. 'But why on earth ask me about *him*? Oh, I see,' she laughed unpleasantly, 'you danced with him in the Paul Jones, and I suppose you imagine he was Charles Boyer?'

Laura coloured up. Dinah smirked. 'Why, you're actually blushing! How terribly quaint. What a little Pollyanna you are.'

Resisting a strong desire to smack Dinah's face and wishing she had kept silent, Laura said, 'I just wondered what became of him, that's all.'

'How should I know, for God's sake? I never saw him again after that beastly dance. I certainly don't keep track of every man I meet. Why should I? In my experience men don't care for girls who run after them.'

'Run after . . . ? But I didn't!' Laura's colour deepened. She felt sick with shame.

'Come off it, Prentiss. Everyone noticed you making

a fool of yourself that night, dancing with your eyes closed and an idiotic smile on your face; trying to make an impression . . .'

'That simply isn't true! You have no right . . .'

'Oh, for goodness sake grow up! You started this conversation. Don't turn it into a slanging match,' Dinah said coldly. 'I can only assume that your friend Flanagan's bad manners have rubbed off on you. But I strongly advise you both to keep a civil tongue in your head from now on. It may interest you to know that my promotion to petty officer has been confirmed.' She half turned, then added as an afterthought, 'A word of advice; keep to essentials in future. I am not at all interested in your squalid little love affairs.'

As Felix flounced away down the corridor, a deep feeling of anger bubbled up in Laura, anger laced with a burning sense of injustice and humiliation. Was it true that she had made a fool of herself at the dance? Had Pierre and Dinah Felix laughed about it afterwards – out there in the garden? *Had* she seemed to be running after him? Tears stung her eyes. Whatever the truth of the matter, it didn't matter a damn now. The memory of that night had been ruined by Dinah's mockery.

'What you need, my girl, is a good night out!' Grace Flanagan made her diagnosis in that forthright way of hers which brooked no argument. 'You've been drooping round like a faded rose far too long. Oh, I know why. It must have been awful for you, seeing that launch blown out of the water. But just think, mavourneen, it would have been a hell of a lot worse if a destroyer had hit one of those bloody mines, and I reckon the guys aboard the launch would say the same if they were here.'

'Please Grace, I'd rather not talk about it.'

'So what are you going to do? Sit here in this lousy common-room, with a face as long as a fiddle? What good will that do? Now look, kid, you've got to snap out of it. So why don't we go dancing? There's a hop at the Olympia Hall tonight. You needn't dance much if you don't feel like it. At least it would be a change of scenery! But I won't go if you don't.'

'That's not fair.'

'Oh come on, Laura. We can't take the weight of the world on our shoulders.'

Laura sighed. 'Very well then. But what about Ruth?'

'Yes, well she's coming too, whether she wants to or not! Honestly, you two are worse than my kid sisters at times, the way they moan and groan when it comes to doing something positive, like washing behind their ears! So you get ready while I find her.'

Rob looked up from the book he was reading as Tim Merrydew knocked and entered his cabin.

'Just popped in to remind you, Skipper,' he said.

Rob frowned. 'Remind me?' The loss of his friends aboard the Air Sea Rescue launch, *Goldie*, had affected him more deeply than the rest of his crew. The captain, Ray Fielding, had been a close personal friend since their university days. He had no idea what Tim had come to remind him of.

'It's Jimmy's twenty-first birthday, sir. We're going

to the Olympia Hall. You said you'd come in later to join us for a celebratory drink.'

'Oh yes, Tim. Thanks. Now I remember.'

Merrydew calling him 'sir' struck Rob as a solecism. It was always 'skipper' on duty when the urgency of a mission brought them together as a team, the way he preferred it; when he wore his second 'blues', battledress jacket, and thick-knit sweater. Then his rank was forgotten by himself if not the members of his crew. Thankfully, Jimmy and the rest of the men knew that his appearance at the Olympia Hall must be on a totally different footing, that of a commanding officer proposing a toast on the coming of age of one of his crew.

'All right, flight sergeant, tell Corporal McGregor I'll be along later. Better have a shave first.'

'Sir.' Withdrawing, Tim Merrydew thought that the skipper had taken badly the loss of Ray Fielding and his crew. He'd never known Peters so cut up before. Cut up and bleeding.

Shaving, Rob thought of a bird he had owned as a boy – a canary, a tiny bundle of yellow feathers. One minute the bird had been fluttering on its perch, the next it had dropped to the floor of its cage. Picking it up he had felt a slight tremor as life departed, and then there was nothing; no movement, no heartbeat; no more song. Small things, dying, made no sound, and yet the silence after the death of that bird had seemed to him a tangible thing: total, profound, lonely and terrible. And that was how he had felt after Caroline died, and now felt about Ray Fielding and the crew of *Goldie*.

*

The Olympia Hall was decked with bunting. A glittering witchball showered brilliant flecks of light on the heads of the dancers. The band played a slow waltz; 'If I Should Fall in Love Again'. Couples moved close together, the women's heads resting on uniformed shoulders. Tears welled up in Laura's eyes. Listening to the music reminded her of the bitter sweetness of life. Soon, she thought, these men and women might be scattered to the far corners of the earth – and beyond.

She saw, in the faces of the airmen and in the eyes of the women, a kind of gallant gaiety masking the heartbreak which tomorrow might bring. Then they would look back on this night, this place, with its soft lights and that slowly revolving witchball, as a time, a place of momentary happiness.

The waltz ended, couples went back to their tables. Suddenly Grace poked Laura in the ribs. 'Hey,' she whispered, 'That flight lieutenant has just come in. He's heading for that table near the bar. Looks like there's some kind of celebration going on.'

The spillage of her drink had been an accident pure and simple, Laura realized, but the flight lieutenant had made no attempt to apologize for his part in the contretemps. He had spoken to her abruptly, sarcastically, pulling rank on her, making her feel small.

The men seated at the table rose smartly at his approach.

'Say, he's very good looking, isn't he?' Grace commented. 'And so is that corporal he's shaking hands with. I wonder what's going on. Let's drift a bit closer and find out.'

There were times when Laura could have gagged Grace.

'Look! There's a table! Come on, you two!'

With her penchant for finding out things, Flanagan might have been better off in the secret service, Laura thought mutinously as they pushed their way through the crowd.

'Yeah, it *is* a celebration! I thought so! A twenty-first birthday party! Gosh, someone should tell the band-leader. Just a sec, I'll have a word with him.'

Laura groaned inwardly. Trust Flanagan to poke her nose in. But then, Grace was Grace. Suddenly she envied her friend's easy, uncomplicated approach to life, that bubbling, infectious charm of hers which carried all before it, while she and Ruth, inhibited and self conscious, seemed destined to remain in the shadows.

And yet Ruth looked quite pretty this evening, in her pin-neat uniform, her newly shampooed hair fluffed about her cheeks, and those enormous pale blue eyes of hers dominating the finely sketched oval of her face.

When the band began to play, 'Happy Birthday', people started singing, although they hadn't a clue whose birthday it was, until Corporal McGregor stood up to take a bow. As the spotlight fell on him, the irrepressible Flanagan hurried up and planted a kiss on his cheek. 'Well, I had to do *something*,' she laughed. 'So happy birthday, whatever your name is.'

'My name's Jimmy McGregor. What's yours?'

'Grace Elizabeth Maria Flanagan.'

'You mean *you* asked the band to play "Happy

Birthday?" ' Jimmy laughed. 'Come on, then, "Irish" – let's dance!'

'OK, "Scottie", what are we waiting for?'

Grace fitted herself into the crook of Jimmy's arm. The band struck up a lively quickstep, 'That's for Me'.

Peters watched as the couple spun away. It was time for him to leave. He had done his duty; wished Jimmy well, and drunk his health. Turning away from the table, saying good night to the rest of his crew, his glance fell on the girl at the next table. The girl who reminded him of Caroline.

Possibly she had forgotten the incident at the *Lord Nelson*, but he hadn't. It had lain like a stone on his conscience ever since. Knowing that he owed her an apology, he approached the table.

'Would you care to dance?'

'No thank you. I'm not a very good dancer.'

'Then may I buy you a drink?'

'No thank you.'

'I see. Forgive my intrusion. Good night.'

Pushing through a crush of people near the swing doors, Rob wished to God he had never set foot inside the Olympia Hall. Sick at heart over the loss of Ray Fielding and his crew, he hated everything about the place; the music, the laughter, the witchball, meeting that girl again, the girl who had refused point blank to dance with him. But could he blame her?

The sound of music carried away on the wind as he walked past the Roxy cinema, the shuttered shops and houses in the town square, the municipal gardens, the *Lord Nelson*!

Dreading the thought of returning to his lonely quarters, he entered the warm, fuggy pub atmosphere.

Wiping the bar counter, the landlady smiled at him as he ordered his usual half of bitter. 'All alone tonight, are we sir?'

Her friendly remark triggered a reminder of Ray Fielding. Thank God the table in the far corner where they had often sat laughing and talking together, was occupied. He could not have borne to sit there staring at Ray's empty chair.

Perhaps it was wrong to grieve so much over the death of his friend. Possibly the pain might have been less had Ray gone out saving the lives of some bomber crew down in the Drink. To have been blown out of the water by some bloody German mine, laid under cover of darkness, seemed a wanton waste of a human life. But if Ray could speak to him now, he would say, in that calm way of his, 'Don't grieve for me. It's not what happens to us that matters so much as what we believe in.'

Since the death of his fiancée, and his best friend, Rob wasn't sure what he believed in any more.

Starry eyed with excitement, holding tightly to Jimmy McGregor's hand, Flanagan told Laura that they had been invited to join 'Scottie's' birthday celebration. 'Oh, this is Scottie, by the way,' she said breathlessly. 'Scottie, meet Laura and Ruth.'

'Pleased to meet you,' Scottie grinned. 'Come on over to our table.'

'Thanks, but I don't think . . .' Laura had a splitting headache.

'Oh, come on!' Grabbing Laura's hand, Grace led her to the next table. Ruth followed automatically.

Laura felt her head swimming as introductions were

made. Names floated together, 'Grace, Laura, Ruth, meet Tim Merrydew, Gavin Truefitt, Jock Campbell, Dick Sutcliffe, John Madden.' Someone handed Laura a glass of beer. 'By courtesy of the management,' Scottie said proudly. 'A pity the skipper couldn't have stayed a little while longer.'

'You mean that flight lieutenant who proposed your health?' Grace enquired nosily. 'But why do you call him "skipper"? I thought you were RAF types.'

'So we are,' Merrydew interposed, 'attached to the Air Sea Rescue service.'

Laura's heart missed a beat. She could still see, in her mind's eye, the *Goldie* skimming the waves, that column of water shooting skyward as the launch hit the mine: heard again the dull crump of the explosion as she had heard it so many times in dreams from which she had awakened to find her body bathed in perspiration, whimpering softly as she remembered the strewn wreckage floating on an empty sea.

As if he knew what she was thinking, Merrydew said quietly, 'We lost one of our craft recently.'

Then the band struck up a catchy quickstep: 'Six Lessons from Madam la Zonga'. Scottie held out his hand to Grace, Gavin Truefitt asked Ruth to dance, Jock, Dick, and John went in search of partners, and Laura was left alone with the coxswain.

Merrydew smiled at her across the table, 'Care for a cigarette?'

'I don't smoke.'

'You should give it a try. It does wonders for the nerves.' Opening his cigarette case, 'Have one of these.'

Reluctantly, Laura accepted; choked as the smoke went down the wrong way.

Tim laughed. 'Don't try to inhale, just draw in the smoke then puff it out again. That's the way.'

Watching her, he thought how pretty she was, how uncanny the likeness between this girl and the skipper's fiancée, whose photograph he had seen in Peters' cabin.

Having reached this conclusion, he said what lay uppermost in his mind. 'By the way, I couldn't help noticing that you refused to dance with Flight Lieutenant Peters. Would you mind telling me why?'

Startled, Laura stopped puffing at her cigarette. 'Why do you want to know?'

'I happen to like the bloke, that's all. Besides, he's had a rough time lately. The captain of the *Goldie* was a friend of his.'

'I'm sorry, I didn't know.' Laura stubbed out the cigarette. 'I saw it happen. Perhaps that's why I don't feel much like dancing.'

Tim regarded her thoughtfully. 'It's a pity you two didn't get together. You have a lot in common.'

'I don't think so. After all, he's an officer. Besides, we got off to a bad start one night in the *Lord Nelson*.'

'Is that so? I didn't realize you'd met before.'

'We didn't exactly – meet.' Laura explained the circumstances of her first encounter with Flight Lieutenant Peters. 'He was rather rude to me, as a matter of fact.'

That figured. It must have come as a bit of a shock to the skipper, coming face to face with Laura, Tim thought, offering her another cigarette.

'No thanks. I'd rather not, if you don't mind.'

'Fair enough. I can see that you are not cut out to be a smoker.' Determined to get back to the subject of Flight Lieutenant Peters, he continued, 'I've known the skipper a long time. We were at Blythe together at the outbreak of war. Then Jimmy McGregor joined the team.'

'You mean – Scottie?'

Tim laughed. 'Yeah, he seems to have made quite a hit with your friend. Jimmy's one of the best, believe me.'

Laura liked this older man with his good-natured face, who obviously cared a great deal about his comrades. 'I'm sorry if I offended the flight lieutenant,' she said, 'but I don't suppose it will make much difference one way or the other. We are hardly likely to meet again.'

The quickstep over, the rest of the party came back to the table, laughing and talking. Listening to the chatter, Laura's headache increased in intensity. Ruth was talking to her partner, Gavin Truefitt, and the other men, whose names she could not remember, had brought back with them from the dance floor three laughing girls in WAAF uniform.

Glancing at Laura, Tim Merrydew sensed her distress. Now he knew why. The poor kid! Seeing the *Goldie* blown up had obviously deeply affected her.

When the band struck up once more, a slow foxtrot this time, and the others got up to dance, he said 'I don't particularly want to stay on; if you don't, I'll walk you back to the Wrennery.'

They walked together into the darkness. Lifting her head to breathe the fresh air, Laura noticed the stars: the Great Bear, the Archer, Orion's Belt – ablaze yet mysterious in the velvet-soft chalice of the sky.

'Feeling better now?' Tim asked.

'Oh yes! Much better!'

Tucking his hand into her elbow, 'I could do with a nightcap. Would you mind if we popped into the *Lord Nelson*?'

Tim had been kind to her. She felt at ease with him; guessed that he was married, a devoted husband and father, the kind of man who would probably show her photographs of his family over a drink. She would have sooner gone straight back to the Wrennery, but to say so would seem discourteous.

'We needn't stay long,' he said with a smile, holding the door for her, playing his hunch . . . And yes, there was the skipper, sitting alone, as Tim had hoped he might be.

Hardly the right shape or size to play Cupid, he thought, grinning to himself as he made his way to the bar, but he wasn't a bad actor. His, 'Oh, good evening, sir,' had sounded quite natural. 'May I introduce a friend of mine, Laura Prentiss? Laura, this is Flight Lieutenant Peters,' even better.

Craning his neck a little, he saw that the skipper had offered Laura a seat. Great. So far, so good.

Scarcely prepared for the encounter, Peters sat down. Presumably Tim Merrydew had stagemanaged the meeting. For what purpose Rob could not imagine. Now, having played the part of liaison officer, Cupid, or whatever, he had disappeared in the direction of the bar.

A matter of an hour ago Laura had snubbed him most effectively. Not a very promising beginning. Or had the girl inveigled Merrydew into bringing her here? Perhaps that was the devious way some women's minds worked – the initial brush off followed by the subtle come on.

Then, looking across the table at her, noticing the way her hand tightened on the strap of her shoulder-bag, he dismissed his suspicions as nonsensical. The girl looked far from well, as if one harsh word might bring tears to her eyes.

Ill at ease in Peter's company, not knowing what to say to him, Laura glanced sideways at the bar, wishing that Tim Merrydew would come back, wondering why he had placed her in this impossible situation. And to think that she had trusted him.

Breaking the silence, Rob asked Laura if she would care for a drink. 'But I thought that Flight Sergeant Merrydew . . .' she began.

'Ah, here he is now.' Rob interrupted, relieved when

he saw Tim coming their way balancing a couple of glasses on a tray. 'Here we are, sir.' Merrydew said heartily setting them down, 'Half of bitter for you, skipper, and a small brandy for the lady.'

'Brandy?' Laura asked.

'I thought it would do you good,' Tim said with a meaningful look. 'Well, cheers sir. I'll get back to my pint now, if you'll excuse me.'

When Tim had gone Rob said, 'I gather that you are feeling unwell?'

'I . . . No, not really. I have a headache, that's all.'

'Perhaps you should report sick?'

'I'd rather not do that. It's nothing really.'

Remembering Caroline, he said concernedly, 'How long have you been feeling off-colour?'

Tears pricked her eyelids. 'Ever since the – accident.'

'Tell me about it.'

She said shakily, 'I was looking out of the window at the time. I saw the launch set off. I thought how wonderful it must be to skim over the water like that, heading for the open sea. A kind of freedom. And then . . .' Her hand trembled on the stem of her glass, 'I heard the explosion; saw the launch blown out of the water. One minute it was there, the next it had gone.'

Now Rob knew why Tim Merrydew had brought the girl to his table. 'I know how you feel,' he said. 'I, too, saw it happen.'

'I'm sorry, sir, I didn't realize.' She paused, not knowing the protocol – a non-commissioned Wren talking to a senior RAF officer – 'Flight Sergeant Merrydew told me the captain was a friend of yours.'

'He was. Ray Fielding and I were friends of long

standing.' Rob guessed that she felt ill at ease with him. 'Would you care for another drink?'

'No thanks. I haven't finished this one yet. To be honest, I don't want it.'

'In that case, I'll walk back with you to base.'

Panic stricken, 'It doesn't matter, sir. I'll be quite all right on my own.'

'Nonsense! Unless you'd prefer me to walk two paces behind you,' he said jokingly.

'No, of course not.' Preceding him to the door, Laura wished her legs would stop shaking.

And that, Rob thought afterwards, had been the moment when his frozen heart had begun to feel warm again, when the memory of Caroline had ceased to torment him, as if her essential sweetness had been resurrected from the ashes of the long lonely time he had spent without her.

He had known, walking Laura back to the Wrennery that night, that he wanted to see her again, to get to know her better, to make discoveries about her.

The voice of wisdom warned him not to rush things. Laura was very young, very innocent; too aware of his rank. It was this innocence of hers he found so devastating.

Walking beside her, he wondered what her reaction would be if he asked her for a date. In all probability, she would refuse. Even so, at the gates of the Wrennery, plucking up his courage, he asked her if she would care to have dinner with him one evening.

When she said yes, he walked down the hill to his own quarters with a singing feeling of relief.

He slept better that night than he had done for ages.

*

Grace, Ruth and Laura were getting ready for their respective dates.

'Here, Ruth, try a dollop of my mascara,' Grace said encouragingly, 'it'll do wonders for your eyes!'

'No, thanks.' Ruth said primly, 'my mother . . .'

'Wouldn't approve,' Grace finished the sentence for her.

Ruth coloured up. 'I suppose you think it amusing to poke fun?' She bit her lip. 'You're always poking fun at me!'

'Gosh. I didn't mean any harm! Honestly, mavourneen. I just wish you'd stop harping on about your mother all the time. After all, what's wrong with wearing makeup? What's wrong with being light-hearted? There's enough doom and gloom in the world without us adding to it.' She pulled a long face. 'Here endeth the first lesson. But take my advice, if Gavin invites you to a fish-and-chip supper, keep off your mother and Methodism as topics of conversation!'

'*Grace!*' Laura said reprovingly, not daring to laugh, thinking that if Flanagan didn't hold her tongue, poor Ruth might burst into tears and say she had decided not to go out with Gavin after all. In any delicately balanced situation, opting out – playing safe – was always a possibility, especially with girls of her own, and Ruth's retiring nature.

Laura had already begun to wish that she might be spared her dinner date with Flight Lieutenant Peters. What if the menu were in French? What if she used the wrong cutlery? Oh lord, just her luck if she made a fool of herself.

Suddenly she envied Grace Flanagan's carefree attitude to life, her lack of pretence, her down to earth commonsense. Grace, she knew, could scarcely wait to see Scottie again, with no soul-searching, no inhibitions; plunging wholeheartedly into the here and now.

But then, hadn't she come to the conclusion, after seeing the Air Sea Rescue launch blown out of the water, that only the here and now mattered a damn? What if Flight Lieutenant Peters regretted his invitation? After tonight, they would probably never see each other again.

The low-slung MG sports car had been a twenty-first birthday present from his parents, Rob explained, opening the door, making sure that Laura was comfortable. 'I brought it with me, from Cornwall, as a means of escape,' he said, slipping into the driver's seat.

'Escape? – from what?'

'Ringley, my job, the war in general,' he said lightly, engaging first gear.

'Don't you like Ringley?' Laura asked the question diffidently, afraid of appearing a fool in his eyes.

'Not much. And you?' Keeping his eyes on the road ahead.

'It's not a patch on Scarborough. That's my home.'

'Tell me about it.'

At least, Rob thought, she had stopped calling him 'sir'. Glancing at her, he saw that she was smiling.

'I'm glad you came,' Gavin held Ruth's arm. 'I had the feeling you might change your mind at the last minute.'

'If that's what you thought, I'm surprised you bothered to turn up yourself.' Ruth spoke sharply to cover her confusion. She nearly had decided not to come.

'I wanted to see you again.'

'I can't think why.' She felt an utter fool. Her first ever date, and it might be her last, the way she was going on.

'I liked you. I kinda thought you liked me.'

'I do. I wouldn't be here if I didn't.'

'Then why not relax and enjoy yourself?'

Just as well it was dark, Ruth thought, so that he couldn't see her face very clearly. It seemed so odd walking beside a man, feeling his hand on her arm, wondering what her mother would say if she could see her now. She thought miserably that Mother might as well be here, walking beside her, rigid with disapproval. Then it dawned on her why she was being so awkward, saying things she didn't mean. Her mother *was* here, putting words into her mouth. Ruth thought desperately she might as well *be* Mother, prim and unyielding, ascerbic, disapproving. And she really did like Gavin, who reminded her of Alan Ladd. Not that her mother knew that she had occasionally slipped into the one-and-nines to see Alan Ladd films when she was supposed to be doing the shopping.

Whirling round the dance-floor to Glen Miller's 'In the Mood', Flanagan knew this feeling she had, the singing, soaring sensation of happiness bubbling up inside her could mean only one thing. She was in love.

She had had many a boyfriend before but Scottie was different – lively, warm-hearted, funny, generous. She loved his looks, his smile, the way his hair quiffed up from his forehead, his accent, the way he kissed her. The only flaw in her happiness, that she might lose him. She knew this could happen at any moment in wartime – the sudden posting, the inevitable separation, the hurried goodbyes.

Looking down at Grace's sparkling face, Scottie knew that he could never let her go. He had never felt this way about a girl before. He loved her infectious gaiety, the way her eyes crinkled up at the corners when she laughed that clear as a bell laugh of hers. He had planned everything very carefully; knew exactly what he would say to her; had rehearsed his proposal beforehand. Asking a girl to marry him was something a fellow did only once in a lifetime – if he were lucky – and he wanted to get it exactly right.

Despite the war, the Carlton had maintained its reputation as the finest hotel in the Ringley area. Not that the clientele remained the same. The elderly dowagers, stoop-shouldered World-War-One colonels and brigadiers, the bishops and their ladies, and members of the golfing and fishing fraternity who had once drifted down the curving staircase to drink their pre-dinner glass of sherry were all gone now. The new clientele were mainly men and women in uniform, whose taste in drink did not include either sweet or dry sherry.

Stepping into the plum-cake rich atmosphere, Laura thought she had no need to worry about being incorrectly dressed. Apart from its lack of gold braid and shiny buttons, her uniform did not stand out like a sore thumb. She was as well dressed as the rest of the women.

They had been given a table in an alcove near the

dance-floor, and the menu wasn't in French. When Rob had ordered the wine, he said, 'Before I go any further, I owe you an apology.'

'Why?'

'It has been on my conscience ever since. That night at the *Lord Nelson*. I spilt your drink, I'm sorry. I don't normally act like a bear with a sore head.'

Laura smiled, warming to him, beginning to relax in his company, liking his looks; sensitive mouth, straight nose, the way his hair curved on to his forehead. 'It was as much my fault as yours,' she said, 'Or rather it wasn't anyone's fault. Just an accident.'

To Ruth's relief, Gavin made no attempt to winkle her into the back row of the cinema. The film was fast moving, exciting. *Destry Rides Again*. James Stewart reminded Ruth of Flight Lieutenant Peters. When she said so, during the interval, and mentioned that her friend Laura was having dinner with Peters, Gavin raised his eyebrows. 'So the skip's having a second bite at the cherry? Can't say I blame him. Your friend Laura's a very pretty girl. Funny, isn't it, that he's gone for exactly the same type?'

'I don't know what you mean,' Ruth said, mystified. 'What – same type?'

'The same type as the girl he was engaged to marry. Tim Merrydew said that Laura looked exactly like her. The poor old skipper's been carrying a torch for her ever since.'

'What happened to her, I mean your skipper's fiancée?'

'The poor kid died suddenly, a week before the wedding. Apparently she had leukaemia; cancer of the blood. Tim said her death fairly shattered Peters.'

As the lights dimmed and the Pathé news came on, Ruth found herself unable to concentrate on the screen. Gavin's words had disturbed her, although she couldn't think why.

Grasping Flanagan firmly by the elbow, Scottie hurried her across the road, through a snicket leading to the seafront, and along the promenade to the shelter he had chosen as the setting for his proposal.

'Hey, slow down! Where's the fire?' Grace wanted to know. 'Why all the rush? We've plenty of time yet! It's only half-past eleven! I don't have to be back at base 'til twelve.'

Oh God, Scottie thought. Suppose the shelter was occupied? He'd have to change his plans if it was. He couldn't very well ask Grace to marry him in front of an audience.

Of course, he might have known it. The shelter *was* occupied. The couple canoodling there drew apart in haste when Scottie blundered in, pulling Grace by the hand. 'Oh, sorry, mate,' he said, 'my mistake.' With that he wheeled round sharply, tugging Flanagan after him.

'What was all that about?' she demanded, bemused by so many changes of direction. 'There was plenty of room in there for us too! Look, do you want to kiss me or not, or are we going to spend the next half hour rushing about like a couple of maniacs?'

'No! I mean yes! Yes, I mean No! Oh hell,' Scottie wailed, 'I dinna know exactly what I *do* mean! The fact is, I – miscalculated the situation!'

'What – situation?'

'Why, asking ye tae marry me! I should've known there'd be someone else in that bloody shelter!'

Grace's heart missed a beat. 'Why? Were you going to get down on your knees?'

'Oh *hell*!' Scottie said, turning to face her, drawing her into his arms. 'No, I hadna planned tae get down on ma knees exactly, but I *had* prepared a speech.'

'And what was I supposed to do? Come over all faint and feminine? Whisper, "Darling, this is so sudden?" ' With a deep throated chuckle, Grace threw her arms round Scottie's neck. 'Of course I'll marry you. I thought you'd never get around to asking.'

'Hang on, I've got the ring here somewhere!' He began searching his pockets. 'Strewth! Don't tell me I've lost it! Och, here it is. I hope you'll like it.'

'Scottie, it's lovely!'

Serious for once in her life, Flanagan held out her left hand to receive the small cluster of diamonds.

Emerging from the cinema, 'Hey, watch your step,' Gavin said easily, slipping a protective arm about Ruth's waist. 'The pavement's a bit uneven.'

'I'm perfectly all right, thanks.'

Gavin held her closer. 'Say, look at the moon. Why don't we take a stroll in the park?'

Staring at the dark cavern beyond the municipal park gates, 'I don't think so,' she said uneasily. 'I'd better be getting back.'

'Why the hurry? You have a late pass. Or perhaps you'd rather pop into the *Lord Nelson* for a drink?'

Faced with the uninviting alternative, Ruth chose the park. Heart hammering, she heard the faint rustle of the trees. Gavin's arm tightened about her waist.

She experienced, for the first time in her sheltered life, the powerful witchery of the night, the unimagined desire that a man's touch evoked in her.

When Rob asked her to dance with him, this time Laura did not refuse.

'With the Wind and the Rain in your Hair', the song reminded Laura of spring mornings long ago; the feel of gossamer light rain on her cheeks; walking on the seashore, the wind tugging at her hair.

Looking down at her, a feeling of tenderness swept over Rob. Bending his head, 'A penny for your thoughts,' he said quietly.

'I was thinking of home.' She glanced up at him, smiling. How odd, she thought, that she had once been afraid of him.

When the music ended, they stood close together in complete silence. Then, taking her hand, Rob led her back to their table, knowing that he had fallen in love with her.

The knowledge neither surprised nor disturbed him. Loving Laura seemed as natural to him as breathing. His only regret, that a man in his position, constantly flirting with danger, perhaps even death, had no right to burden any girl with the responsibilities of marriage.

As much as he loved Laura, as much as he wanted her physically, and in every other way, he could not ask her to marry him just yet.

In any case, he thought wryly, what right had he to assume that Laura would want to marry him – now, or at any time in the future?

Ruth and Laura were getting ready for bed when Grace

burst into the cabin, too excited to keep her voice down.

'Guess what?' she cried ecstatically, 'I'm engaged! Scottie has asked me to marry him! Look!' She wafted her ring for inspection.

The other inmates of the cabin, already in bed, slipped into their dressing gowns and gathered round Grace, full of congratulations. There were cries of, 'Oh, isn't it lovely!' 'When are you getting spliced?' 'What did he say?' 'Did he get down on one knee?'

'Did he heck as like,' Grace said merrily, 'the silly so-and-so raced me uphill and down-dale so fast I scarcely knew if I was coming or going!'

'I'm so happy for you, Grace,' Laura said, hugging her.

Only Ruth seemed lacking in enthusiasm. 'But you hardly know him.'

'I know all I need to know. I'm in love with him. That's all that matters,' Grace retorted, 'and we're getting married as soon as possible.'

I I

Unable to sleep, Laura re-lived her memories of the evening.

The sound of music had floated away in the distance as they walked towards the hotel car-park. The unmistakable tang of autumn was in the air. Stars glimmered, coldly brilliant, in the dark arch of the sky. The half-moon, as yellow as a pumpkin lantern, hung suspended above the treetops; crinkled autumn leaves lay thickly on the paths. She had felt strangely uplifted, sensing that something miraculous was about to happen.

It had seemed natural to stop walking. Then Rob drew her into his arms and kissed her, tenderly touching her lips with his. Afterwards came the sensation of drifting away into another dimension. She had felt the strong beating of his heart against hers; the lean strength of his shoulders beneath his uniform jacket; his hands cupping her cheeks, pressing her temples. 'Oh, Laura,' he whispered, and then his lips were on hers once more, and the second kiss was far deeper, more searching than the first.

She remembered, too, what they had talked about over dinner; telling him funny, secret little things she had never dreamt of telling anyone before – about her visits to Wiltshire, the way she had felt in Salisbury Cathedral, as though all the people who had gone before had somehow imbued the building with the essence of holiness, of spiritual grace.

Then, afraid that she was talking too much, boring him perhaps, she had asked him about his home in Cornwall: what he had done before the war.

'Nothing very spectacular, I'm afraid. I taught English literature at a small private school near Reading, but I didn't care for the place. The Thames Valley is very lovely but I felt constricted there, as if I couldn't breathe properly away from the sea. I couldn't wait to shake the chalk-dust from my feet and get back to Cornwall during the vacations.'

His home, he said, overlooked the sea, with steps leading down to a beach where he could read for hours on end, if he felt like it. The house itself, little more than a cottage with bits tacked on to it, was invariably untidy; filled to overflowing with fishing-tackle, wellington boots, and books – masses of books, collected by his father who had owned an antiquarian bookshop. Then, when war came, when nobody wanted to buy books any more, his father had closed the shop and volunteered for the local Civil Defence Service.

'What about your mother?'

Rob laughed. 'Mum's quite a character. An artist by profession. Now she's driving an ambulance.' He paused to offer Laura more wine. 'But tell me more about your family.' And she had told him about her father taking on the fire-watching job to make ends meet, about her grandmother's rheumatism, and her cousin Meggie, whose decision to join the WAAF had not met with her parents' approval.

When Laura said wistfully, 'I feel partly to blame for that,' Rob covered her hand with his.

'I know. It's a rotten war, isn't it? But if it hadn't happened, we wouldn't be here together, and Meggie might have ended up marrying a man she wasn't in love with.'

German attacks on Allied shipping increased the workload at naval stations the length and breadth of Britain. Ringley was no exception. Messages flooded relentlessly into the teleprinter room.

The older Wrens had warned the newcomers of the dreaded 'Waterloo': morning watch followed by a week of night watches.

'Honestly, my dears, it's simply ghastly!' Daphne King, a full-bosomed Wren with enormous brown eyes and an Oxford accent, took up the thread. 'Whoever thought of it should have been keel-hauled! Just imagine, a whole week of night duties following a morning watch! And trying to sleep with all that row going on downstairs is just about impossible! We hang, "Wrens sleeping" signs on our door-handles, of course, but no-one takes a blind bit of notice. In fact, I'm sure the stewards make more noise than usual, just to annoy us. God, it's frightful the way they clang the dustbin lids when they chuck out the rubbish, and stamp up and down the corridors whistling and singing. I stuff cottonwool in my ears, but it's no use. So one goes on night watch feeling rather like a zombie.'

Laura discovered that what King had said was true. The more she tried to sleep during the day the more sleep eluded her. It wasn't just the whistling and singing and the clash of the dustbin lids that disturbed her, but the distant ringing of telephone bells, the whine and throb of aircraft overhead, and the bellowing of the Marine colour sergeant on the parade ground behind the dormitories. Besides, there was something unnatural about sleeping during the day when other people were up and doing, with daylight coming in through the edges of the drawn blackout curtains, as though one were living life the wrong way round.

And yet, inevitably, around three o'clock in the morning, when the pundits said that the human spirit was at its lowest ebb, came a thinning of the signals picked up by the wireless operators in their room across the landing, as if the Germans, too, had grown weary of the war-game at that godforsaken hour.

Then the girls took time off to spend a penny, titivate their faces in the cloakroom, gossip, drink coffee, and enjoy much needed cigarettes. During this brief respite, they would discuss their latest love affairs; what had gone wrong, and why; what he had said to her, and she to him. The unlucky ones would come to the conclusion that most men were rotters anyway, after only one thing. 'Up with the lark, to bed with the Wren', as the saying went.

It was during one such lull that Grace thought to ask Ruth how she had got on with Gavin Truefitt.

Immediately on the defensive, Ruth blushed to the roots of her hair. 'We got along quite well,' she said stiffly. Wild horses would not have dragged from her that she and Gavin had walked together in the municipal park. Grace would probably hoot with derision if she knew that.

'Got along quite well?' Grace prodded relentlessly. 'That's not saying much, is it? Come on, tell all! Did you sit on the back row of the pictures?'

'No, we did not! Gavin behaved like a perfect gentleman!'

'God, how bloody boring for you,' Daphne King remarked. 'What is he – a sky-pilot? A padre? A man of the cloth?'

Tears of humiliation welled up in Ruth's eyes. 'No, he isn't. He's a medical orderly, if you must know, if it's any of your business!'

At that moment the door banged open and a new sheaf of signals arrived via a sailor called Eddie, who thumped them down on the sorting table and beat it back to the W/T room, before the teasing began.

Poor Ruth, thought Laura, awaiting her allocation of messages. If only she could learn to laugh at herself, to dismiss awkward questions with a smile and a mysterious 'Ah, wouldn't you like to know' or, 'That would be telling.'

Thinking about it as she tapped her way through a complicated five-figure signal, Laura realized that she had learned a valuable lesson from Leading Wren Felix – never to divulge one's innermost feelings.

Thankfully, since her promotion to petty officer, Dinah had been transferred to another watch; had removed herself and her belongings to a different cabin, so that they seldom saw each other, except as ships that pass in the night and did not talk in passing.

Meanwhile, Ruth, tapping away at the next tele-printer, turning her thoughts to the film she and Gavin had seen at the Roxy, said to Laura, 'I think that Flight Lieutenant Peters looks a bit like James Stewart, don't you?'

Laura considered the question. 'No, not really. I

suppose they're about the same height, but Rob's hair is much fairer, and . . .'

Ruth appeared not to be listening. Interrupting Laura's reply, she continued, 'It must have been *awful* for him.'

Laura frowned, wishing that Ruth would shut up. 'What must? Oh Lord!' Now she had made a mistake, had hit the stuttering D key instead of the figure-five.

'Losing his fiancée. Didn't he tell you?' Ruth asked in all innocence. 'Gavin said you look exactly like her. Apparently she died a few days before the wedding and your flight lieutenant's been carrying a torch for her ever since.' She sighed deeply, then, catching sight of Laura's frozen expression, 'Is anything the matter?'

'No,' Laura said stiffly. 'I'm a bit tired, that's all. I didn't sleep very well.'

Ruth sniffed. 'Neither did I with all that noise going on.' She paused, not understanding that her careless gossip had shattered Laura's happiness. 'When are you seeing him again, by the way?'

'I'm not sure.' Laura, at that moment, wished she could run away, from this stuffy room, the sheaf of signals confronting her. God, what a fool she had been to imagine that Rob . . . that she . . . He must have been thinking of that other girl all the time, even when he'd kissed her. And she had believed, when they had talked about his family and hers, that they had somehow drawn closer together. Now she thought, that all he had done was to project a carefully edited image of himself on to the screen of life.

Perhaps, she thought dully, Ruth had been right after all in her criticism of Flanagan's engagement. What did Grace really know about Scottie when all was said and done? How easy it was to imagine one self to be in love in this spurious, reckless, wartime atmosphere, not knowing what tomorrow might bring. How easy to kiss beneath the hypnotic influence of the bright, inconstant moon, living to a heightened awareness of danger, when love seemed a kind of talisman against fear and loneliness.

That night German bombers crossed the south-east coast, wave upon wave, engines droning, to wreak havoc upon London.

Next morning came news of the worst raid so far. St Paul's Cathedral had been hit, the high altar destroyed. By some miracle, the great dome had survived the attack, that onslaught of Nazi high explosive and incendiary bombs.

Sick at heart, Laura rang home to find out if her mother had had word of Aunt Madge, Uncle Herbert and Joanne, who were not on the telephone.

Dad answered her call. Relief washed over Laura when he told her that Uncle Herbert had been in touch to say they were all safe and well. 'But what about you, Laura?' her father asked urgently, 'Are *you* all right?'

'I'm fine. You mustn't worry about me.' Her voice roughened with unshed tears. As the pips carved up their conversation, she blurted desperately, 'I love you, Dad.'

'And I love you . . .' The line went dead.

She stood there for a little while before hanging up the receiver. Love, she thought; such a simple little word, and yet it was, perhaps, the most important word in the English language. A word not spoken often enough.

Now that the time had come to meet Rob again, Laura knew she must not shirk the meeting. But this time she would remain calm, not let her emotions run away with her. Remembering Dinah Felix's remark: 'Men don't care for girls who run after them', Laura supposed that she was too naive, ready to give her heart at the touch of a hand, a smile, a kiss, taking things far too seriously. Well, from now on she had better stick to her screen heroes viewed from the safety of the one-and-nines. In any case, Rob came from a different kind of background to hers. Moreover, he had been in love . . .

Suddenly, the thought of him holding another woman in his arms, kissing her, filled Laura with a dull feeling of jealousy. What a fool he must have thought her to turn starry-eyed over an embrace which had meant little or nothing to him.

According to her fellow Wrens, all men were after only one thing. Mum had said much the same. It was this one thing that troubled Laura.

Standing alone in the deepening twilight, she wished she possessed enough courage to tell Rob to go to hell, considered asking the guard to give him a message saying she was ill.

At that moment, his MG turned the corner.

'Sorry I'm late,' he apologized, opening the door for her. 'I had a meeting with the CO.'

He had been waiting for this moment all day, seeing Laura again after her week of night watches. 'I thought we might dine at the Carlton.'

'I'd rather not.' She could not bear the thought of dancing with Rob again. Nothing in earth or heaven comes as it came before, she thought, sitting beside him, wishing that she had not been told about Rob's fiancée.

'Just as you like. Perhaps you'd prefer to dine somewhere else?'

'Thank you. I'm not hungry.'

'Fair enough. The cinema, then?' He wondered what had gone wrong, why Laura seemed so defensive.

When she turned down the cinema as an alternative, quickly making up his mind, Rob pointed the car in the direction of Marine Parade, the more affluent area of Ringley with its fine Victorian houses overlooking the harbour, and a quiet park crowning the summit of a hill – the town's highest vantage point from which, on a clear day, one could see the rugged coastline stretching from Deal to Dungeness.

This area was new to Laura. She wondered where he was taking her. As if reading her thoughts, he said, 'This is a favourite place of mine. I come here occasionally when I need to be alone. There's something so solid and comforting about Victorian architecture, don't you think? I like to imagine the days of the British Raj: the people who would have lived here in Victorian times, all those eminently respectable ladies and gentlemen parading along the esplanade on their way to Sunday service.

'There's a gem of a park up there on the hilltop, as different from the municipal as chalk is from cheese. The residents, I gather, clamped down hard on nine-hole putting greens, kiddies' paddling pool, Wall's ice-cream carts, and the like. Snobbish of them, perhaps, but I admire their sense of environment.' Drawing up at the entrance to the park he suggested, 'Let's walk, shall we?' He had his reasons for wanting to be alone with Laura in a place conducive to conversation. Whether or not this was the right time, he couldn't be sure, but he wanted to tell her about Caroline, to set things straight between them.

Darkness and trees enfolded them as they entered the park. Walking silently, allowing herself to be led, Laura felt her resolve to remain calm and aloof beginning to weaken. The touch of his hand on her arm unleashed that tide of emotion she was fighting hard to control. She knew that she had fallen in love with him. There was a feeling of strength about him which she needed. She had begun to notice and absorb little things which touched her heart with unexpected joy or pain. The way his smile lit up his face, a certain expression in his eyes which came and went so fleetingly that she could not quite capture its significance: tantalizing facets of a man she scarcely knew at all. A man she might never come to know as that other girl had done, the one he had loved enough to want to marry.

Even now, walking beside him, anchored to his side by the firm, warm clasp of his hand on her sleeve, she felt isolated, lonely, adrift on an unfathomable tide of longing. Her mother's voice came back to her: 'Never cheapen yourself, Laura,' she'd said severely. With Mum, Laura thought rebelliously, it was never what one *should* do, faced with a difficult situation, always what one should *not* do. At the time of her first period: 'Now, Laura, don't mention this to anyone else.'

Choosing what he hoped was the right moment, Rob drew Laura gently towards a deserted Victorian bandstand set among the trees. 'Let's sit down,' he said. 'I have something to tell you.'

He began hesitantly. Speaking of Caro was not going to be easy. He said, 'The first time I saw you, you reminded me of someone. Her name was Caroline Westlake. We were engaged to be married.'

Incapable of subterfuge, Laura said dully, 'I know, someone told me.'

So that was it. He might have guessed. This explained everything that had puzzled him concerning Laura's silent withdrawal, her dismissive attitude towards him. 'Was it Tim Merrydew?' he asked quietly.

'No. In any case, does it matter who told me?'

He drew a deep breath. 'No, not really. What matters is that you are upset, that you heard about Caroline from someone else when I wanted to tell you about her myself.'

'You needn't tell me about her at all,' Laura said. 'After all, why should you?'

'Oh, my dear girl!' He ran his fingers impatiently through his hair, blurting out the truth, 'Because I love you.' He had not meant to say it. Now that he had, he felt an ineffable sense of relief.

'Love . . . ?' In her wildest imaginings, this was something Laura had not dreamed possible. She should have felt elated. Instead, she felt stunned.

'I'm sorry, I shouldn't have told you. I didn't mean to. I have no reason to suppose that you feel the same way,' he said ruefully.

'Not feel . . . ? But I *do*!' She felt suddenly weak, faint with happiness. The relief was almost unbearable. Her muscles, tight with tension, suddenly relaxed. She wanted to laugh and cry at the same time, to say something important and tremendous. Instead she sat there tongue-tied, incapable of movement, looking at Rob. Then she laid her hand gently on his, and he held it tightly as if he could never bear to let go.

'Caroline and I grew up together,' he said slowly. 'Our families took it for granted that we would get married one day. We were very fond of each other.' He gripped Laura's hand more tightly. 'But, possibly because we knew each other so well, we never experienced an overwhelming passion for each other. Our marriage would have been – how shall I put it – a continuation of our lifelong friendship?'

Memories of the way it had been with Caro surged up in Rob's mind, the laughter and camaraderie they had shared since childhood days, their love of riding, swimming, sailing. Re-living the dark days of her illness, he went on, 'A few weeks before the wedding, Caroline complained of feeling off-colour. That in itself was unusual. She was normally a vivacious, happy person.'

'Don't tell me any more if you'd rather not,' Laura said, her fleeting jealousy of Caroline washed away.

'Thank you, darling, but I'd rather you heard the whole story.' He paused. 'We knew, of course, that she had consulted the family doctor. What none of us knew at the time was his diagnosis, confirmed by a Harley Street specialist. In other words, Caro didn't tell us that she had been given a short time to live. She simply said, "I think we should cancel our wedding plans until I'm better".'

'Oh Rob, I'm so sorry.'

He continued quietly, 'I was with her at the hospital

an hour before she died. Her courage was amazing. Afterwards, I felt as though a hole had been torn in my life. All this happened just before the outbreak of war. When the funeral was over, I volunteered for the RAF, received my commission, and went into the Air Sea Rescue Service. From then on it was a matter of throwing myself into my work – until that night in the *Lord Nelson* when the door opened and you walked into my life.

'At first I thought . . . In that first moment of shock, I almost convinced myself that you *were* Caroline. It was a stupid reaction. I left my drink on the bar and went out to the yard to pull myself together. When I came back, we bumped into each other, and I behaved badly. But I knew even then that I wanted to see you again . . .'

'Because I looked like Caroline?'

'Partly that,' he admitted, wanting to be entirely truthful. 'But you must believe that never, at any time since that night, have I thought of you as Caroline. I knew, when I kissed you, that my feelings for you were entirely different.'

Turning her head, she thought that this bandstand reminded her of the one in *Top Hat*, only smaller. Ginger Rogers and Fred Astaire danced briefly on the screen of memory.

'Look at me, Laura! Don't be unhappy. When the war is over, I shall ask you to marry me – if you'll have me.'

'When the war is over? Why not now, if you love me?'

It was difficult to put into words his feeling of presentiment, that he might not survive the war. If he did not, how could he bear to leave Laura a grieving widow with possibly a child to bring up? Married, he would want children, but not yet. Not until they had a reasonable future to grow up in.

'It wouldn't be fair to you, darling, that's all.'

'Is that all you have to say?'

'It's the way I feel.'

Laura said, 'Married or not, it won't make any difference to the way I'll feel whenever you leave harbour.'

12

Standing in the potato field, shading her eyes against the bright October sunlight, Meggie watched the convoy of tanks as it rumbled towards the village.

A platoon of soldiers, detailed by the War Ministry to help with the harvest, straightened their backs and hallooed derisively as the procession of armed monsters roared past, raising clouds of dust, shaking the ground, scarring the chalky road beneath their tracks.

A week ago, posting a letter to Laura, Meggie had listened to the complaints of the elderly postmistress, Clara Hedley, that one of 'they tanks', bound for Salisbury Plain, had flattened the sunflowers growing in her unfenced front garden, and had come close to flattening herself when she rushed out to see what was happening.

'I suppose my flowers didn't matter tuppence to them,' Clara said tearfully, 'but they mattered to *me*! I grew those sunflowers from last year's seed, and they measured nine inches across.'

Meggie knew exactly how the old postmistress felt. This war had brought out the worst in some people. Even quiet villages like this had suddenly become battle-grounds.

Yesterday, everyone in Hazelwitch had turned out to attend the funeral of three evacuee boys from

London, killed outright when a German plane had dropped a stick of bombs near the schoolhouse. And to think that those kids had been sent here for safety.

Standing silently beside the communal grave, listening to the parson intoning the words of the burial service, a burning sense of anger had welled up in Meggie, a strong feeling of injustice that the war had taken the lives of those children, that the senseless killing, and the despoilation of the land itself, had brought the war closer to home. The school she had attended as a child now lay in ruins, and bomb craters scarred the fields awaiting the sowing of next year's harvest. Ugliness and sudden death had replaced beauty and the quiet continuance of daily life in a place where most people died simply because they were too old to go on living any longer.

The past few weeks had been anything but pleasant for Meggie, faced with her parents' disapproval and Fred Briggs's hostility when she had announced her intention of joining the WAAF.

Thankfully, she had received word that she had been accepted for service, sent a travel warrant and been told to report to York on the 27 October, to begin her training as a cook.

At least, Meggie thought, watching the tanks pass by, she would be doing something she liked and was good at. As for Fred Briggs . . . come to think about it, she had never cottoned on to him even as a schoolgirl. He had always been a bully, chasing smaller boys in the playground, pulling the girls' pigtails and pinching their bottoms. She must have been mad to even consider going to the pictures with him; had done so, perhaps, because she was tired of being teased over not having a boyfriend. To be fair to her parents, they must have felt relieved when Fred had started taking her out, pleased at the prospect of her becoming an asset rather than a liability, a means of settling the continual wrangles over the stream that knotted itself in queer convolutions between the two farms, which Fred's father reckoned was his by right.

When Fred heard that Meggie had been to Devizes to enquire about joining up, the stream had assumed the importance of the Suez Canal. 'Right, my girl,' he blustered, 'you've made me look a right fool, but your dad will look a bigger fool when my father starts charging him for the use of the water. Or mebbe he'll tek it into his head to throw a dam across it. A right mess you'll be in then!'

Hating the gloating expression on Fred's flabby face, Meggie said coolly, 'Oh yes? Well think on, Fred Briggs. If your father starts making life awkward for us, I'll make it awkward for *you*. I happen to know that you haven't complied with the new slaughtering regulations, so you needn't start playing silly beggers with me!'

'Why, you rotten little bitch! Huh, and to think I might have made the mistake of marrying you! Mind you,' he added nastily, 'my dad was never in favour of that idea from the start. "Why choose a plug-ugly lass like her," he said, "when you could take your pick of the girls?" And he was right. I could take my choice of any girl in the village, at the drop of a hat!'

'Could you, Fred? Could you *really*?' Meggie viewed the situation clearly at last. 'You never had any intention of marrying me, I know that now. You made your mistake when you thought that a plug-ugly girl like me would be glad to drop her knickers for you. Well, you were wrong. I may not be very good-looking, but I'm not soft in the head. That's why I'm joining up, to get away from you. In any case, I wouldn't marry you, Fred Briggs, if you were the last man on earth. And *you're* no oil painting either, so clear off!'

Later, in her bedroom, she had stared earnestly at her reflection in the swing mirror, laid her head on her arms, and wept. What Fred said was true. She *was* ugly: overweight, with crooked front teeth, frizzy hair, and broken fingernails from all that potato lifting.

Even so, despite her physical defects, she felt cleansed now that she had sent Fred Briggs about his business. And then she thought, drying her eyes, Laura still loved her; soon she would be doing a job of national importance, and daresay there'd be lots of other fat, plug-ugly girls in the Women's Auxiliary Air Force, too.

In any event, it was too late to withdraw. The die was cast. She had made her decision. If only she could feel certain that her parents understood her urgent need to make a new life for herself far away from Fred Briggs. But that was hardly likely since she had never told them how much she disliked him. They simply thought that she was being awkward and bloody-minded, wanting to leave home for no good reason; leaving them in the lurch at this crucial time of the year with the fruits of last year's toil being harvested and next year's harvest about to be sown.

One bright spot lay in the fact that she would be able to visit her Uncle Will and Aunt Mary occasionally. York wasn't all that far from Scarborough. Perhaps she'd be able to get there by bus on her day off. As for Fred's threat that his dad might dam the stream, Meggie knew she had nipped that crack-brained notion in the bud. Fred and his father were up to their eyes in the black market: killing more than their quota and selling the meat to butchers' shops as far afield as Bristol and Exeter. She knew because Fred had got drunk in the village pub one night and started bragging about his nefarious activities to one of the young soldiers billeted here, a decent lad, Johnny Smith, who had told her quietly about his conversation with Fred and asked her what she thought he ought to do about it.

'You must do whatever you think best,' Meggie replied seriously, liking his looks, admiring his honesty, wishing that he, not Fred Briggs, had taken her to the pictures to see *Wuthering Heights*. They had been standing knee-deep in potatoes at the time. 'I'll be leaving home soon. You know I've joined the WAAF?'

'Yeah. Can't say I blame you. This isn't exactly women's work, is it?' He smiled sympathetically. 'I know girls are joining the Land Army these days and doing a good job, but you are worth something better than lifting bloody potatoes all day long. I beg your pardon, I didn't mean to swear, it just slipped out. Well, thanks for listening, I'll give the matter some thought. I can understand why you might not want to be involved. Someone told me that you and Fred Briggs are going out together.'

'Are you – going – with anyone?' Meggie asked wistfully. 'Anyone special, that is?'

'Well, yes and no,' he said awkwardly, wiping the sweat from his forehead with his left hand. 'Her name's Mavis, but I don't know exactly where I stand with her, though she writes to me occasionally. She's in the ATS.'

'Are you in love with her?'

Johnny grinned. 'I don't know for sure. I might be if she'd stand still long enough for me to find out.'

'Is she – pretty?'

'Yes. Too pretty for her own good, if you want my opinion, and that worries me. I mean, what would a girl as pretty and attractive as she is, want with a chump like me? Well, I'd best be getting back to work.' He added, as an afterthought, 'Say, Meggie, I don't suppose *you'd* care to write to me once in a while? I'd kinda like to keep in touch. Not that I'd want to put Fred Briggs's nose out of joint if you two are serious about one another.'

'We're *not*,' Meggie replied huffily. And that was that. Johnny had gone back to his potato lifting; she had gone back to the farmhouse to help her mother cook the evening meal, and he had made no further mention of letter writing, which added up, Meggie supposed, to the fact that he hadn't been serious about it in the first place.

That night, after supper, she had gone alone to the pictures to see Robert Donat and Greer Garson in *Goodbye, Mr Chips*, a film she had seen twice before, a tender love-story of which she imagined herself to be the heroine. Greer Garson was so beautiful, standing on the deck of that steamer looking down into the dirty River Danube which only lovers saw as blue.

Tears filled Meggie's eyes. She didn't even trouble to wipe them away surreptitiously this time as she usually did, but allowed them to flow down her cheeks when Greer Garson looked down at the river and murmured, 'But, Flora dear, it *is* blue.'

Grace had received a letter from her mother which she tossed aside in disgust. 'Blow that for a lark,' she muttered, tucking into a bowl of lumpy porridge. 'Scottie and I have made our plans, and I intend sticking to them!'

'Why, what's happened?' Laura went on buttering a slice of caught toast, scraping off the burnt bits.

'Ma's kicking up a fuss about my getting married, playing pop 'cos she and dad haven't met Scottie. Huh, I know what's upsetting dad's apple cart. Scottie isn't a Catholic. I thought Ma would throw a fit on the telephone when I told her I was engaged. Now she knows I'm getting married in a registry office the balloon's really gone up. She says in the letter that I'm to have a proper wedding with bridesmaids, and a reception at the church hall.'

Pushing aside her empty porridge dish, Grace set about demolishing a plateful of bacon and fried bread. 'I know what's on her mind. She thinks I'm rushing to get married because I've something to hide – something that wouldn't stay hidden for very long, if you see what I mean.' Flanagan grinned. 'She thinks Scottie's "deflowered" me. If only she knew . . .'

'Knew what?'

'Never mind. I'll tell you one of these days. Hey, this bacon's salty. Ugh, the food here gets worse instead of better.' Grace pulled a face and returned to her theme. 'Ma just doesn't understand that Scottie and I don't want to hang about to get married. The sooner we get spliced the sooner we'll be able to find a place of our own to live.'

Laura swallowed a mouthful of tea to take away the taste of the toast. 'You mean you'd be allowed to do that?'

'Yeah, sure. Married couples are given special permission to live together, off duty. Scottie and I have looked at a couple of places already. There's one we particularly like, a flat in the town square. It isn't very big, just a bed-sitting room, kitchen, and use of bathroom, but the furniture's not bad, and the landlady seemed nice. Said we could have it if we wanted, after we're married, as long as we can show her a copy of our marriage licence. She didn't exactly say, "No hanky-panky on my premises," but that's what she meant. So you see why we want to do the deed as quickly as possible? Say, hand me a slice of bread, please, to sop up this dip.'

If Rob and I got married, we might have a place of our own, Laura reflected wistfully. The thought of waiting until the war was over, depressed her.

'You've got a funny look on your face,' Grace remarked. 'Is anything the matter?'

'Well yes, but I can't talk about it now.'

'Fair enough. What say we have tea together this afternoon after squad drill? We could go to that café in the town square. They might even have some home-made scones if we get there before the crush starts.'

'Sorry dear. We hadn't enough fat to make scones today,' the elderly waitress-cum-part-owner of the Blue Bird Tea Shoppe told Flanagan. 'But we could

163

make you some toast, couldn't we Sybil?' poking her head through the serving-hatch.

The invisible Sybil's voice floated back to them. 'Yes dear, and we have plenty of plum jam.'

'Right. We'll have toast and plum jam then. Come on, Laura, let's grab those seats near the window.' Flanagan, as usual, led the way, this time to a blue-tiled table on which stood a small vase of purple asters. 'God, I'm ready for a sit down, my feet are killing me! Hey, wasn't it a hoot when that Marine colour sergeant told us to halt, and we all concertinaed together when that silly cow, Daphne King, didn't quite catch what he said and stopped dead in her tracks to say, "Pardon?". No wonder he turned blue in the face, the poor man! Bet he's praying to God he won't be in charge of us at the Victory Parade!'

'You think we are going to win this war, then?'

'I sure as hell do!' Grace looked surprised. 'Why, don't you?'

'Yes, of course. It just seems to be going on such a long time.'

'What's eating you, Laura?' Grace puckered her forehead. 'You can tell me. I know I act daft at times, but I'm not really. Are you in love? Is that it?'

'Yes.' Laura needed to tell someone.

'Flight Lieutenant Peters? I thought so. And – he's not in love with you?'

'Yes, but he doesn't want to get married until the war's over.'

'Did he give you a reason?'

'Something about it being unfair to me!'

'Well, I admire his concern. He's obviously a caring bloke, but I can't quite follow his reasoning. If you're in love, the tension's going to be there anyway. It's the same for me and Scottie. Do you imagine that we haven't thought about it, too? If that bloody launch of theirs got blown up, you and I would be in the same boat! Sorry, I wasn't trying to be funny. I've never been more serious in my life. The only difference, if that happened, Scottie and I would have made the most of our time together.'

'Then you believe that being married is the best that life has to offer?'

'Yes. Don't you?'

'I don't know. My mother doesn't seem to think so. I have the feeling that she and my father never . . .'

'Enjoyed sex?' Flanagan said bluntly. 'Well, some people don't, but I'm not one of them! Remember our conversation at breakfast? I said I'd tell you something one of these days. Well, I lost my virginity when I was sixteen. His name was Tony Marshall. We'd been to a dance together, had had a drop too much to drink. We did it in a railway compartment with the blinds drawn.' She shrugged her shoulders dismissively. 'I'm not proud of it. Now I'm in love with Scottie, I wish it had never happened, but it did, and I liked it. Mind you, I worried myself sick afterwards, wondering if Tony had made me pregnant, knowing that my father would take a strap to me if he had. I lived in a state of nerves until my next period arrived.' She smiled suddenly. 'Funny, you're the first person I've ever told. Odd, isn't it?'

'Why – odd?'

'Well, let's face it mavourneen, you're not exactly the forward hussy type, are you? The kind who enjoys stripping off your clothes; not like Blodwen Thomas, for instance. I could tell by your face, that first night at Armley House, that you'd never had sex. Remember when she started on about having had "it" four times in one night? I gained the impression that you weren't even very clear what "it" entails. I guess you still don't. Am I right?'

Laura nodded.

'I thought so. Bet your ma never told you the facts of life. Well, neither did mine, which is why I decided to find out for myself. But you can take it from me, kid, that sex, properly done, with the right person, must be pretty darn wonderful.'

A platoon of soldiers marched into view at that moment, arms swinging, forage caps correctly tilted, accompanied by a young subaltern: boots ringing on the cobbles, obviously on manoeuvres by the amount of gear they carried with them. From where she was sitting, Laura could see the houses of Marine Terrace; church spires probing the sky, the crown of trees which marked the Victoria Park. Everything looked different by day, more clear cut and prosaic. Night held the mystery, the romance, the magic. Darkness, stars, the moon.

Talking about sex – an ugly word – had little bearing on the way one felt in the darkness, the almost unbearable longing, seeking, striving, yearning. Never would she regret falling in love with Rob. Regret lay in the thought of unfulfilment if their time on earth ended suddenly; never to have experienced the full measure of love for some altruistic motive beyond her power to understand or accept. Flanagan was right when she supposed that she had no clear idea what the act of love entailed. Fed on half truths, blinkered by her mother's uncompromising attitudes towards love and marriage, she remembered, as a child, that day on her Uncle Bob's farm; being dragged away by her mother when a massive, lumbering boar was being led to the pigsty. Intrigued and curious, she had never understood the reason why she was hustled away so roughly or her mother's words: 'I won't have you watching that kind of thing. It isn't decent!'

What kind of – thing? Meggie had told her later, in bed, that her father had brought the boar over from a stud farm, near Salisbury, to make the pig have babies. They were very young at the time, speaking in hushed voices.

But why had Mum made such a mystery of the whole affair? Why hadn't she taken the chance of explaining the facts of life to her then? Now, because of her hidebound attitude towards sex, she had imbued her own daughter with a feeling that love was not a natural instinct at all, but something of which to feel ashamed, something – indecent. So what would Mother say if she knew that she had fallen in love?

It seemed wrong, to Laura, that she felt closer to Grace Flanagan than her own mother.

13

The air-raid siren wailed its third warning of the night; the wafer-thin mattress of the bed-chair had ridged, like sand, beneath Will Prentiss's back. If this war went on for very much longer, he too would be seeking the pain-killing properties of wintergreen lotion. Inching forward between the chair's confining arms, he felt for his torch and called to Sid Bumby, his fire-watching partner, to wake up.

'Christ! Not again!' Bumby, a truculent individual at the best of times, scrambled up and reached for his tin-helmet, cursing the bloody Jerries who never gave a man a minute's peace. Listening with half an ear, Will thought how different the store seemed at night – empty, echoing, eerie. He felt suddenly lonely and vulnerable stuck up here in this cold eyrie near the roof. The thought crossed his mind, as he fumbled his way to the fire-escape door, that he was too old for this job, and yet he owed it to Mary to make certain they had enough money for rent and rates. His earnings from hairdressing would scarcely keep them in shoe-leather these days.

A sudden blast of wind almost snatched his breath away as he pushed open the door and stared into the pitch blackness. Shivering in the brittle November air, he saw, in the far distance, beams of light criss-crossing the sky near Flamborough Head. Strangely, he drew comfort from those anti-aircraft beams combing the darkness. Bumby, as usual, was keeping well back, stamping his feet, moaning about his lack of sleep, embarking on his well-worn theme, what the hell would they do if the place went up in smoke? Will's patience snapped. 'We'll have to do the best we can. That's what we're paid for.'

Since Laura went away, Will's world had narrowed like diseased arteries. Mary provided little comfort when he came home to snatch a couple of hours rest before starting his day's work. Customers may be fewer but they still needed his attention; deserved the best he had to give. If Mary only realized that what he wanted most, after long uncomfortable spells of duty, was a smile, a word of sympathy, the touch of her hand in his. But he knew, by the hunching of her shoulders beneath the bedclothes, that she feared, as she had always done, his invasion of her body. He tried to make allowances, knowing she was going through a difficult time for a woman. Would things have been different, better between them had he not, on their honeymoon, somehow disgusted her with his ardour? He should have been more patient, more forbearing. It had never occurred to him that a bride, on her wedding night, would not want the physical proof of her husband's passion.

The hairs at the nape of his neck began to prickle. The sound was unmistakable, the irregular droning beat of approaching enemy aircraft.

The explosions happened with shattering suddenness. In a split second Will realized that the German planes, returning from some inland bombing mission, nearing the coastal anti-aircraft batteries, about to run the gauntlet of those probing searchlights, had jettisoned their left-over bombs haphazardly before heading out to sea.

'*Christ!*' Pale and shaken, Bumby backed further down the fire-escape stairs. 'The buggers! The bloody buggers! Let's get downstairs. I'm not staying up here on this bloody roof.'

'For God's sake, pull yourself together!' Will was thinking of Laura, when a whistling sound filled the air, faint at first, then becoming louder, more terrifying, akin to a shrill human scream of anguish as the bombs came hurtling down. He thought I am going to die. There was nowhere to run to, nowhere to hide. Strangely, he experienced no sensation of fear or regret. He simply stood there waiting, as if frozen, his eyes fixed on the searchlight beams raking the darkness, and began praying. 'Our Father . . .'

It was like being back in the trenches: hearing the roar and thunder of the guns; the whine and crump of exploding shells about his ears, so that the world seemed filled with nothing but sound and fury as the shells ripped through the darkness. God, it was dark. Why was everything so dark? Where was he? He tried to move his legs, found that he could not. He was trapped and yet he could hear voices, hoarse voices, a long way off. He made a scrabbling, crab-wise exploratory movement with his right hand, and tried to call out. The voices were coming closer. Staring into the pitch darkness, he saw faint, wavering blobs of light, like Jack-o-Lanterns. Tears coursed down Will's cheeks.

Grace and Scottie had finalized their wedding

arrangements, and the landlady had agreed to reserve the flat for them even without sight of their wedding lines. By this time Mrs Dalton had become swept up in the romance of the situation; almost motherly towards the bride-to-be when she realized that her house was not to be a hole-in-the-corner meeting place after all. A pillar of the local Methodist Church, a thin, brisk widow whose husband had been 'taken' during the Great War, Mrs Dalton possessed one secret vice, a passion for romantic fiction; tales of starry-eyed heroines and strong, silent heroes, which she borrowed weekly from the Ringley public library, taking a quick, furtive glance over her shoulder to make sure that no-one was watching when she shuffled the books onto the counter to be stamped. Now a real-life romance seemed far more interesting than any amount of fiction, especially since Grace had confided, with that bubbling charm of hers, that she was flying in the face of her Catholic upbringing to marry the man she loved.

They were having tea at the time, in Mrs Dalton's sitting-room, surrounded with heavily-framed photographs of the late Arthur Dalton, in and out of uniform, hand-embroidered texts, and a plethora of ornaments – presents from Cromer, Southend-on-Sea, the Cheddar Gorge, Bonnie Scotland . . .

'My hubby and I were great travellers, in our time,' May Dalton explained, starry-eyed with her memories of the modest holidays she and Arthur had spent together in what seemed to her far-flung outposts of the British Empire. 'Have another piece of cake, dear. It's home-made. Arthur was always so fond of my home-made cakes.'

'Thanks, I will! It's really delicious. So you don't mind if Scottie and I bring round a few more of our wedding presents? The girls of No. 4 watch have given us silver coffee spoons, and a cut-glass vase . . .'

'Your parents, and Scottie's, *are* coming to the wedding, I suppose?' Mrs Dalton interrupted wistfully. 'I mean, it would seem such a pity if . . .'

'Oh, yes, they're coming right enough,' Grace assured her, biting into the cake. 'I've been running round like a scalded cat, these past few days, fixing up accommodation.' She pulled a wry face, 'And to think that Scottie and I wanted a quiet wedding.'

'Ah yes, but you seem to forget that a girl's wedding day is the most important day of her life, an occasion to be shared, at least it used to be. *I* was married in white, for instance, at the Lime Street Methodist Church. Just before the outbreak of the First World War, that was. I shall never forget, until my dying day, the way Arthur looked at me as I walked down the aisle.' She sighed deeply, 'But things are different now, I suppose.'

'Yes, I suppose they must be,' Grace admitted, wishing that the wedding was over and done with, longing for the moment when she and Scottie would be alone together. Nothing else mattered. She could not have cared less about the wedding ceremony, the joining of hands, the exchange of rings. All she wanted was the feel of Scottie's arms about her in the long hours of the night: to give herself to him, body and soul; to blot out the rest of the world; to live for today, forget about tomorrow.

*

Laura's eyes met Rob's across the crowded room.

'To the bride and groom.'

They raised their glasses of sherry.

The girls of No. 4 watch had formed a guard of honour outside the register office. People had stopped to watch as Grace and Scottie received their full complement of confetti.

Honouring the toast, Laura felt that the old Grace Flanagan had somehow slipped away from her, that a far more mature person had taken her place.

Eyes shining, skin aglow, holding on to her husband's arm, it seemed as though Grace and Scottie were somehow set apart in a world of their own, beyond the clamouring crowd of well-wishers.

Deeply aware of Rob's presence, Laura thought how wonderful it would be if they, too, might slip away together . . .

But perhaps he did not love her enough to take a chance, a calculated risk of happiness, however fleeting, based upon the belief that they would survive this war, as Grace and Scottie had done.

'Laura! Is that you?' Painfully, Will Prentiss opened his eyes.

'No. I am Ward Sister Dawson. Just lie still, and try to relax. You are quite safe now, and your wife is here to see you, but try not to talk too much.'

Pat Dawson held back the curtains about his bed as his wife rustled through, holding a handkerchief to her eyes. Christ, she thought angrily, what on earth was the bloody woman up to, worrying the poor man with money problems at a time like this? The woman he referred to as Mary. So who was Laura?

Whoever she was, Pat decided, she must be sent for immediately.

Shakily, Laura replaced the receiver. Beside herself with worry, she went along the corridor to the duty office. Felix was not there. So where the hell was she?

The office telephone shrilled suddenly. Dinah emerged from the inner office.

'Please, Dinah,' Laura blurted, as she picked up the receiver, 'I must speak to you! It's very urgent!' Anger bubbled up in Laura as Dinah took her time answering the call. She could have throttled the girl with her bare hands.

Her father lay desperately ill in hospital. He may be dying, and all Dinah Felix could do was burble away on the telephone. Well, to hell with Felix! To hell with the Women's Royal Naval Service! She intended going home to see her father, and no power on earth could stop her!

'Just a minute, Prentiss! You said you wanted to speak to me. What about? And must I remind you that if you wish to speak to me, you should refer to me by my proper title?'

'Don't you understand, I must go home!'

'There is no "must" about it. You will fill in the usual request for compassionate leave, then it is up to the first officer to decide. I suggest you calm down, Prentiss, and stop behaving like an hysterical child. Nothing can be done now, in any case. Report to the duty office first thing in the morning.'

Grace and Scottie had been on honeymoon two whole days, and it hadn't stopped raining. Not that they cared. The hotel was warm, comfortable, not too expensive and owned by friends of Rob Peters who had recommended it to his wireless operator. 'I think you'll like it there,' he said. 'It's on the promenade, facing the sea, and there's a dance-floor. Of course things may have changed since I last stayed there, but the Lansings still keep hens, and they grow their own vegetables. I think you'll find it a perfect place for a honeymoon.'

'Thanks, sir. It sounds just the job.'

Despite the rain, he and Grace had been out walking; had wandered down to the harbour, hand in hand, to watch the cobles come in, and leaned on the railings to look at the sea washing up on the deserted beach. The skipper was right, Scottie thought happily, this was a perfect place for a honeymoon; the Lansings perfect hosts, providing late breakfast for himself and Irish; plenty of eggs and bacon, toast and marmalade. The war might be on another planet. He had never believed such happiness was possible. As for Grace, his funny, beloved Irish . . . he had never imagined that she would give herself to him so fully, with not a trace of shyness, that she would respond so eagerly to his lovemaking.

Knowing Rob Peters well, the Lansings naturally wanted to know how he was faring. On the first night, after dinner, Mrs Lansing, who happened to be in the bar serving drinks when Grace and Scottie went in for a nightcap, brought up the subject of Flight Lieutenant Peters. 'He and his fiancée intended to come here on their honeymoon,' she said. 'Of course, they had often been here before, just for weekends. Miss Westlake was a lovely girl. My husband and I were shattered

175

when she died so suddenly, and so was Rob. He wrote to us, cancelling the honeymoon. I still have that letter.'

Later, in the bedroom, Grace said reflectively, 'I hadn't the heart to tell Mrs Lansing that Rob has fallen in love again. What beats me is, why is he hanging back? Did you notice the way he and Laura looked at each other at our wedding reception? So why won't he marry the girl?'

'I don't know,' Scottie said seriously. 'The skip's a funny kind of bloke, at times; kind of twisted up inside as if he knew . . .'

'Knew – what?' Grace asked, half afraid.

'Oh, nothing!' He smiled suddenly, 'Do you realize that you haven't kissed me for the past half hour?' He drew his wife into his arms, and buried his face in her hair. 'Know what? You smell of oatmeal soap and fresh air!'

'Huh,' Grace kidded, 'so why did I waste my money on that bottle of "Evening in Paris" perfume?'

14

The week that followed seemed to Laura like an out of sequence movie; a compacted space of time in which she moved through a surrealist, fog-bound landscape.

Sitting in a crowded railway compartment, staring out at the fields and trees shrouded in a thick November mist, she thought about her father; could almost feel his hands, firm and warm, holding on to her the day she took her first donkey-ride, ready to catch her if she happened to fall.

His touch had given her confidence. 'Gee-up, Neddy,' she'd cried gleefully, grasping the reins. Then dad had laughed up at her as the donkey trotted away, and walked beside her, one hand lightly on the saddle, just in case . . .

Rob had seen her off at Ringley Station. She had telephoned his quarters early that morning to say she had been granted a week's compassionate leave. She knew he must have moved heaven and earth to be there, to make sure she had everything she needed for the long journey home – her travel warrant, chocolate, magazines. It was he who suggested sending a telegram saying she was on her way home.

They clung together at the last moment, and she watched his tall figure gradually diminishing as the distance between them lengthened.

There was no-one at Scarborough station to meet her. She had scarcely expected there would be. The fog seemed even thicker near the coast, and the town lay blanketed beneath what the inhabitants euphemistically termed a sea-fret.

Picking her way from the station in the foggy darkness, scarcely able to see her hand in front of her, Laura worried about her father.

Her mother's greeting was perfunctory. 'Gran and I are going to the hospital,' she said. 'The taxi will be here in a few minutes.' She added, ungraciously, 'I suppose you'd better come with us.'

What had upset Mum? Something obviously had. Laura watched, frowning anxiously as her mother banked down the fire, put up the guard, hustled Nell through to the kitchen, and pinned on her hat.

If she lived to be a hundred, she would never forget the smell of the place; a queer, sickly smell compounded of, what, she scarcely knew. Disinfectant? Cooking? Death?

Hospitals were depressing at the best of times, even worse in wartime and winter; wreathed in mist, with blacked out windows.

Walking with Gran, she tucked her arm into the crook of the old lady's elbow to help her up the stairs, while Mary forged ahead, a ramrod figure in her brown coat and hat, her shoulders rigid with disapproval. Of what? Laura wondered. She soon found out.

Their entrance to the Haldane Ward was barred by the slim figure of the ward sister. 'I'm sorry, Mrs Prentiss,' she said coolly, 'but I cannot possibly allow my patient three visitors at a time.'

'Your patient, indeed!' Mary Prentiss retorted. 'May I remind you that I am his *wife*?'

'Frankly, Mrs Prentiss, I couldn't care less if you were the Queen of England! Is this your daughter? If so, she had better come with me. I'm sure you ladies won't mind waiting in the corridor.'

As the swing doors closed behind them, the ward sister smiled, 'Your name's Laura, isn't it? Sorry about that, but your father's been asking for you. Mind you, no questions, no soul-searching, is that clear? I don't want him upset.' A pause. 'When did you last eat, by the way?'

'I had some toast for breakfast; chocolate on the train.'

'Been travelling all day?'

'Yes. I left Ringley at eight o'clock this morning.'

'Not about to pass out, are you? Not thinking of bursting into floods of tears?'

'No, I don't think so.'

'Good girl.' A warm, sympathetic smile; the squeak of rubber-soled shoes on the lino. 'He's going to be all right, you know. Your father is going to pull through. He's still a bit hazy after the operation, but his heart is strong and he's responding to treatment.' A hand on her arm. 'Don't expect a miracle, that's all. He's had a pretty rough time. OK?'

Will opened his eyes at the sound of her voice. 'Laura? Is that you?' He held out his hand to her.

'I came as soon as I could,' she said, holding his hand.

'You look tired, love.'

'No, I'm not tired. I'm fine.'

Sitting beside him, she scarcely knew what to say to

him, her own father. She knew what she wanted to say – how much she loved him. It was then she noticed the tiny crop of threadveins beneath the surface of his skin, the grey hairs at his temples, the fine network of worry lines about his eyes, the ash-grey stubble of his beard.

'Is it raining out?' he asked. She nodded. He smiled. 'I thought so. Remember how we used to walk together in the rain when you were a little girl?'

'Yes, Dad. I remember.'

'They thought we were barmy, didn't they, your mum and gran, when we went walking in the rain?'

'Gran's here with Mum,' she said. 'They're waiting in the corridor.'

'Oh, I wonder if Mother thought to bring my shaving tackle. I feel a bit rough.'

So much for those Hollywood movies, Laura thought, in which bedside reunions took place to soft background music played on violins. There was nothing in the least romantic about the stubble on a man's face when he needed a shave.

Her father said hoarsely, 'I thought I was going to die. Funny, I wasn't afraid.'

Tightening her clasp on his hand, 'Don't think about that, Dad. The ward sister said you mustn't . . .'

The curtains about his bed billowed out suddenly with the force of her mother's entry.

The scene remained fixed in Laura's memory; her mother's angry face; the ward sister's restraining hand on her arm. Then the briefly held image faded. Laura got up from her chair, kissed her father and walked down the ward and through the swing doors to where her grandmother was waiting, chewing her false teeth, saying, 'I tried to talk sense to her, but she wouldn't listen. Oh no, off she went, like a mad woman. Eh, I don't know. As if things weren't bad enough! I mean, that night of the air raid, I've never been so frightened in all my life! We heard those bombs coming down. Whistling bombs, they were. I thought my end had come. The house fairly shook. I was shaking, too, I might tell you. Just to think, if they had landed a bit nearer, we might all have been killed. I wish now I had been. The way things are, I'm nowt but a nuisance. I'd be better off dead.'

'Don't, Gran! Oh, please, *don't*!'

Laura scarcely remembered the journey home. On their return, Nell licked her hands in a frenzy of delight; Mum stalked backwards and forwards from the kitchen to the living-room, clattering plates, cups and saucers on to the table. No-one spoke; there was only the sound of rain on the windows, the spurting of the coal in the grate, until Gran, tired of holding her tongue, blurted, 'If you think I'm eating *that* stuff, you've got another think coming! *Brawn!* Ugh! You know how much I hate it!'

'All right, Gran, *you* do the shopping from now on,' Mary said. 'If you think you can manage better than me on the money I have coming in these days, you go ahead and try!'

'Yes, well, I may be old and decrepit, but I wouldn't have done what you did tonight! Making a damn fool of yourself! You're a stupid woman, Mary, causing all that fuss and bother. Well, I'd have had more pride.'

'You dare talk to me about pride? I had no intention of letting that jumped-up ward sister get the better of me! I shall write a letter of complaint to the hospital authorities first thing in the morning!'

'More shame on you, then! The woman was only doing her job. I quite liked her, as a matter of fact. What's her name? Ward Sister Dawson? You lost your temper with her, but she didn't lose hers. Did you notice, Laura? I could have laughed my hat off when she said she couldn't care less if you were the Queen of England! Served you right! *That* took some of the starch out of your pinny . . .'

Lying in bed, Laura wondered how she would be able to survive her week's compassionate leave with Mum and Gran at each other's throats all the time. Loneliness engulfed her. She missed Rob.

Rain pattered on the windows. Getting up, she drew back the curtains. Not a glimmer of light anywhere. Thoughts tumbled through her mind disjointedly.

What if those bombs *had* fallen nearer the town centre? What if the blast which had blown in shop windows in Westborough, the shell splinters that had holed the roof of Barry and Jackson's store, trapping her father beneath a welter of slates and timber, had landed squarely on this house? What if her family had been wiped out, if there had been no house to come back to, if this room of hers, along with all the other rooms, and the staircase, had simply collapsed in a heap of smouldering rubble?

Her mind seemed incapable of grasping what might have happened if that enemy aircraft had released its bombs a split second sooner. No wonder Mum was so on edge. Gran, too. She must make allowances for them, be more understanding.

Getting back into bed, shivering, she thought of

Rob, imagined herself locked in the safety of his arms, conjured up his smile, his voice, and longed to see him again.

Mum was cleaning the grate next morning when Laura came downstairs; riddling ashes, brushing away dust, plumping a floor-cloth in hot, soapy water, washing the hearth, her forehead puckered in a frown of concentration, sleeves rolled up to her elbows.

Filled with pity, Laura wondered why Mother made a fetish of housework, why she gave priority to cleanliness rather than the things that really mattered. Love for instance. Why she waged this eternal war against emotion of the softer kind, as though gentleness, even laughter, might pierce the armour of her angry self-containment and weaken her brittle shell of resistance to life and happiness.

Thinking to help, she went through to the yard, followed by Nell, to bring in coal and sticks from the shed. 'There was no need,' Mary said shortly, when she returned, 'I'm not quite incapable, you know.'

'I'm sorry . . .'

'So, they've given you a week's compassionate leave? Well, you can go to the hospital alone this afternoon. I daresay that will please your father – and that ward sister he's so fond of!'

It was then Laura realized that Mum was jealous of Sister Dawson.

She went to the hospital alone, every afternoon after that, with her mother at night. The afternoon visits were the more successful. Dad seemed much brighter then, more relaxed, especially when Sister Dawson was on duty.

At first Laura put aside as nonsensical her flash of knowledge that mum was jealous of the sister. What possible reason could she have? True, the woman was younger than Mum; attractive, with dark, closely cut hair, a generous, full-lipped mouth, possessed of abundant energy and resourcefulness. Possibly her mother would resent any woman called upon to perform duties of an intimate nature so far as Dad was concerned. If so, she was being ridiculous. Her father would never look at another woman. And yet . . .

As the week wore on, Laura could not fail to notice the rapport which existed between Dad and Pat Dawson; the way his eyes lit up whenever she bustled into the ward, the laughing, light-hearted quality of their relationship.

Strangely, Laura felt the same kind of empathy towards the trim, energetic woman who had done so much for him.

Unknown to Mum, she and Sister Dawson had talked together in her office one morning about Dad's future; what would happen to him when he left the hospital.

'He'll need plenty of rest,' Pat said. 'Above all, no anxiety.' She paused to glance keenly at Laura, 'Will your mother be able to manage that?'

Laura knew what Sister Dawson was driving at. Mum had nurtured her martyrdom for such a long time that nagging had become second nature.

'I'm sorry, I shouldn't have asked that question,' Pat said. 'It's a matter of needs must. Your father will be sent home in due course, in a fortnight or so, I imagine, when he is fit enough to walk. Then he'll come here as an out-patient two or three times a week for physiotherapy.' She sighed deeply, 'I'm afraid I crossed swords with your mother the first time she came to visit. I'm too outspoken, that's my trouble.'

'So is my mother.' They exchanged glances.

Pat laughed. 'That much I gathered. One thing is certain, you have done him a world of good. He's been much brighter since you came.' She paused to straighten a pile of folders which did not need straightening, as if there was more she wanted to say but didn't quite know how. Keeping her eyes lowered, she said softly, 'I care a great deal about your father's welfare.'

'Yes, I know. And I want to thank you for all you have done for him.'

'Nonsense!' Squaring her shoulders, Pat looked up, 'It's just that one becomes attached to some patients more than others.'

The telephone rang. Picking up the receiver, Pat answered the call. Turning away from the desk, Laura stared out of the window at the steadily falling rain. The telephone conversation over, Pat said briskly, 'I understand that you are leaving tomorrow?'

'Yes, I'm afraid so.'

'I know how you feel, believe me. But you mustn't worry. And when you say goodbye to your father, remember to keep smiling.'

Laura walked home in the rain, needing to think, to get her life into perspective.

Lifting her face to the driving rain, she thought about her father, and Rob. Loving them both, it seemed to her that a torch of love had been handed down from her father into Rob's keeping.

The blow had fallen unexpectedly. When she arrived

home her mother was waiting for her. Laura knew from her face that something was wrong. 'What is it?' she asked.

Mary pursed her lips disapprovingly. 'I have just answered a telephone call from a man – someone you apparently know well. A Flight Lieutenant Peters, to say he'll be waiting for you at Ringley Station tomorrow night: wanting to know the time of your train, sending you his love! Well, what have you to say?'

'Rob . . . ?'

'Oh, so it's "Rob" is it? Now we're getting down to brass tacks! Who is this man?'

'I – he's a friend of mine.'

'A *friend*? He sounded more than a friend to me. Where did you meet him? I want the truth!'

Suddenly, Laura felt like a child again, caught in the act of doing something wrong, the way she had felt when her mother had read her diary, and poured scorn on its contents.

Mary continued, 'Have you made yourself cheap, Laura?'

'It depends on what you mean by "cheap".' Laura found her tongue at last. 'I wish you'd tell me! What's wrong with being in love? Because I *am* in love! So now you know, and I'm glad!'

Words came tumbling forth in a torrent, as if a river had suddenly burst its banks. 'The trouble with you, Mother, you don't know the meaning of love! Never once have you told me you love me! It's the same with Dad. Why do you do it? Why have you always turned away from our love as though it meant nothing to you?'

Mary Prentiss turned on her daughter in a fury. 'Because men are after only one thing! All they want is sex! I know. Your father wouldn't leave me alone until he'd lumbered me with a child . . .'

'No, Mother! You're wrong! I won't listen! I can't believe that my father . . .'

'Oh, yes,' Mary said scornfully, 'you've always thought the sun shone out of him. But I know better. He's like *all* men. Selfish. Inconsiderate.'

'Don't say another word! I'm warning you, Mother! Say one more word against my father, or Rob, and I'll never set foot inside this house again. *Never!* You have poisoned your own life, and dad's, but you won't poison mine! I won't let you! I have nothing to be ashamed of. I love Rob. We intend to get married one day, and when we do, I shall be proud to have his child!' Laura continued hoarsely, 'I never realized until now, that you didn't want me to be born. I suppose that explains why you have never loved me!'

The mist had not lifted throughout the journey to Ringley. Sitting in a train packed from end to end with servicemen and women, most of whom were standing in the corridor, almost asleep on their feet, not talking or laughing, simply enduring the discomfort, Laura remembered taking leave of her father. Smiling. Not wanting him to guess how she really felt.

But he had sensed there was something wrong. In the final minutes *he* had been the strong one. 'Mum and I will be all right,' he said gently, 'try to remember that she is going through a rough patch, too.'

'Yes, Dad. I'll remember.'

But her mother had remained unforgiving. She had

not even kissed her goodbye. Gran, on the other hand, had wept openly, and hugged her, standing near the front door in her dressing gown, her grizzled hair sticking out in two plaits beneath her green slumber helmet, while Nell had whined softly, and jumped up to lick her hands.

And now the train was about to enter Ringley Station.

Laura's heart lifted. Rob would be there to meet her. Within minutes she would be in his arms, his lips on hers.

But he was not there. She waited on the platform until the carriage doors had all slammed shut and the train was nothing more than a memory.

Then, beneath the dim blue station lights, a figure in Wren uniform appeared.

'Flanagan!'

Laura hurried forward. 'Oh, Grace! Thanks for coming! You'll never know . . .' She stopped suddenly. Delight died away at the sight of her friend's face seen dimly through the mist and rain, a face devoid of happiness. 'What is it? What's wrong?' she asked, her heart skipping a beat.

'It's the *Rosie*,' Grace said bleakly. 'She's missing! Feared lost!'

15

They stood together in the foggy darkness, speaking in disjointed sentences, overwhelmed by the enormity of what had happened.

'I had to come. I didn't want you to find out the way I did!'

'What? I mean – how?'

'A mayday call. Quite early. Scottie and I had been together at the flat.'

'Oh, Grace!'

'I watched him go. I remember thinking . . . it was as if the fog had swallowed him. You know? I could hear the engines, but I couldn't see the launch any more. Well, no use standing here, I suppose.'

They walked slowly towards the barrier. 'We were going dancing tonight,' Grace said wistfully. 'Funny, Saturday nights always seem so special.'

Laura remembered the Blue Bird Tea Shoppe, Grace's words: 'If the launch gets blown up . . .' And yet, sitting there at that tile-topped table, watching a squad of soldiers setting off on manoeuvres, noticing the seagulls, the glowing colours of the asters, they had not really believed that this could happen.

'When it dawned on me that Scottie had been gone a long time, I rang the base.' Grace's voice roughened. 'I don't suppose whoever answered the phone meant to sound offhand. I just stood there, staring at that bloody poster. You know the one I mean? "Your Cheerfulness, Your Resolution . . ." Oh, God!'

'What do you think we should do now?' Laura asked. They stopped uncertainly outside the station.

'What time are you due back?'

'Eight o'clock. That's when my leave ends officially.'

'I don't think I could face the Wrennery right now.' Grace dried her eyes. 'Why not come to the flat? I could make some tea.'

'Yes, I'd like that.'

'It's so bloody impersonal! The Wrennery, I mean. That overhead lighting. The chatter! "In the Mood". Honestly, I'll smash that bloody record over somebody's head one of these days!'

Laura had not been to the flat before. The homely touches surprised her. Grace had covered the bed, in one corner of the room, with a brightly coloured patchwork quilt. The standard lamp, the quilt, and the coffee table in front of the plopping gas-fire had been wedding presents from her parents, she explained.

A photograph of Scottie and Grace, taken outside the registry office on their wedding day, stood in the centre of the mantelpiece – the surrounding ornaments belonged to the landlady – a brass spill-holder and pipe-rack, a 'Present from Cromer' vase, two smug-looking Staffordshire dogs. Grace's Aunt Elizabeth Maria – Aunt Em for short – had given them a sheepskin rug, an Irish linen tablecloth and matching serviettes, various other members of her family, and Scottie's, the canteen of cutlery on the sideboard and the teaset. The toasting fork and fruit dishes had been a present from her brothers and sisters, paid for from their pocket-money.

Grace moved among her treasures as the chatelaine of some great Elizabethan house might have moved along a Holbein hung gallery, justifiably proud of her home, this overcrowded, multi-coloured oasis which she and Scottie had managed to create together, despite the war.

When the tea had been brewed, the toast made, Grace said forlornly, 'I can't imagine my life without Scottie. Not now.' She was kneeling on the rug, her face flushed from the fire. 'Oh, Christ! Perhaps this is my punishment.'

'Punishment? For what?'

'Oh, you know . . . not taking my religion seriously enough. Getting married in a registry office. Not going to confession!'

'No, Grace. You mustn't think that! After all, I'm not a Catholic, but this has happened to me too! Or do you believe that there is one God for you, another for me?'

'I'm not sure. I'm not sure of anything any more, except that . . .' Grace bowed her head, tears streamed down her cheeks, 'if Scottie comes back to me, I will light a candle to Our Lady every day of my life from now on.'

Laura wondered what she would do, by way of contrition, if Rob came back to her. Write a letter to Mum, saying she hadn't meant all those things she'd said to her in a fit of anger; things better left unsaid, driving a further wedge of misunderstanding between them?

She knew now that anger, like jealousy, demeaned the human spirit. It had taken this war, the blossoming of love, her father's brush with death, the loss of the

Rosie, to make her realize that she was no longer a child but a woman. That if, by some miracle, Rob came back to her, she would try to behave as a woman. To make amends. And if he did not . . .

'What are you thinking?' Grace asked.

Staring at the glowing gas-fire, spreading out her hands to the warmth, Laura remembered those April days of her youth, when Nature seemed dedicated, not to death, but re-birth. 'Whatever happens,' she said slowly, 'I shall never regret loving Rob. If I keep faith, we will meet again – one day!'

The fog had cleared away when she left Grace's flat. The sky was brilliant with stars, shining like diamonds in the dark vault of the sky.

She reported to the Wrennery, stowed away her belongings, applied for a pass, and went out alone, with no clear idea of where she was going.

She needed to be alone, to come to terms with her grief. Grace was right about the Wrennery. The glaring neon lights, the comings and goings, the shrilling of telephone bells, the noise from the common-room where someone kept on playing the same Glenn Miller record over and over again at full blast, had seemed unbearable. She knew she should ring home, speak to mum. But she couldn't. Not yet.

Walking on blindly, she heard, borne on the searching November wind, the faint sound of music from the Olympia Hall. The Saturday night dance was in progress. She recognized the tune, recalled the words: 'I'll be seeing you in all the old familiar places . . .' And then she knew where she was going. The music faded away on the wind as she walked towards Marine Parade, that hilltop crowned with trees from which, on a sunny day, one could see the coastline from Deal to Dungeness.

Looking up she saw how bright the stars were, strung like jewels or fairy-lights above the trees. Entering the park, following the path, she came at last to the Victorian shelter. Sitting down, she touched with her fingertips the empty bench beside her, conjuring up the essence of the man she loved; his warmth, his smile, the way she had felt when he told her he loved her, as though the stars were hers to gather, to hold in her hands.

Silently she began to pray, 'Dear God, bring him back to me.'

Sitting there, hands clasped, looking up at the stars, she waited.

Ruth Maple lay shivering in her bunk, her face buried in the pillow. News of the *Rosie* had filtered into the common-room after supper.

She had been sitting alone, as usual, pretending to read, thinking about Gavin, wondering if he would ring her when he came off duty; suggest a visit to the cinema perhaps, or the Olympia Hall, when Daphne King and two other girls came in.

At first, Ruth had not caught the gist of their conversation. King always spoke in italics anyway, dramatising situations. Everything in her book was 'simply ghastly' from the stewards to squad drill. Now, apparently, the adjective applied to some occurrence or other connected with the Air Sea Rescue base. Possibly one of her many boyfriends had broken a date with her, Ruth thought contemptuously, until Daphne said dramatically, 'Poor Grace McGregor. How simply ghastly for her. So soon after the wedding.' Then one of the other girls had chimed in, 'Prentiss, too. Am I mistaken, or has she something going with the skipper of the *Rosie*?'

Ruth scarcely remembered getting up from her chair, but she must have done. All she clearly remembered afterwards was standing there, white-faced, confronting Daphne King, speaking to her in a high-pitched voice demanding to know what had happened; Daphne and the other two girls staring at her as if she had gone mad; Brenda White saying, 'Oh, Lord! I'd forgotten that you were seeing – what's his name? The medical orderly, Gavin Truefitt?' At least she'd had the grace to apologize. 'I'm sorry, old girl, we just didn't think, that's all. The fact is, the *Rosie*'s missing, presumed lost.'

'I don't believe it! It can't be true! *No*. Don't touch me!' She'd shrugged away violently from Brenda's outstretched hand. 'Of course you had forgotten about me!' Ruth knew she was shouting, making a fool of herself, but she didn't care. 'Because none of you care tuppence about me; my feelings. Poor, dull Ruth Maple! That's what you all think, isn't it?'

'No, honestly. You're just upset . . .'

'Why shouldn't I be upset? The only people you really care about are yourselves! Never mind about me! I suppose you think I haven't got any feelings to hurt? Just because I keep myself to myself, because I don't fit in with the rest of you when you start boasting about your boyfriends. Well, I'm sick and tired of the lot of you!'

Turning on her heel, tears streaming down her cheeks, she rushed out of the room, slamming the door behind her, and ran blindly to the refuge of her cabin.

Lying face down, her thin body heaving with sobs, she thought about that night in the municipal park, the way she had felt with Gavin's arms around her, his lips on hers, her initial nervousness tinged with pride that he found her desirable; remembered his lips against her hair, whispering, telling her not to be afraid, to trust him not to hurt her.

And she *had* trusted him; trusted him enough to let him unfasten her blouse, to cup her breasts in his hands. She had started to shiver then, had felt a burning hot tide of passion run through her like a living flame, a strange yearning in the pit of her stomach.

She had cried out with the pain of it, and he had whispered to her not to worry, that what he was doing to her would not hurt at all the next time. Face buried in the pillow, Ruth remembered the rough feel of the tree trunk digging into her back, the searing pain he inflicted on her, the curious rhythmical jerking of his body, the way his breath came in deep, uneven gasps; that final, convulsive breath; his sudden grunt of pleasure, the relaxing of his body, the wet feeling between her legs.

'Was it . . . ? I mean, was I all right?' She'd asked the question diffidently, wondering why she felt so wet and uncomfortable, why whatever had happened for him had not happened for her too. 'Sure,' he had said, combing his hair and straightening his tie, 'you were great, kid, and it'll be even better next time, when you learn to relax more.'

'There will be a next time then?' She'd had the strangest notion that he was in a hurry to go, that he'd had enough of her for the time being. But she didn't want him to go. With a deep feeling of guilt at her wantonness, she had clung to him, throwing her arms round his neck, begging him to kiss her again, not understanding his sudden withdrawal.

'Oh hell, sure there'll be a next time. Just don't crowd me, that's all. Look, if we hurry, we can nip into the *Lord Nelson* before the landlord calls time. OK?'

Crying into her pillow, Ruth Maple knew that she would never love anyone as she loved Gavin. 'Oh, God,' she whispered, 'don't let him be dead. Please don't let him be dead. I can't live without him. I can't live without him!'

The *Rosie* limped home slowly on her one remaining engine, her super-structure, aerial mast, gun turret and lookout hatch destroyed by enemy gunfire.

At last the fog was lifting, Rob thought wearily, rubbing his eyes with the back of his hand, that blessed, marvellous fog which had miraculously covered their retreat after the crew of the fishing vessel were safely aboard.

The odd thing about miracles, no-one really believed in them. But had it not been for that grey bank of mist rolling across the Channel, those enemy planes would not have turned back towards the coast of France, and he and his crew might have died in the concentrated fury of their attack: that deadly accurate hail of machine-gun bullets relentlessly raking the *Rosie* from stem to stern, biting into the fabric, the very guts of her, intent upon destruction.

The aerial mast gone, they had lost contact with

base; drifting out of control until, stripped to the waist, sweating profusely, the two fitters had coaxed that one remaining engine back to life. By that time they were long overdue and the *Rosie* was battling to stay afloat in rapidly worsening weather conditions, floundering in the trough of heavy waves, shrouded in fog, with rain whipping obliquely across the surface of the sea.

Then *Rosie*'s engine had picked up and they had made their way slowly back to base.

Rob thought about Laura, how she must have felt when her train arrived and he wasn't there to meet her. God, what an idiot he had been not to realize, not to . . .

Smiling grimly as the Aldis lamp flashed out its call signal to shore base; screwing up his eyes to catch the signalled reply, he threw back his head and laughed. The message read: '*Well done, you chaps. Welcome home.*'

Too tired to think any more, Grace had tucked herself in bed with a hot water bottle, and curled up, her head resting on Scottie's pillow.

Drifting up from the Olympia Hall came the strains of a dance-tune. Scottie's favourite, 'Indian Summer'.

In her light, uneasy sleep, she sensed Scottie's presence, dreamt that he was standing near the bed, looking down at her, telling her to wake up; shaking her gently by the shoulder.

Opening her eyes, she could scarcely, in that moment of awakening, differentiate between her dream and reality. 'Scottie?' she whispered uncertainly. And then, with a cry of joy, she was in his arms, and he was holding her tightly, telling her how much he loved her.

Tears ran unheeded down her cheeks. 'Oh, Scottie! I thought . . .'

'I know what you thought – but you were wrong! Oh, Irish . . .' He held her even closer, kissing her hair, wiping away her tears. 'Did you think I would give up on us so easily? I'd have come back to you if I'd had to swim home!'

Slipping into bed beside her, naked, warm, unshaven, smelling of oil and salt air, he fastened his mouth on hers.

Between kisses, he said hoarsely, 'Sorry about the dance, sweetheart, that I couldn't quite make it in time.'

'It doesn't matter, Scottie. Nothing else matters except your being here.'

'Christ, I'm tired,' he murmured, falling asleep in her arms.

Desperately sorry that she had unwittingly hurt Ruth Maple, Brenda White went up to her cabin to tell her the good news.

'Look, old thing,' she said in her jolly hockey sticks voice, 'sorry if we upset you. The fact is, word came through a few minutes ago. The *Rosie* got back safely after all. No casualties.'

Ruth sat up jerkily, like a marionette, clutching her wet handkerchief. 'You mean . . . ?'

'Your boyfriend?' Brenda smiled reassuringly, thinking what a wreck Maple looked; eyes swollen with weeping, her nose red. 'Yes, I'm pretty sure he's OK. Why not come down and find out for yourself?'

'Has he left a message for me?'

'That I don't know. You'd better ask the duty officer.'

'Yes. Thanks, I will!' Ruth shuffled out of bed to dress, and comb her hair.

News of the *Rosie*'s safe return had been pinned up on the notice-board. Edging past a crush of girls near the duty office, Ruth asked the petty officer in charge if there had been any message for her.

'No message,' the young woman said briefly, turning away.

How long she had been sitting there, Laura had no idea. Everything was still. Numb with cold, she knew how the stars must feel, cold and solitary in that vast, mysterious sky.

She also knew that peace came hand in hand with solitude. Peace. Acceptance. A deeper awareness of life. Now it was time to go back to the noise, the clamour, the urgency of the world beyond this place; this tiny oasis of calm, this spiritual refuge where she had struggled so hard to bring her life into focus.

Rob had spent the past hour with his commander-in-chief, making his report, going over the details of the mission as he explained, graphically, what had happened out there; the initial difficulty of pin-pointing the position of the fishing vessel; the appearance of the German fighter planes; the strafing of the *Rosie*.

The official business over, he went to his quarters to bathe, shave, and change his gear, keeping an eye on the time. Almost ten o'clock. He hadn't eaten since breakfast. The mayday call had come just after. The *Rosie* had been on standby, refuelled, checked, cleaned, ready for action. The mayday signal received, the crew had scrambled, leaving the meal unfinished. He knew that there would be hot food awaiting their return, but what did food matter? He must speak to Laura, the sooner the better.

The anxiety of waiting for her to answer his phone call seemed marginally worse than the misery he had endured when Jock and Dick were wrestling with that bloody engine.

When the duty officer came back on the line she said, 'Sorry, sir, Wren Prentiss isn't here at the moment.'

'Not there? You mean she hasn't returned from leave yet?'

'No. She reported back at twenty-hundred hours. Then she applied for a late pass, and went out again.'

'I see. You don't happen to know where?'

'Afraid not. Sorry, sir. Any message?'

'No. Thanks, no message.'

Lighting a cigarette, he pondered the situation, trying to put himself in Laura's place, wondering what she would have done, where she might have gone when she knew the *Rosie* was missing.

Then suddenly he knew. Loving her so much, knowing her so well, he guessed where she would be. Stubbing out his cigarette, he made for the place he would have chosen, had their roles been reversed.

He must go to her, tell her how he had felt as the *Rosie* limped home to base, that blinding moment of revelation when he knew that he wanted her for his wife, not in some unforeseeable future, but now.

Laura walked towards the park gates. The wind had dropped, the stars hung brilliant in a cloud-threaded sky. She could hear the lullaby of the sea on the rocks below the promenade.

Sharing Rob's love of the sea, she understood his reasons for wanting to be a part of it, the decks of the *Rosie* beneath his feet, battling against tremendous odds. If he were dead, he would have wanted it that way, but how could she go on living without him?

He saw her as a shadow beneath the trees, a formless blur until she came towards him, silhouetted against the starlight. 'Laura,' he called softly. 'Laura!'

She looked at him disbelievingly as though he were a figment of her imagination. Then, quickening her footsteps, she ran into his arms.

Time had no meaning as they clung to each other. The taste of her tears were on his lips when he asked her to marry him.

Looking into his eyes she asked, 'Are you quite sure?'

Tracing the outline of her face with his fingertips he answered, 'I have never been more certain of anything in my life.'

Part Three

16

Meggie turned up the collar of her greatcoat and clung on to her cap. Rounding the Pavilion Corner seemed akin to facing a cavalry charge as the wind came tearing up the funnel of Westborough, straight from the sea, bringing with it a fusilade of hailstones. Almost breathless, leaning into the wind, she battled her way across the road towards her Aunt Mary's house, half wishing that she had never set off, but these visits to Scarborough had become a regular occurrence since she joined the WAAF.

Not that Aunt Mary appeared to derive much enjoyment from her visits. But it was difficult to know what her aunt thought about anything these days. She seemed to exist in a kind of limbo, seldom smiling, speaking when spoken to, moving from room to room like an automaton. Perhaps she was going through a bad time, Meggie thought. Some women did go queer at a certain stage of their lives, and it couldn't have been easy for her – or poor Uncle Will either – when he was forced to give up hairdressing. After his operation last year, that was. The wonder was that he hadn't been killed in that air raid. Luckily, he'd been able to find a more suitable sitting-down job at the labour exchange, but Meggie had noticed a change in him too.

Apart from the fact that he now used a walking

stick, his hair was rapidly turning white. Shock, she supposed. Some people's hair turned white overnight. She'd read about that somewhere. Truth to tell, she'd always liked Uncle Will better than Aunt Mary. He was such a kind man; patient, gentle, humorous, in direct contrast to her aunt who had never been the gentle, loving type; always a bit bossy and straight-laced. As for humour – huh – she never saw the funny side of anything, Meggie thought, hanging on to her cap for dear life.

Turning into the crescent, she thought that Laura getting married must have come as a shock to Aunt Mary. Now it was as if Laura had died, or done something dreadful like pinching money from the mess funds. Aunt Mary wouldn't even talk about her.

Poor old Laura. Meggie kept one letter she'd written, in her pay-book. The way she'd explained about wanting to make the most of life while she and Rob still had the chance, had made Meggie cry. It was so romantic.

Thank God. Here was the house at last. Seizing the bell, Meggie stood shivering in the biting wind, stamping her feet, then she heard footsteps coming along the passage, the scrape of the key in the lock. 'Hello Aunt Mary,' she said cheerfully.

'Oh, it's you, Meggie.'

'Weren't you expecting me?

'Yes. Come in.'

'How are you?'

'Well enough. And you?'

'I'm fine. Just fine.' Oh Lord, Meggie thought, she's in one of her moods.

'Come through to the sitting room. I'll put the kettle on.'

'Thanks. By the way, mother sends her love.'

'How is she?'

'Fine.' Strewth! Why did she keep on saying fine all the time? What a daft expression, especially on a day like this. Divesting herself of her cap and greatcoat, Meggie bent down to make a fuss of Nell. Even the poor dog was showing signs of age.

Aunt Mary might have gone to Laura's wedding, Meggie thought mutinously as Mrs Prentiss rustled through to the kitchen. Holding her hands to the fire she wondered how any mother could have kept away from her own daughter's wedding. Uncle Will couldn't have gone anyway, he was in hospital at the time, having had three shell splinters removed from his legs. And Gran couldn't have travelled all that distance alone.

Perhaps it was time to slide out of these trips to Scarborough. Difficult to know what to talk about nowadays apart from the weather, everyone's state of health, and her job in the cookhouse. Trying to make conversation with Aunt Mary was like talking to a brick wall. It had been different when Uncle Will was at home, coming through from the saloon between customers to chat to her. Now the house seemed like a mausoleum.

Gran hobbled into the room. 'Oh, it's you, Meggie. I thought I heard the bell.' She had always been fond of Meggie. 'My, what a day! Just hark at the wind!' She pulled a face. 'It's playing hell with my rheumatism!'

Aunt Mary was still in the kitchen. 'Have you heard

from Laura?' Meggie whispered, feeling like a criminal. Gran nodded. 'I had a letter from her yesterday. She's settling down fine. They've moved into a new flat. Ssshhh!'

Mary came in with the tea things. She had always been thin, Meggie thought, getting up to clear a space on the table, now she looked like two boards clapped together, and her hair wasn't as neat and tidy as usual. But then, it must have made a hell of a difference when Uncle Will's saloon was dismantled; his hairdressing equipment sold. Aunt Mary wouldn't be able to have her hair shampooed and set every Friday as she used to.

Helping as best she could, feeling lumpish and out of place as she spread the cloth and put the teapot on its pokerwork stand, Meggie wondered what her Uncle Will had ever seen in her aunt. But she hadn't been as thin and irritable in the old days as she was now, although she had always been narrow-minded. Meggie recalled the incident of the boar being led to the sty to do its stuff with the sow. What a kerffuffle there had been that day. The way she had dragged Laura away. As if there was something indecent about the poor old boar doing what came naturally to animals and human beings alike.

'Oh, I almost forgot,' Meggie said quickly, 'I've brought something for you. They're in my great-coat pocket. I was waiting for the bus when I noticed a queue outside a greengrocer's. I'll just get them!'

Bustling to the hallstand, she returned with a bag of wizened bananas. 'They're not much cop, I'm afraid,' she said apologetically, handing the bag to her aunt, 'but I daresay the brown bits won't show if you cover them with custard.'

'Bananas!' Gran said avidly, 'It's months since I tasted a banana! I'll have mine now! Never mind the custard!' Meggie laughed as the old woman stripped off the mottled skin and dug her teeth into the over-ripe fruit.

'Really!' Mary wrinkled her nose in disgust. 'There are times when you make me feel sick!'

'Oh – *you*!' Gran stared up at her belligerently. 'What a stick of a woman you are to be sure! I rue the day I came to live under your roof. I'd have been better off in an old people's home!'

'Don't be so ridiculous!'

'Well, I would have. You never wanted me here in the first place. And while we're on the subject, what kind of a mother are you to turn away from your own flesh and blood?'

'I hardly think that this is the time or the place . . .'

'Oh, isn't it? What would be the right place for you, then? A nunnery?'

Oh, God, Meggie thought desperately, wishing she had never come.

Gran returned to the attack. 'I felt ashamed of you, Mary Prentiss, not going to Laura's wedding! Making silly excuses the way you did! Well, all I can say is this; the girl has found herself a good man to take care of her! And I know she's happy because she has told me so in her letters!'

'If Laura chooses to write to you and her father, not me, that's her affair, not mine!' Mary said coldly, pouring the tea, unwilling to reveal that Laura had written to her several times, and she had burnt the letters unopened.

'That's all very well, but *why* doesn't she write to you? I'll tell you why! Because the poor girl knows you never wanted her to be born. My God, when I think how you treated her on her last leave, when Will was in hospital! You didn't even say goodbye to the lass. The dog showed her more affection that you did!'

'Hold your tongue, you stupid old woman!'

'You see how it is?' Gran's face crumpled suddenly as she appealed to Meggie for support. 'You see what I have to put up with, day in, day out!'

Meggie did see. 'Yes,' she said stoutly, 'I'm sorry, Aunt Mary, but I agree with Gran! I think I had better be going now, if you don't mind. I – I won't come again. There's really no point, is there?'

'Do as you please,' Mary said stiffly.

Planting a kiss on Gran's cheek, Meggie put on her coat and cap, opened the front door, and staggered once more into the teeth of the gale.

Battling her way to the bus station, she thought that the past half hour was the worst she had spent in her entire life. Worse even than her row with Fred Briggs.

Why it had happened, she scarcely knew, except that she had felt it her bounden duty to make some kind of statement on Laura and Gran's behalf. But now the statement had been made, now that she had virtually closed the door of Aunt Mary's house behind her for the last time, she wondered what real satisfaction lay in that hollow kind of victory, when the more realistic approach to emotional problems lay, not in running away but standing one's ground; attempting to sort things out. Besides, going off in a huff meant that she had disclaimed the right to know what would happen next. Oh, damnation!

Climbing aboard the bus, Meggie thought perhaps it was time she applied for a posting. Not that she disliked York, she was simply fed up with being in one place. The war was getting her down. If only she could see Laura again. As the bus set off, staring out of the window, she thought about the old times: sitting with Laura in the cinema in Devizes; crying their eyes out over some romantic film or other.

What a bloody life. Nothing ever worked out quite right. She had really believed, for instance, that that nice lad, Johnny Smith, had meant what he said about wanting to keep in touch with her, but she had never heard another word from him since that day in the potato field. He had simply mizzled into thin air.

As for Fred bloody Briggs . . . the last letter she'd received from her mother contained news of his forthcoming marriage to Dolly Blewett, one of those lasses he used to chase round the school playground.

'It was very good of you to come,' Will Prentiss said haltingly.

'Nonsense! I take an interest in my patients.' Pat Dawson smiled at him encouragingly. 'I simply came over to . . .'

'You know that I am in love with you?' he blurted out. Throwing caution to the wind.

'Yes,' she replied softly. 'At least, I – I hoped you might be.'

'You know I'm married' What a stupid remark. Of course she knew.

'The nicest men usually are,' she said lightly.

'I have nothing to offer you.'

'I haven't asked for anything.'

'That's the worst part about it. You have given me so much – my life . . .'

'Don't talk nonsense! You'd have pulled through anyway.'

They were standing together in the out-patients' waiting room of the physiotherapy department.

'Perhaps, but not with so much – joy, so much hope . . .'

'I'm not a very moral person,' she said. 'I've had lots of men friends. Just thought I'd tell you. This is a nurse's cap I'm wearing, not a halo.' Her lips trembled. He saw that her eyes were bright with tears. 'But I've never been in love before the way I am now. I'd just like us to be together once in a while. I don't mean sexually. That's why so many people come unstuck. The first fine careless rapture never lasts. When it's over, friendship is what really matters.' She laughed self-consciously. 'Hark at me!'

'Pat, my dear . . .'

'What I'm really trying to say is, I'm not young anymore. Forty-three next birthday. I live alone. When my mother died four years ago, I decided to keep the house. The solicitor advised me to sell it; move into a self-contained flat, but I didn't want to. One puts down roots. Besides, I love the garden . . .'

'I couldn't come very often,' he said slowly, 'and even if I did . . .'

'I know.' She touched his hand; a gesture of affection which moved him deeply. 'You needn't worry. I wouldn't try to lure you into bed. I know the score.

Perhaps that's why I love you, because you wouldn't want me to.'

Looking at her, the man he used to be shone through. He felt suddenly alive again. Reborn, recharged with energy and life. The unloving shadow of his wife rustled, reed dry and sterile, across the screen of his memory, bringing with it the old feeling of sourness and regret that he had never made her happy.

At least Laura was happy. She had sent him photographs of the wedding. He liked the look of Rob Peters: regretted that he had not been there to give Laura away; knew that Laura regretted it too, but he did not blame her for making the decision to go ahead with the wedding. She had explained, in a long, deeply personal letter, which he had never shown to anyone else, her reasons for doing so. She had not wanted the fuss and bother of white dress and flowers, just a simple church ceremony. 'All that matters,' she had said, 'is being together. I love Rob very much. That doesn't mean I love you any the less. It's just a different kind of loving. Please tell me you understand. I couldn't bear it if you felt that anything had changed between us, that I am shutting you out.'

How different his own life might have been had he married a woman like Pat Dawson. A woman with stars in her eyes, not ice water in her veins. He had never been unfaithful to Mary. He belonged to that generation of men who believed that family life is all important. Until this moment, he had never even considered the possibility of having an affair. Telling Pat how he felt had been a spur of the moment impulse born of necessity. He thought wryly that he might have chosen a better place, a better time. This out-patients' waiting room was scarcely the setting for a declaration of love. Nothing had been planned, he had simply said what lay in his heart because it seemed important that she should know. There had been no ulterior motive no overriding sexual urge. He doubted his ability to satisfy such an urge had it existed. Faithfulness remained a part of his makeup. He had not for one moment imagined embarking on a passionate physical love affair. Now the thought of being alone with Pat, however fleetingly, stirred in him a deep awareness of his need for affection – the quietude and peace of understanding.

His brush with death, and Laura's marriage, had brought to him the realization that to love and be loved, however altruistically, remained the bedrock of his existence. Time brought about inevitable physical changes in every man's life; the fear of impotency, the waning of sexual desire. These changes he had recognized and learnt to live with. What he could not accept was the coldness, the paucity of spirit, the acute sense of failure which overshadowed his life with Mary, the remorseless pursuance of an old worn out theme that men were beasts, marriage a kind of legalized rape.

This was the doctrine which had soured his life, and Laura's. Happiness lay in the knowledge that Laura had not succumbed to her mother's abortive philosophy.

The physiotherapist popped her head round the door at that moment. 'Ready for you now, Mr Prentiss,' she said briefly.

'Coming.'

Pat smiled. 'Be seeing you?'

He knew what she meant. The question lightly

asked, anticipated a refusal. A rare human being, this. A woman with no illusions.

Drawing in a deep breath, smiling back at her, 'Yes,' he said, 'I'll be seeing you.'

The war, enemy air raids, the shelling of Channel convoys; the Japanese attack on Pearl Harbor in December, the sinking of the *Repulse* and the *Prince of Wales*; the Japanese invasion of the Philippines; the fall of Rangoon; soap rationing, the sheer bloody business of day-to-day living in this fraught spring of 1942 seemed suddenly eased by the knowledge that he had something to live for, after all.

Dinah read the letter disbelievingly. Giles was coming home! Not that he'd said so directly, but she knew what he meant.

'So looking forward to our wedding, darling,' he'd written in his firm, upright hand. 'You'll wear white, of course, and carry roses'.

Roses? She hated roses!

'Start thinking ahead, darling. After all, the war can't last forever'.

God, that meant he was on his way, that he would be home any day now. At one time the letter would have thrilled her. But now . . . ? What about Neville?

Swept off her feet by her new affair, she recalled the night when she and Neville had first made love, how she had taken off her engagement ring and thrown it dismissively on to the bedside table when he told her, with a quizzical raising of his eyebrows, that he would find it more than a little off putting to make love to her with that blasted ring on her finger. 'Ah, that's better. Much better,' he'd said lazily, pressing her back against the pillows; smiling down at her, stripping off his dressing gown to reveal the sublime length of his strong, naked young body, his purposeful erection.

Then, very slowly and deliberately, he had come into her, making her cry out with the power and passion of his lovemaking, his untender exploration of her body; the unexpectedness of his various approaches to the art of making love, turning her first this way, then that; changing direction; altering his stroke; first delighting, then frustrating her; holding back at the last moment; confusing her; knowing exactly when to end her torment.

But never once had he told her he loved her. Never, during all those weekends thay had spent together at the Carlton Hotel, those passionate hours locked in each other's arms, had he mentioned the word love. When, angrily, after a blazing row brought about by his seemingly careless approach to their relationship, he had told her that he could not afford the luxury of falling in love with any woman, however desirable, she had told him to go to hell.

'What makes you so sure that I am not there already?' he'd asked bitterly.

'What kind of an answer is that? Do you love me or not?'

'Dinah, my sweet, I love you as much as I am capable of loving any woman under the present circumstances.' He smiled wearily. 'Perhaps it is time to start wearing your engagement ring again; forget about me.'

Picking up her overnight case, she had stormed out of the room, marched down to the reception desk, ordered a taxi, and returned to the Wrennery.

Now she knew that Giles was on his way home, she simply had to get in touch with Neville. Picking up the telephone in the duty office, she rang Ringley Aerodrome, and asked to speak to Squadron Leader Jackson.

Waiting, tapping her foot, gulping the smoke of a hastily lit cigarette, cursing the delay, she waited, rehearsing speeches in her mind. She would say she wanted to see him as soon as possible; arrange a meeting. He couldn't simply write her off. 'Forget about me,' he'd said. As if she could forget. And she did not believe that he could forget about her as easily as all that. Dinah's self-confidence would never allow an admission of failure. It had just been a storm in a teacup, a lovers' tiff. The poor darling was probably tired out; in need of a rest from flying. He would think differently when he knew Giles was coming home. She would *make* him think differently; tell him she had decided not to marry Giles after all. Then everything would be all right between them. They could get married without fuss. The poor lamb was probably jealous of Giles anyway, the thought of her belonging to another man. Oh God, why didn't somebody answer?

A man's voice came on the line. 'Neville darling, is that you?' she cried impatiently. 'Dinah here!'

'Dinah Felix? Ah yes, my dear. I thought it might be you. Ralph Stacey speaking. I'm afraid I have bad news. The fact is, Neville failed to return from his last mission. He was a good friend, a very gallant gentleman. We shall miss him . . .'

Blindly, Dinah replaced the receiver, remembering that her last words to him had been spoken in anger.

A very gallant gentleman! A burning sense of injustice ran through her like a flame. Neville was a fool, a bloody egotistical fool! How could he have left her now, when she needed him so much? What use was a dead hero? Oh Christ! He *couldn't* be dead! He simply couldn't! What she felt was not so much grief that Neville was dead, more an overwhelming feeling of self-pity that he had made her unhappy, had left her with this feeling of something unsettled, undecided, unfinished. How dare he have told her to forget about him before she was ready to do so? How dare he assume that the affair meant more to her than it had done to him?

The duty officer came in at that moment. Glancing at Dinah, noticing the curious mask-like expression on her face she asked, 'Anything wrong?' thinking that the usually confident Felix appeared to be in a state of shock. 'Bad news?' She had seen that kind of expression before, on the faces of colleagues when they had lost their husbands or boyfriends.

'Bad news? Good heavens, no!' Dinah said, 'Quite the reverse! I have just received news that my fiancé is on his way home. He's Sir Giles Pritchard, you know. We're to be married very soon . . .'

'Congratulations!' Christ, the duty officer thought, watching Felix's unsteady progress along the corridor, there'll be no talking to her when she's Lady Pritchard, the stupid bitch! Did she really imagine that no-one knew about her affair with that handsome young squadron leader? That no-one had noticed she had stopped wearing her engagement ring recently? The trouble was, girls like Dinah Felix, the snobbish offspring of wealthy jumped up little Jacks in Office, educated at the best public girls' schools, finished in Switzerland, France, or wherever, lacked the advantage of breeding, and this, she supposed, was the reason why nobody liked her.

17

The flat on Marine Parade came as a surprise to Laura. Rob had kept hinting for a couple of weeks beforehand that he had something up his sleeve, but she couldn't think what it was. When he asked her to guess, 'A Mizpah brooch,' she said eagerly, remembering the one she'd seen on that market stall at Armley.

'A – *what*?' he'd asked, mystified. 'What on earth is a Mizpah brooch?'

'It's a kind of Victorian love token,' she explained, keeping an eye on the gas-stove in the tiny kitchen of the two-room flatlet they had moved into after their brief honeymoon in Cornwall. 'I'm not sure what the letters stand for, but they must mean something romantic, like SWALK on the back of a love-letter.'

'No, darling, it's not a Mizpah brooch. It's a bit more practical than that,' he said, smiling down at her, not caring tuppence if the potatoes on the stove emerged as soft mush, or if the sausages she was cooking burnt black. 'As a matter of fact, sweetheart, I've discovered a much nicer place than this. I think you'll like it. It's on Marine Parade; a self-contained flat overlooking the sea.

'Oh, Rob! How wonderful! When may I see it?'

'Now seems as good a time as any other.'

'But what about the sausages, the potatoes?'

'I have a much better idea. When we've looked over

the flat, we'll have dinner at the Carlton and a bottle of wine to celebrate.'

'To celebrate what?'

'Not having to eat sausages and mash!'

'I knew you were going to say that!' She took a swipe at him with the tea-towel, loving the teasing quality overriding the tenderness of their relationship; her husband's sense of fun which had lain dormant for so long.

Laura wandered from room to room in a kind of dream, loving the view of the sea from the sitting-room windows; the wide Victorian skirting-boards and high white marble mantelpiece; the comfortable armchairs and sofa. The bedroom overlooked the back garden with its budding apple trees and borders of daffodils. She laughed with Rob at the size and depth of the claw-footed bath, remarked on the spaciousness of the airing-cupboard and the workmanlike kitchen with its white-painted dresser and shelves of pots and pans.

'Well, what do you think of it, darling? Could you be happy here?'

'Oh yes, Rob.' She thought how close she had come to losing her chance of happiness, what might have happened had not the *Rosie* returned to harbour that momentous November night; had not Rob changed his mind about getting married in wartime. Now, every moment they spent together seemed a moment to treasure, a garnering of memories, so that one day, pray God, encompassed by long years of happiness, in a world at peace, growing old together, they would be able to look back and say 'Do you remember when . . . ?'

As if he knew what she was thinking, Rob held her fiercely, tenderly in his arms, and kissed her. 'Loving you,' he whispered against her hair, 'is the best thing that has ever happened to me.'

Glancing at her wedding ring, Laura thought how lucky she was that Rob's parents had accepted her so gladly, that she had discovered, in Rob's arms, how deeply thrilling the act of love could be when the two people involved really cared for one another.

She had felt diffident, at first, about spending their honeymoon with Rob's parents, imagining every mother to be a mass produced facsimile of her own. She could not have been more wrong.

Marjorie Peters had welcomed her warmly, without undue fuss or ceremony, wearing her ambulance driver's uniform; a tall, slim attractive woman with greying hair worn in a straight bob, a mobile mouth, splendid teeth, and blue-grey eyes. Laura remembered, with gratitude, that she had said directly, without embarrassment, 'I'm glad my son has found someone to make him happy. High time he settled down. Now, come and look at the house. No, not you, Rob. You wait here for father. I want to get acquainted with my daughter-in-law.

'I've given you and Rob the bedroom in the west wing,' she said, leading the way. 'It's virtually self-contained, so you won't be disturbed. Father and I get up quite early, as a rule, eat breakfast in the kitchen, then go our separate ways. I want you to feel quite at home here. We've always been an easy come, easy go kind of family. No need to see my husband or me at all if you'd rather not.'

Her son had chosen well, she thought. 'We usually

have a meal around seven. Rob will tell you I'm not much of a cook, but you'll be welcome to join us.'

'We'd love to.'

'Take a look at the view. One can see the whole of Mevagissey Bay from this window.' Marjorie held back the curtain. 'Can you see the steps leading down to the beach?'

'It's perfect. Just perfect!' Looking out at the glorious panorama spread before her, the sloping lawns leading down to the beach, the line of trees at the garden's edge; catching the scent of seaweed from the rocks below; the tang of salt air borne inland on the breeze, she knew that Rob could not have chosen a better place for their honeymoon.

She walked across the landing from the bathroom, smelling fragrantly of White Windsor soap and Evening in Paris perfume.

Forever afterwards, she would remember Rob's tall figure silhouetted against the moonlight, the sea glistening like silver beyond the open windows, the way she felt, nervous yet excited, as he held her in his arms and drew her gently to the window-seat.

How she loved him for giving her that breathing space, that interlude of peace and relaxation. Resting her head against his shoulder, she felt the strength of his body through the light cotton robe he wore, the warmth of his arm about her waist. She would be eternally grateful to him for making their love a thing of tenderness as well as passion; his understanding of her shyness; holding back until, aroused by his gentleness and strength, she had turned to him, wanting to give herself to him.

When that happened, when he knew the right time

223

had come, lifting her in his arms, he carried her over to the bed.

Next morning they wandered down to the beach together, hand in hand, looked back to see their footprints in the sand, and threw pebbles into the sea.

Thereafter, they had spent their days in a drifting, hazy, mellow mood of delight, the evenings with Rob's parents, the nights in each other's arms.

Now, looking round the new flat, Laura wished that she might make up the quarrel with her mother.

Spoiling her happiness, lay the corrosive thought that, in taking what she wanted from life, she had somehow diminished Mary's happiness.

When Rob knew what was troubling her, he begged her to go home to visit her parents.

'Not without you, darling,' she said.

'I'm afraid that's impossible, sweetheart. I've used up all my leave. But you go. I want you to. I can't bear to see you unhappy.'

'You're – sure?'

'Of course, darling. I'll be here when you return.'

The train to Scarborough was late arriving. Walking from the station, hurrying up the path to the house, Laura thought, as she rang the bell, that perhaps it was unfair of her to have come with no prior warning.

Mary moved slowly along the passage, wondering who could be calling at this time of night, almost nine by the sitting room clock.

Standing on the doorstep, heart thumping, Laura heard the familiar scrape of the key in the lock. When the door opened a fraction, 'Hello, Mum, it's me,' she said softly.

'Laura?' Mary stared at her disbelievingly. Then, 'What is it?' she said. 'What do you want, coming here at this time of night? Why can't you leave me alone?'

'May I come in?'

'Please yourself. I can't stop you. But there's nothing to eat in the house, and your bed's not aired . . .'

'That doesn't matter! Aren't you pleased to see me?'

'Huh, as if you cared one way or the other! Bone selfish, you are, just like your father! He thinks I don't know what's going on, but I do! After all the years I've spent looking after him, this is how he repays me!'

'I don't understand,' she said desperately. 'We have to talk.'

'Push your way past me, then. I can't stop you. You are young. I'm old. Tired out. Finished and done with. I wish I were dead!'

'You're not making sense, Mum.'

'Nothing makes sense any more,' Mary said bitterly. 'So there's nothing to talk over. Nothing to say that will make any difference.' Turning away, she walked along the passage to the sitting room, shoulders hunched.

The dog, hearing Laura's voice, bounded to greet her, creating a momentary diversion.

'I'll put the kettle on,' Mary said dully, shuffling towards the kitchen.

'No, Mum,' Laura said, 'I don't want any tea. Not just yet. We'll have some later. Sit down and get warm.'

Their roles appeared to have been reversed as she guided her mother to her chair by the fire. 'Please tell me what's happening. Where's Dad?'

'With that woman, that ward sister. They're having an affair.'

'I don't believe it! How do you know? How can you be sure?'

'Do you think I've lived with him all these years without knowing? He doesn't give a brass farthing for me now.'

Mary's attitude puzzled Laura. For so many years, Mother had been the uncaring one. 'If what you suspect is true, why do you suppose it has happened?' she asked.

Mary covered her face with her hands. 'Oh, yes, that's right, blame me.'

'No-one is blaming you.' Kneeling on the hearthrug, Laura held her mother's hands. 'It's just that you have never shown Dad much affection.'

Mary shrugged aside Laura's hands, 'I was brought up to shun affection by my mother who showed little or none for Lally, Madge and me,' she said. 'She used to slap my wrists if I tried to kiss her good night. That kind of treatment rubs off on a child.'

'I know,' Laura said, 'it has rubbed off on me. I expect it has rubbed off on other people, too.'

'If you mean your father, yes, I expect it has,' Mary admitted. 'Perhaps I married him for the wrong reasons, but I've tried my best to make him a good wife.'

'Despite not loving him? The way you have never loved me?'

'You have no right to say that.' Suddenly, Mary remembered the night of the air raid; the way she had gone up to Laura's room to tell her she loved her; her distress when she knew that Will had been injured.

226

The feeling she had now that she had left everything too late.

'I'm afraid I can't stay long.' Guiltily aware that he should not have come at all, Will Prentiss glanced round Pat Dawson's sitting room.

Kneeling at his feet, 'Where are you supposed to be right now?' Pat asked lightly, smiling up at him.

'Playing dominoes.'

'Poor darling,' she said softly, 'this can't be easy for you. I'm flattered that you came at all. Shall I make some tea?'

'No! Don't move! Let me look at you!' Leaning forward he touched her face, her hair, gently with his fingertips. Then, with an imperceptible sigh, he found her mouth and kissed her, very tenderly at first, then more and more passionately until, breaking away, running his hands over his face, he said despairingly, 'It's no use, I'm not cut out for this kind of thing.'

Drawing away, 'You'd better leave then, hadn't you?' Pat said.

'Yes, I suppose so. I'm sorry, Pat.' He felt suddenly conscious of his own limitations, his age, his deeply held views on fidelity within the sketchy framework of his marriage; above all, Laura's belief in him as the one person on earth beyond reproach. 'Can you ever forgive me?'

'There's nothing to forgive. What, after all, has happened? Nothing of any consequence. You came to visit me. I was happy to see you. Now you are leaving. So what?' She laughed. 'Christ! There should be violin music at this point. An orchestra playing the theme tune of a Hollywood movie! "Just One of Those Things".'

'I've hurt you very deeply.' Moved almost to tears by her gallantry, her light-hearted refusal to admit defeat, Will rose to his feet.

'Don't you believe it,' she kidded, 'the end of a love affair that never happened isn't the end of the world for an old battleaxe like me!'

'Pat!'

'No,' she said. 'I think I knew all along the way things would be if we got around to admitting our feelings for each other. But there'll always be a kind of joy in thinking what might have been. Now you get on with your life and let me get on with mine. No, don't kiss me again. Just – go!'

Speaking quietly, Laura said, 'I love you, Mother. So does Dad. If you only realized how much.'

Mary fixed her eyes on the clock. 'Is that why he comes home at all hours?'

The front door closed. They heard the click of the key. Will came in, leaning heavily on his stick.

'Oh, so you've come at last, have you? About time, too! A quarter past eleven! Have you no shame?'

'Mum, don't say anything you might regret . . .'

'Be quiet, Laura. This is between your father and me!'

'Mary, I . . .'

'And don't bother to lie to me, Will Prentiss. I know where you've been. With that – woman. That – whore!'

'Stop it Mary,' he said wearily. 'You are right. I *have* been with Pat, but not for the reason you imagine. I

228

have not been unfaithful to you. I had to talk to her . . .'

'Lies! All lies! Why can't you tell the truth. You're in love with her!'

'Yes,' Will said quietly, 'I do love her, because she's hopeful and – understanding. Because she makes me feel hopeful, too.' He paused. 'I'm sorry, but you wanted the truth, now you have it . . .' He turned to Laura. 'For what it's worth, the "affair", if you can call it that, is over and done with. Can you ever forgive me?'

Mary's anger erupted. Believing that it was his daughter's forgiveness Will was seeking, not hers, she shouted hoarsely, 'That's right, ask *her* forgiveness, not mine! Well, Laura may forgive you, but I never shall! *Never!*

18

Sir Wilfred Felix knew precisely where to purchase the food and wine for his daughter's wedding. A man accustomed to the best that money could buy, he brushed aside shortages as nonsensical evidence of poor government.

Dinah, on a month's compassionate leave, arrived home to find her parents immersed in preparations for what her mother would insist upon calling, 'the Great Day'; wedding presents arriving by every post, trestle tables in the drawing room, the kitchen a hive of activity, and the wedding gown she had bought in London and ordered to be delivered to her home, hanging, swathed in white cotton, in her dressing room. The sight of the dress, sheeted, white, ghostlike, had a strangely depressing effect on her. She did not even want to try it on and wandered about the house like a lost soul, evincing little or no interest in the frantic activities of Lady Felix, trying valiantly to cope with seating arrangements, telephone calls, and the maddening ineptitude of the staff she had engaged to help with the catering.

'Dinah, darling, I do wish you would show a little more enthusiasm,' Lady Felix said chidingly. 'You might at least start writing thank you letters.' Later, to her husband, 'Dinah *is* very highly strung, of course, just like me. Do you remember how nervous I was on the eve of our wedding?'

Wilfred grunted a reply which might have meant anything. The only thing he remembered about his wedding day was the weather. It had poured with rain when they left the church and had continued to do so for a week afterwards. In any event, he had no wish to remember the exigencies of those days; the financial insecurity, his courtship of, and subsequent marriage to Mabel Smithers, his secretary at the time.

At dinner that evening, Lady Felix's brightly determined conversation served to deepen Dinah's depression as she picked at her food. When she said archly, 'Darling, you've scarcely eaten a thing since you came home. Is anything the matter?' Dinah pushed back her chair in exasperation.

'I'm tired,' she snapped. 'If you'll excuse me, I'm going to my room.'

'Yes, of course, darling.' When she had gone, 'What do you suppose is wrong with her?' Mabel Felix asked her husband. 'I've never known Dinah so moody before. Did you notice the way she flounced out, the way she flung down her serviette? You don't suppose she's having second thoughts about marrying Giles?'

'Don't be so bloody ridiculous! Dinah knows which side her bread is buttered,' Wilfred blustered, irritated by his wife's continual harping on about the wedding. 'Pritchard isn't a jumped up nobody. One of these days he'll inherit his father's title, take his place in the House of Lords. You mark my words. No, she's probably at that time of the month when all women seem to go haywire.' He added fiercely, 'Damn it all woman! *You're* her mother. *You* should know.'

Dinah bathed quickly, slipped into a white towelling robe, and lay disconsolately on her bed, willing the telephone to ring, realizing with a feeling of despair, that the voice she wanted to hear would never come again. Never again would she answer a 'phone call and feel the sudden uplifting of her heart, knowing that Neville would be on the other end of the line.

For the first time in her life she thought about love in a different way. Nothing whatever to do with conquest or even physical desire, simply the way she had felt when she knew that Neville was dead, that she would never see him again, never again experience that soaring, magical sensation of happiness whenever they met; that undercurrent of excitement as powerful and heady as if she had drunk several glasses of Bollinger champagne in quick succession, as if they were somehow encapsulated within the radiant bubble of that private and special relationship which she had believed to be love.

The bubble had burst suddenly the night he would not tell her that he loved her; the night when, hurt and angry, she had walked out on him, so sure of her power of attraction, her dominion over him, she had believed that he would telephone her straight away to make up the quarrel. Why hadn't he? Just one word, his voice on the other end of the line would have healed her wounded pride. One word, 'Sorry.'

Instead, he had flown to his death, that one word left unspoken. Ever since, she had imagined him striding across the tarmac towards his waiting Lancaster, heavily kitted out in flying gear; climbing into the cockpit, signalling chocks away; the plane taxi-ing, engines roaring; lifting from the solid earth into the dark loneliness of the night sky.

What had been in his mind at that moment of take-off, as the formation headed out to sea, crossing the French coast into enemy territory? Had he been thinking of her? Wishing their quarrel had never happened, meaning to ring her the minute he returned? If only she *knew*, if only she could feel certain that their love affair had meant as much to him as it had to her. And this was the worst thing that had ever happened to her – not knowing; the reason why she dreaded the thought of tomorrow; of marrying Giles. And yet . . .

When the 'phone rang Dinah's cool selfish core of commonsense came to the fore. 'Hello, Giles darling,' she said breathlessly. 'Where am I? In bed, actually, having an early night. Hmmm, yes, of course I've thought about tomorrow night. The hotel sounds fabulous. Oh, by the way, darling, thank you for the flowers. I adore roses. Yes, they are beside me, now,' she lied, 'and your card is under my pillow. What? Oh yes, of course. You know Daddy. Everything's organized down to the last truffle! No, you may *not* have a description of my wedding dress. Wait and see.' She laughed delightedly, shrugging aside the ghost of her dead lover. 'Oh, very well, you – baby. If you insist.' Pressing her lips against the receiver, she whispered, 'I love you.'

Later, she retrieved the flowers from the waste-paper basket where she had thrown them, along with the message: 'To my beautiful bride to be. See you in church? All my love. Giles.' She felt happy then, aglow with renewed happiness, secure in the knowledge that Giles loved her as she deserved to be loved.

Stretching luxuriously, she thought of the Lake District, Windermere; the hotel overlooking the lake in which she and Giles would spend the first week of their honeymoon before travelling to Oxfordshire where Giles would assume command of an RAF station near Stanton St John. The thought of being the commanding officer's wife, Lady Pritchard, holding sway over the other women at various dances and mess parties, apart from the private dances and dinner parties they would be invited to attend, did wonders for her ego. What the hell was she doing worrying about a burnt out love affair anyway? Giles knew, better than most men, how to make love to a woman, besides he was so gloriously rich, and quite devastatingly handsome.

God, she thought, getting out of bed to stare at herself in the mirror, had her nightmares over Neville sketched ugly little worry lines on her face? How beastly! Unscrewing the lid of her night cream, she began repairing the ravages with firm upward strokes of her fingertips.

Out of breath, Meggie heaved her duffle-bag over her shoulder and climbed aboard the transport bound for Ringley Aerodrome.

The journey from York had been a nightmare, the train so packed that she had been obliged to stand in the corridor all the way. Now rain was coming down like stair-rods, and she was so hungry she could eat a horse. The only bright spot in her existence, that she would soon be seeing Laura again. This

Ringley posting had been a stroke of luck pure and simple.

'All right, you lot, look lively!'

Meggie cast a withering glance at the RAF corporal standing in the rain, hand extended to help herself and six other girls from the transport.

'I wonder how lively you'd look if you'd been on your feet for the past ten hours,' she said tartly, refusing to take his hand. 'Don't bother. I can manage on my own!'

Gavin Truefitt slicked back his hair with Brylcreem, straightened his tie, and ran a duster over his shoes.

Frankly, he didn't want the war to be over. Let the married blokes do all the worrying and fretting. Let them spend their off duty time writing letters to their wives and children. The single guys had it made. No strings and no connections. Women fell for the Alan Ladd look hook line and sinker these days. OK, so he wasn't very tall, but neither was Alan Ladd. At least he wasn't short where it really mattered, so let snide buggers like Tim Merrydew kid him about his lack of inches, about his affair with Ruth Maple, too, if they felt so inclined.

He knew what they were driving at – why bother with a plain looking girl like her? As if they didn't know. Plain girls were easy, fairly begging for it, glad of the chance.

Take Ruthie, for instance. She knew which side her bread was buttered right enough, had quickly learned what he wanted of her. Let him do it as often as he wished. No messing. He'd warned her that sob-stuff was out. He didn't want involvement, commitment of any kind. Pity she wasn't a bit better looking. But then, what did looks matter in the dark?

Now for the Saturday night hop. He experienced an intense feeling of pleasure at the prospect of a new crop of women. Ruth would be jealous, of course. She always pulled a long face when he danced with other girls. He couldn't care less. Her jealousy added a fillip to what came later.

As long as she lived, Ruth would never forget the Olympia Hall, which she had come to associate with deep feelings of loneliness and humiliation, knowing that sooner or later Gavin would leave her on her own, and she would watch him swagger across the floor to ask someone else to dance the tangoes and quicksteps she had never been able to master properly. She wished she possessed the pride and dignity to put an end to the affair. If he knew how cheap she felt, the way that all plain girls must feel watching with hungry, jealous eyes, the man they loved dancing with more attractive women; flirting, laughing, holding them far too close.

Worst of all, knowing what would come later, the sapping of her willpower beneath the trees of the municipal park, when, feeling his body warm against hers, his hands at her breasts fumbling with the buttons of her blouse, she would submit helplessly to his lovemaking when every instinct prompted her to cry out, 'No! This has got to stop!'

But if she did she would never see him again. The thought was unbearable. No more telephone calls, nothing to look forward to. Life would cease to have any meaning. There would be no purpose in living.

Memories of the night she knew the *Rosie* was missing remained branded on her mind, when she had faced the possibility of never seeing him again. So terrible was the anguish she had lived through then, that she had gone on with this meaningless charade of loving: giving him all that lay within her power, as long as he continued to want her.

Sod it, Gavin thought bitterly, trust those bloody Americans to get in first! Ordering a pint of beer at the bar, a port and lemon for Ruth, he watched, jealously, the Wren with long legs gazing intently into the eyes of an American Air Force sergeant. No youngster, by the look of him, greying slightly at the temples, yet possessed of that lean, brown, healthy look apparently inherent in all American servicemen, as if every last one of the bastards had spent a lifetime soaking up the Californian sunshine.

He'd smiled at her a couple of times. No response. She had looked through him. Or perhaps she *had* noticed him, and this lovey-dovey business with the American was just a come-on. The next dance was a jitterbug. No use asking Ruth, she couldn't jive for toffee, far too stiff and unbending. He'd ask one of those Waafs lined up near the entrance. The one with the red hair looked a lively type. No doubt about the come-on there. She was smiling, tapping her feet, dying to dance.

Leaving Ruth at the table with her glass of port and lemon, he eased his shoulders, straightened his tie, took his comb from his breast-pocket, slid it furtively through his hair, and walked over. 'Care to dance?'

'You bet!' She grinned, 'Say, you remind me of someone.'

'Don't tell me. Alan Ladd?'

'Yeah, as a matter of fact.'

He'd just known it. This girl was born to jive. Other couples stopped dancing to watch when Gavin and the redhead went into action. Gavin relished that triumphant moment of being the centre of attention, the star attraction. The more the girl responded, the more daring he became, the more chances he took with her. They couldn't go wrong. Whoosh! Between his legs she slithered as the trumpets rose to a final crescendo and the watching couples burst into spontaneous applause. He had never known anything like it before. The spotlight had picked them out as they danced, concentrating on that area of the floor where he had unerringly sent the girl spinning away from him, then drew her back, legs moving like pistons, accurately, rhythmically, filling him with a heady sense of elation.

'Christ, that was marvellous!'

'I'll say it was.' The redhead linked arms as they walked off the dance floor. 'What's your name?'

'Gavin. Gavin Truefitt. What's yours?'

'Susan Daley.'

'Look, Susan, I'm with someone right now. Perhaps we could get together some other time? How about Wednesday? Say eight o'clock?'

'Sure. Where?'

'Here. I'll wait for you outside.'

'OK. Fine. Be seeing you, then.'

'You won't forget?' He felt reluctant to leave her, to go back to Ruth and her bloody port and lemon, her long face, lack lustre hair and damp personality. But when he went back to the table, Ruth had gone, leaving her drink untasted.

She walked alone into the night. The air felt fresh on her face. She knew now that it was all over, finished and done with at last. She felt strangely at peace. No more torment. No more pretence. She thought of home, of her mother; wished she could write her a letter explaining how she felt at this moment, telling her how the affair had begun and why. Because she was thin and plain and lonely and needed someone to love her, someone to make her feel important and special; to break down the barriers of an insular upbringing, those hidebound precepts of the Methodist religion in which the plainer women of every congregation could expect little more than a lifetime of service to a tea urn.

Then the war had happened, thrusting her into a world of agonizing choices and decisions, bringing with it an acute awareness that love was possible even for herself, the plainest of girls. But when had love entered into her relationship with Gavin? He had used her, humiliated her. She saw that clearly, in this moment of reckoning.

Now all she needed was courage, even more courage than it had taken to walk out of the Olympia Hall a few moments ago, when she had watched him dancing with that other girl.

The church was packed with guests, well-wishers, and those common-or-garden sightseers intent on witnessing a really posh wedding, despite the grinding weariness of the war news – Rommel's offensive against the Allied Forces in the Libyan desert; the threat of fuel rationing; the idiocy of that 'Bare legs for patriotism' edict issued by some smart-arsed Jack

239

in Office. As if the women of Britain weren't doing enough already: queuing for food; packing their kids off to the country for safety; coping with air raids; helping to feed the hungry and the homeless; working in munition factories; worrying about their sons, husbands, and fiancés, without going bare-legged into the bargain!

When Dinah floated down the aisle in her white satin wedding dress, a few of the sightseers exchanged meaningful glances. 'Huh, no shortage of clothing coupons there,' muttered one of them spitefully. 'No shortage of food, neither, I'll be bound. Amazing, isn't it, how some folk manage?'

'Oh, do shut up, May,' breathed another ecstatically, 'it's just like a movie, isn't it? Just like Madeleine Carroll and Ronald Colman in *The Prisoner of Zenda*! Cor, what a handsome bloke! A real toff. Oh, do shut up and listen.'

'I, Giles Edmund George, take thee, Dinah April Elizabeth to my wedded wife, to have and to hold from this day forward . . .'

The woman called May began, suddenly, to cry. Her husband was with the Eighth Army in Libya.

'You'll like my cousin Meggie,' Laura promised Rob, cutting the egg and cress sandwiches. 'Meggie's happy and uninhibited, and I love her. Oh, there's the bell!'

Laura ran down the stairs. Meggie was on the doorstep, beaming. They flung their arms round each other. 'Meggie! I'm so pleased to see you!'

'Me too. Gosh, it's been ages! Let me look at you. Oh, I've missed you. I'm sorry I couldn't come to your wedding. There was a bit of a flap on, and I couldn't get leave.'

They walked up to the first-floor landing, chattering nineteen to the dozen, arms linked. Rob was there, waiting, smiling. 'Meggie, this is my husband.' Rob kissed her. Meggie blushed.

'How do you do? I've heard a lot about you.'

Rob laughed. 'Laura has told me about your trips to the pictures in Devizes. How much you enjoyed a good cry together.'

'Well, I never!' Meggie had felt nervous about meeting Laura's husband, a flight lieutenant no less, afraid he might be difficult to talk to; too posh for the likes of her. How silly of her. She might have known that Laura wouldn't have married someone stuck-up.

Listening as they talked over tea, Rob observed and understood the rapport between them and thought that, one of these days, on that inevitable day when he could no longer be a part of Laura's life, she would need someone kind, generous and warm-hearted – someone like Meggie – who loved her – to ease the pain of his departure.

He had no death wish. He simply could not envisage himself growing old, living out his threescore years and ten. The war had altered all that – his innocent, childhood belief in the Bible, the communion of saints, the forgiveness of sins. He held no feeling of pity for men who machine-gunned, without mercy, the helpless survivors of sinking aircraft.

Yet, curiously, he still believed in miracles; in love, in nature, laughter, valour, ideas, books, music, all the worthwhile things of life. But here and now, not in some nebulous heaven beyond the clouds.

Never had he regretted marrying Laura, who had brought an unexpected depth and meaning to his life, in this home she had created, which he returned to after arduous spells of duty as to a haven, a refuge. Sometimes, inevitably, their watches conflicted. Often he came home to an empty flat to find the notes she had left for him propped up on the mantelpiece, in the kitchen, or on the bedside table; funny, loving little messages – 'I love you. See you around seven,' or, 'Look under your pillow. I've bought you a present. Hope you like it. All my love.' He, too, would leave notes for her. Or, if she happened to be sleeping when he came home, he would move quietly about the flat so as not to disturb her. When she awakened, he would make her a cup of tea, and slip into bed beside her.

And then, for a little while, he would forget the world beyond these four walls.

19

A courting couple discovered Ruth lying near a 'Strictly No Entry' area of the promenade, where concrete tank traps and barbed wire barriers had been erected on an old coble-landing leading down to the beach.

How she came to be there, they had no idea. She must have been walking along the cliff top and lost her footing too near the edge. There had been a kind of landfall as far as they could make out. Loose rocks and an uprooted bush lay close by. At first they thought she was dead. When they discovered she was still alive, the girl stayed with her while her young man hared up the cliff paths to 'phone for an ambulance.

Later, Second Officer Palliser and the station medical officer went to the hospital to find out what had happened. The girl was lucky to be alive, the doctor told them. Something must have broken her fall, otherwise she would most certainly have been killed outright. He had suspected a skull fracture, but the X-ray plates had proved him wrong.

'Any other damage?' the medical officer asked concernedly.

'Two broken ribs and a fractured collarbone, apart from severe bruising of the kind one can expect from a fall of that nature. She's also lost a great deal of blood from the head wound.'

'But she will recover?'

'Oh yes, I think so. We have given her a blood transfusion. Her condition has not deteriorated so far. As I said before, she's a very lucky girl. She's still unconscious,' the doctor added.

'We had better inform her next-of-kin,' Palliser said on the way back to the Wrennery, mistakenly believing that the girl's mother would fly to her daughter's bedside.

It was not as simple as all that. For one thing, Mrs Maple was not on the telephone – an instrument which she considered an invention of the devil. Whichever way Palliser turned in her efforts to get hold of Mrs Maple, she came up against a stone wall of resistance. Even the Manchester Police, who sent a constable to the house to inform Ruth's mother that her daughter had met with a serious accident, had reported no success.

'Frankly, ma'am, the old lady seems completely out of touch with reality,' the head of the Manchester Police department concerned, told Palliser. 'All she did was witter on about her own health, saying she was too poorly to travel. In other words, she didn't want to know.'

'I see,' First Officer Gantry said crisply, when Palliser made her report. 'So where do we go from here? Has Maple any special friends that you know of?'

'I gather she's quite chummy with Peters and McGregor.'

'In that case, you'd better get hold of them. We can scarcely leave the girl in limbo. She'll need someone there when she recovers consciousness.'

Gantry tapped her pen. Looking down at the

patterns the ink stains had made on the blotter, she said thoughtfully, 'I wonder how the accident happened? It seems an odd thing, to me, a nervous girl like Maple walking alone on the cliffs after dark.'

Ruth opened her eyes painfully. Laura and Grace were at her bedside. 'Don't worry, mavourneen,' Grace said cheerfully. 'You're going to be all right.'

Tears trickled down Ruth's cheeks. She had not expected to open her eyes, or weep, ever again. Never to feel pain or unhappiness. And now . . .

'Don't try to move. You're all strapped up. Gosh, you gave us a fright, didn't she, Laura? We can't understand how the accident happened.'

'It wasn't an – accident.' Ruth's voice came in a cracked whisper.

Grace and Laura exchanged glances. 'You mustn't say that.' Grace looked round the room to make sure that no-one had overheard, thinking that Ruth's bump on the head must have done something to her brain. 'You can't believe that someone tried to kill you?'

'No-one tried to kill me. I tried to kill myself!' She turned her face away. 'I wanted to die. I wish I had.'

Leaning forward, clasping Ruth's hand, 'You haven't told anyone else?' Laura asked anxiously. 'Grace and I are your friends. You can trust us to help you.' In a low voice, 'Was it because of Gavin?'

No time for prevarication. They had been warned by the ward sister not to stay too long. In any case, she knew she was right. Poor Ruth had seemed so unhappy of late, coming back to the Wrennery after visits to the dance-hall or cinema looking utterly miserable, unwilling to say what kind of a time she'd had, whether or not she had enjoyed herself. Unlike the other girls who would either float on watch in a state of euphoria, or complaining bitterly they'd had a lousy evening.

Laura had guessed why Ruth seemed so dejected. Gavin was using her. Grace had reached the same conclusion. 'I could strangle that Alan Ladd character with my bare hands,' she'd said recently. 'Ruth will have a nervous breakdown if she doesn't watch out. Why can't the cocky bastard leave her alone?'

Understanding Ruth's dilemma, 'Perhaps she doesn't want him to leave her alone,' Laura suggested.

Now, tightening her clasp on Ruth's hand, Laura said, 'I know how you must be feeling, but you are still alive, and there is so much in life worth living for.' She wanted to cry out, 'He isn't worth it!' But to do so would be both cruel and insensitive. No woman wanted to hear the truth about the man she loved. But perhaps Ruth already knew, and that was why she had attempted to take her own life.

The ward sister came in at that moment, brisk and cheerful in her starched cap and apron. 'Time's up!'

'We're just going.' Grace bent down to kiss Ruth's tear-stained cheek. 'Don't worry, mavourneen. Remember, there's as good fish left in the sea as ever came out of it.'

'Goodbye, Ruth.' Laura withdrew her hand. 'Remember what I said about living. It really *is* true.'

Ruth's mouth worked pathetically. 'You will come again?'

'Every day, I promise.'

Ruth closed her eyes.

'Heavens above! Whatever made me say what I did

about there being as good fish in the sea?' Grace exploded as they walked down the drive.

Laura laughed. 'Because you have a way of saying what other people are thinking.'

'Huh, don't I just. But you know me, always going in at the deep end! I'm just an insensitive idiot!'

'Not you.' Laura knew that Grace had kept her promise to light candles to the Virgin Mary. Since Scottie came back to her she had gone to church, every day, to honour that vow.

Slaving over a hot stove, Meggie thought that she might as well have stayed in York. One cookhouse was very much like another when all was said and done.

And yet there were certain compensations. That RAF corporal, whose offer of help she had dismissed so abruptly on the night of her arrival, had asked her for a date tomorrow night to the Roxy to see *The Fleet's In*.

Well, there was no accounting for taste. Perhaps he liked fat girls, Meggie decided, inspecting a tray of roast potatoes. Not that *he* was any oil painting. Still, a date was a date, and no woman could resist the compliment of being asked out. But if he imagined, for one moment, that his flattery would outweigh her commonsense, he had another think coming.

George Butterworth, his name was. Butterworth indeed! Why couldn't his surname have been Raft? She didn't even like him very much. Still, a visit to the cinema didn't mean she'd have to marry the guy. Or perhaps he was already married? He looked the type. In which case, if he tried to take liberties with her, she'd kick him hard on the shins. Then what would his butter be worth?

Generally speaking, Meggie held a low opinion of men. Blessed is she that expecteth nothing, had been her doctrine, following her disappointment over Johnny Smith.

Meggie's date with George Butterworth was not an unqualified success. She couldn't help wondering where the catch lay: if he would expect her to pay, later, for the bar of chocolate he had given her, in some dark cliff-top shelter. It was only a two-ounce block anyway, and he hadn't even treated her to a seat in the circle.

She'd felt self-conscious entering the cinema with him, thinking they must look like Laurel and Hardy. Oh God, why had she come?

The trouble with cooking was that she had to do a lot of tasting. Not that she minded. She'd always liked food; lots of meat and veg, and Yorkshire puddings smothered in onion gravy, steamed puddings and custard. Working about the farm, it hadn't mattered much how she looked. Now she felt envious of trim waistlines and tight bosoms. George, on the other hand, looked as if a good meal would kill him. Still, he had a good head of hair, slicked down with Brylcreem, and what appeared to be his own teeth.

Aw, what the hell? At least he hadn't tried to unfasten her suspenders. Nor, to her surprise, had he attempted to winkle her into a shelter for a necking session after God Save the King.

By this time, she had begun to wonder why not? What was the matter with him anyway? Perhaps he just didn't fancy her. A queer sort of bloke. A bit on the glum side, not very chatty. Not the kind to give you his life story in ten minutes, nor the sort to throw his money about.

'Thanks for a pleasant evening,' he said politely, on their return to the aerodrome, not even attempting to kiss her good night.

'Don't mention it, I'm sure,' she replied coolly. 'Thank *you*.'

'Next Wednesday night then?' he suggested. 'Same time, same place?'

'If you are quite sure your wife won't mind,' she said tartly.

He stared at her uncomprehendingly. 'Wife? What wife? I'm not married, never have been. Hey, what kind of a man do you take me for anyway? Oh, I get it, you thought I was playing fast and loose with you? Well, I'm not. So let's forget about it, shall we?' He turned away from her, uptight and angry.

'George,' she called after him. 'I – I'm sorry!'

Too late. Perhaps he hadn't heard her. At any rate he didn't turn back. He simply continued walking away from her, leaving her standing alone in the moonlight.

She went back to her quarters, took off her uniform, and got wearily into bed, thinking that, no matter how hard she tried, she could never get anything quite right, especially where men were concerned.

It had been a fantastic honeymoon. Giles had proved himself to be a perfect husband. A bit predictable in bed, compared with Neville, but generous, attentive and masterful. She hated saying goodbye to him, the thought of returning to Ringley without him.

At the last moment, before the train moved away, Dinah flung her arms round his neck in a passionate embrace. 'Oh, Giles,' she murmured tearfully, 'I can't face going back without you.'

He looked slightly embarrassed. 'I know, darling. But it won't be for long. Remember I love you.'

But even at that poignant moment of goodbye she could not help thinking of another angry leave-taking from the man she wished with all her heart she might see again in reality, instead of in her many muddled dreams and nightmares of the past.

20

Dinah returned to Ringley in a volatile state of mind, making her presence felt. 'Behaving like bloody Lady MacBeth,' someone was heard to mutter. 'Who the hell does she think she is, anyway?'

The weather had turned hot. There had been a thousand bomber raid on Cologne. Maisie Castleford went in to the cabin one evening to find Dinah lying on her bunk covering her ears to shut out the drone of the bombers from the aerodrome flying out on their latest mission, crying hysterically that she couldn't bear the noise.

Nor, apparently, could she bear to listen to certain songs on the wireless: 'All The Things You Are', 'Fools Rush In', and 'Room Five Hundred and Four', in particular seemed to upset her. Maisie wondered if Dinah had started a baby, if this could be the reason for her unpredictable moods and crying spells?

'Why the hell can't you leave me alone?' Dinah had snapped when Maisie tried to comfort her. 'If you want the truth, I'm sick and tired of this bloody place. I just want out.'

Meanwhile, Maple, due to leave hospital, had burst into tears when Second Officer Palliser told her that she was being given a month's sick leave.

'Please don't send me home,' she cried. 'Let me stay here. I want to be with my friends.'

First Officer Gantry raised her eyebrows disbelievingly. 'You mean to tell me that Maple actually refused sick leave? God! Now I've heard everything. But why? For what reason?'

Palliser explained.

'I see. Well, we can't force the girl against her will. But is she fit for duty? I'd better have a word with the MO, find out what he thinks.'

'Oh, by the way, ma'am, Petty Officer Pritchard has put in a request to see you. I gather she wishes to apply for a commission.'

Gantry pulled a face. 'I rather thought she might. I gather she's been throwing her weight around since she became Lady Pritchard – or should one say Lady MacBeth?'

The Medical Officer gave his consent to Maple's return to duty on the understanding that she would, for the time being, be spared the rigours of night watches which might prove too much of a strain, and providing a bed could be found for her in the sickbay, away from the main building.

Faced with going home, Ruth had known she could not bear the squeezed, inhospitable atmosphere of the house in Manchester, her mother's carping criticism and questioning. She could never explain how the 'accident' had happened, what she was doing alone on the cliffs at night. Second Officer Palliser had tried to pump her about that but had given up when Ruth said stonily that she couldn't remember anything about it. Her foot must have slipped or the ground given way. The latter tied in with the courting couple's report of a landslide; lots of loose stones lying about; an uprooted bush nearby. In the event, Palliser felt it better not to pursue the matter. Probably Maple had been with someone – a boyfriend perhaps. Possibly they had quarrelled and he had stalked off, leaving her to find her own way home. A queer sort of girl, Maple, Palliser considered on the way back to the Wrennery to make her report: a bit of a dark horse, as plain as the proverbial pikestaff, not the kind that men went for as a rule. But stranger things had happened in this war. She had learned from the doctor's report that Maple was not a virgin.

Relief flooded Ruth when she knew that her request to go back on duty had been granted. Grace and Laura had pulled her through the traumatic aftermath of her suicide attempt, visiting her every day in hospital, talking to her, building up her self-confidence, willing her to get better. Now she clung to them as a lifeline, afraid of what might happen if she was parted from them, frightened of slipping back into that state of black depression which had caused her to do what she did. Not that she remembered anything very clearly, except standing there, on the cliffs, hearing the sound of the sea on the rocks below, wishing she were dead, willing herself to take a step forward in the dark.

What happened afterwards remained a jumbled nightmare. Whether or not she had taken that step, she could not remember. Suddenly, the ground had not been there beneath her feet and she had fallen into space, clawing wildly at the air, aware of a strange rumbling sound close at hand, and then – silence, merciful silence.

At first, in hospital, suffering the agony of her self-inflicted injuries, she had lain sleepless, night after night, when the effects of the pain-killing drugs had worn off, seeing in her mind's eye Gavin dancing with that redhead; recalling her bitter jealousy, knowing what would eventually happen between them in the park, beneath the trees.

Walking out of the Olympia Hall had not been an impulsive gesture. Sitting there at the table, she had realized quite clearly that to walk out would mean the end of their relationship. Her decision to leave had been the hardest decision of her life. Her mother had drilled into her since childhood that pride was a sin. Perhaps it was, but pride had stiffened her backbone that night. Wonderful, sinful pride had given her the courage to do what she did: to make that bid for self-respect.

Now she no longer cared about Gavin and the redhead. The long weeks of her illness had washed away all the pain and jealousy, as if her mind had healed along with her bruised and battered body, because of the understanding of her friends who had talked her through the darkness into the light.

Generally speaking, George Butterworth had had a rough passage through life so far as romance was concerned. The youngest of four brothers, the one they jokingly referred to as 'Georgie-Porgie' or 'the Runt', he had usually managed to end up with their cast-off girlfriends. When Ralph, Henry or Bert had moved on to fresh fields and pastures new down at the Darlington Palais de Dance in Skinnergate, 'You take care of Sibyl, Daisy or Nancy,' they would say, knowing that he would hand back the goods, un-damaged, if they changed their minds. And so he had found himself stuck with a variety of tearful young females, none of whom he had fancied very much, acting as a kind of nursemaid.

Unfortunately, Nancy had fancied *him*. 'You're much nicer than your brothers,' she'd told him confidentially one Saturday afternoon, in town. 'More understanding, like.' (She ended nearly every sentence with 'like') 'Oooh!' Dragging him towards a jeweller's window, 'Look at all them lovely engagement rings!' she exclaimed. Warning bells had jangled in his brain.

Later, over tea and toasted crumpets in Binns' Café, he'd really got the wind up when she had started on about those nice semi-detached houses in Neville Road, saying she fancied living there one of these days. He knew what she was driving at. Well, let her get on with it. He was sick and tired of his brother's cast-offs. He wanted a girl of his own choosing, a petite blonde for preference, instead of which he'd landed himself with a fat little lass in Waaf uniform. Petite blondes, apparently, weren't interested. He had been forced to settle for what he could get.

Not that he hadn't looked forward to their date, but things hadn't worked out right. Meggie had seemed on edge, suspicious of his motives. Now he knew why. She thought he was married! Married! His pride stung, he had taken the huff and pretended not to hear when she'd called after him. Let her stew in her own juice! Meanwhile, he had stewed in *his* juice, unable to find anyone else to go out with him. The girls he'd asked had made excuses: they were too busy, otherwise engaged, or frankly disinterested. One of them had told him to get lost.

Only one thing for it. He'd wait for Meggie outside the cookhouse, try his luck once more. Then, if she didn't want to go out with him again, fair enough. Ah, there she was now.

'Hello, Meggie.'

'Oh, hello George.'

He couldn't tell if she was pleased to see him or not. 'Do you fancy going to the pictures tonight?'

'I don't mind.'

'Same time? Same place?'

'Yes. All right. Fine!'

'Great! Fine! See you later, then!'

Returning to the Wrennery had been, at first, a small triumph for Ruth Maple as the girls crowded round her, saying they were pleased to see her, asking her how she was feeling after the accident. All except one.

Dinah Pritchard stared at her as if she had just crawled out of the woodwork. Too involved in her own emotional entanglements to care tuppence about anyone else's, she said coldly, 'I gather that you are to be given preferential treatment from now on. The trouble is, the senior service is being ruined these days by unselective recruitment – girls with no backbone, no breeding.'

'That remark was uncalled for,' Laura said angrily, springing to Ruth's defence. 'Ruth has just come out of hospital.'

'One cannot help wondering why it was necessary for her to go into hospital in the first place,' Dinah remarked.

'Why you sanctimonious . . .' Eyes blazing, giving vent to her anger, doing what she had felt like doing for a long time, Laura struck Dinah on the cheek.

Dinah flinched, then smiled. 'You do realize that

assaulting a senior officer is a serious offence? I shall report this matter to the station commander.'

Incensed, 'Yes, why don't you do just that?' Grace broke in excitedly. 'And while you're about it, don't forget to tell her why you got a well deserved smack on the kisser. I'll tell you something else, your ladyship. Stick around here much longer, and I'll give you a kick up the arse.' She grinned wickedly. 'Now what price unselective recruitment? I guess that threatening a senior officer with assault is a crime too. But I'll tell you this for nothing, you jumped up example of so called good breeding, I'd face a court martial for doing what I'd like to do to you right now!'

A complaint had been lodged, a petty officer physically and verbally assaulted. Now First Officer Gantry was faced with the unpleasant task of considering the evidence and administering justice.

Seated behind her desk, she asked Palliser to call into her office the three girls involved in the fracas, and ask the witnesses, Maple, King, and Watts, to wait outside for the time being.

Dinah entered first, followed by Grace and Laura. Pritchard, Gantry noticed, seemed elated as though she were revelling in the proceedings, this bringing to book of her colleagues. Leafing through a sheaf of papers, tapping her pen on the blotter, Gantry doubted her ability to remain impartial, so deep was her dislike of Pritchard. Despite her expensively bought education, the girl would make poor officer material.

The assault occurred, according to the petty officer, after she had made some jocular remark to Wren Maple.

'What was that remark?'

'I scarcely remember, ma'am, it was so un-important.'

'And then what happened?'

'Wren Prentiss struck me.'

'Prentiss?' Gantry gazed coolly at Dinah. 'You mean Wren Peters?'

Dinah's face betrayed her anger at being corrected. Longing to have her say, Grace broke in, 'Excuse me, ma'am, but if Petty Officer Pritchard doesn't remember what she said to Ruth, I do.'

'That's enough, McGregor. You may speak when requested to do so, is that clear?'

'Perfectly clear. Sorry, ma'am.'

Later, Gantry asked Palliser, over a cup of tea, what she had made of the affair.

'Speaking from a purely personal viewpoint, I thought that Pritchard deserved a slap on the face. All that nonsense about unselective recruitment, girls with no breeding, no backbone. Just who the hell does she think she is?'

'Lady MacBeth?' Gantry suggested, tongue-in-cheek.

Palliser laughed. 'Quite so. Thank heaven there were witnesses. I rather think that her ladyship came out the loser on this occasion.

'Strictly between ourselves, I'm rather pleased that she did,' Gantry confessed, pouring herself another cup of tea. 'Quite frankly, I felt inclined to dismiss the matter when I had heard all the evidence, but the fact remained that she had been struck on the face – that much was evident – her cheek was still quite red – and I was duty bound to take that fact into consider-ation when I meted out punishment to Peters and McGregor.'

'I'm sure they realize, ma'am, that forty-eight hours confined to base was the lightest punishment that you could possibly have inflicted,' Palliser observed, filled with admiration for her senior officer's sense of fair play.

As if she knew what her liaison officer was thinking, Gantry said wryly, 'You might change your mind about me when I tell you that I have decided to withdraw my letter of recommendation to the Officers' Selection Committee on Pritchard's behalf, for the simple reason that I believe her to be unsuitable officer material. In my opinion, the girl is a trouble maker.'

'Well, this isn't too bad, is it, all things considered,' Grace said cheerfully. 'Forty-eight hours confined to base. We'll be free the first thing Monday morning.' A thought struck her. 'Oh, Lord, Scottie and I will miss the Saturday night dance! What about you, Laura? Had you and Rob made any plans for the weekend?'

Laura said wistfully. 'Not really. We were just going to have a lazy time together at the flat; Saturday evening at the pictures, perhaps; Sunday morning reading the newspapers and listening to the wireless before Rob went back on duty.'

'Never mind,' Grace said consolingly, 'there'll be other weekends.' She sighed deeply. 'Know what? I wish now that I *had* given Dinah a good swift kick in the pants.'

Laura smiled, but Grace sensed that she was troubled. Not by the extra duties they had been given as part of their punishment. No, it was more than that.

She kept on looking out of the window at the sea, the way she had done that day after the *Goldie* was blown out of the water.

'Cheer up,' Grace counselled. 'After all, we're both in the same boat. Hey, now what have I said wrong? Where are you going?'

Heart thumping, Laura raced downstairs to the duty office. 'Please, may I make a telephone call? It's terribly important.'

'Sorry, old girl. You know the rules. No outgoing or incoming calls, I'm afraid,' the duty officer said sympathetically, 'not while you're undergoing discipline.'

'But you don't understand, I *must* speak to my husband.'

'I'm sorry, Peters. I'd be in hot water myself if I let you make a phone call.' The duty officer wavered. 'Mind you, there's nothing to stop *me* ringing the number, leaving a message.'

'Oh, thank you.' Laura waited. The duty officer picked up the telephone in the outer office, asked for the number she had been given. Laura waited. The seconds ticked by. The duty officer shook her head. 'Sorry, there's no reply.'

'Thanks for trying.'

In the same boat, Laura thought bleakly, hurrying back to the T/P room. In the same boat. Rob must have already left the flat on his way to the harbour. If she hurried she might catch a glimpse of him. She could not have explained to anyone her deep sense of foreboding.

'All aboard, Skipper,' Tim Merrydew reported briskly.

'Fine. Let's get going, then.'

'What this time, sir?'

'An enemy aircraft down in the Drink. Any more questions?' Rob grinned at his second in command.

'On a Sunday. They've got a bloody nerve.' Tim grinned back at him. 'OK, sir. Theirs not to reason why . . .'

As the *Rosie* gathered speed, Rob raised his hand, just in case Laura happened to be watching from one of the Wrennery windows. All she could see, from that distance was the launch setting out to sea. Even so, blinded with tears, she lifted her hand in a gesture of goodbye.

They spotted the crew of the *Dornier* just before sunset. The sun, going down in a blaze of glory, had turned the sea to molten gold. Liquid fire ran swiftly beneath the bows of the *Rosie*. The order came: 'Throttle back the engines, lower the scramble nets.' The *Rosie* trembled gently in the shimmering gold water as the Germans came aboard, shrugging aside help. On deck, the captain of the *Dornier* clicked his heels and gave the Nazi salute. Right arm extended, 'Heil Hitler,' he barked defiantly.

Jimmy McGregor clenched his fists, Tim Merrydew spat out a choice swear word. Rob's lips tightened. 'Signal base,' he told Jimmy, briefly. 'Mission accomplished. We're coming home.'

The *Rosie* heaved slightly in the swell. The sea darkened as the blazing sun sank beyond the horizon. The mine, detached from its moorings, drifted slowly to the surface. *Rosie*'s engines throbbed into life. Her bows cut gracefully through the water. The mine struck the launch amidships. The sea shimmered blood red once more, this time with the glow from the blazing fuel tanks.

There were no survivors, British or German.

Gantry broke the news to Peters and McGregor. Sending for them, she told them calmly, but with obvious sympathy, what had happened. The wreckage of the *Rosie* had been spotted early that morning by a reconnaisance aircraft.

They listened in silence. No tears. No hysteria. Gantry felt proud of them, these girls among those whom Petty Officer Pritchard had demeaned as lacking in breeding and backbone.

Quietly Laura entered the flat. She could almost taste the silence. Slowly she crossed the hall and went into the bedroom. Rob's uniform was on its hanger. He would have worn his second blues and a pullover on duty last night. His shaving gear was in the bathroom; the shaving brush still slightly damp; his bathrobe behind the door. Putting her arms around it, she stood there for a little while, her cheek nestled against the folds; catching the intangible fragrance of soap and pine crystals, too stunned to weep, her grief too deep for tears, as if her tears had frozen somewhere in the region of her heart.

Presently, she went into the sitting room and stood by the window looking out to sea. Rob was somewhere out there, resting in peace; forever a part of those restless tides he had loved; a brave man who had fought and lost his final battle against an implacable foe. And yet, on a day like this, with sunlight shining on the waves, the horizon calm and still beneath a peerless summer sky, the sea seemed more friend than enemy.

She could not believe that he was dead, that never again would she hear his voice, feel the touch of his lips on hers, when everything she saw and touched reminded her of him – the roses he had given her, his library books on the table near the window, the Sunday papers beside his favourite chair.

Looking at the telephone, she remembered that she had been allowed to ring him when she knew she was being confined to quarters, recalled his understanding words: 'Never mind, darling, these things happen.'

'I didn't stop to think.'

'I would have done the same thing, my love.'

'You don't blame me, then?'

'Blame you? I'm proud of you. You stood up for what you believed in. That takes courage.'

'I'm sorry about our weekend.'

'There'll be other weekends. Cheer up, darling. Remember, I love you.'

At least she had those last three spoken words of his to cling to, and yet . . . if only she had been with him on that Sunday morning. Now she must live with the thought that her loss of control had cost her those final moments with Rob. She would never forgive herself, or Dinah.

Bitterness lay in her heart like a stone as she walked across the room. Bitterness intermingled with the dead weight of her unshed tears; a feeling of loneliness, so intense that she wished she could die.

It was then she noticed the envelope and the tiny package on the mantelpiece. Opening the box, she saw the brooch embedded in a soft nest of cottonwool. The note read:

> My darling Laura,
>   Eventually I found it! Knowing how much you wanted one, I scoured every antique shop in Ringley. The letters MIZPAH stand for – 'The Lord watch between thee and me when we are apart from one another'.
>
> Eternally yours,
Rob

Her tears came slowly at first, not gently but harshly. Tears of grief caught in sobbing intakes of breath, welling up from the misery and pain buried deep within.

Later, when she felt calmer, she rang the Scarborough labour exchange and asked to speak to her father.

'Laura? What's wrong?'

'It's Rob . . . '

'When? When did it happen?'

'Yesterday.'

'I'll come at once!'

It was as simple as that. No unnecessary questions, no fruitless expressions of sympathy, no telling her to 'keep her chin up'. Merely a lifeline of love thrown out to her across a stormy sea at a time when she needed her father's love and understanding to help her through the difficult days ahead.

Part Four

21

Paris sweltered beneath a cloudless sky. Balconies had been draped with the blazing red white and blue of the Tricolor – the flag of France, of Liberty, Equality, Fraternity; Swastikas torn down in defiance of the Germans.

Trees in the gardens and boulevards were in full leaf, the pavements packed with people surging towards the throbbing artery of the Champs-Elysées. Victory scented the air like blossoms as they trooped joyously, singing and cheering, to welcome their liberators.

Word had spread like wildfire; news of the great Allied advance, the tide of men and armoured vehicles sweeping triumphantly across the whole of France; news of General Patton's capture of five of the bridge-heads across the Seine; news of the imminent arrival of General Leclerc's victorious Free French armoured columns probing westward from Versailles.

Several thousand German troops were still in Paris, fighting from desperately defended pockets of resistance throughout the city. The sound of sporadic firing and explosions could be heard above the laughter and movement of the crowds, but nothing could dampen the high-spirited forward surge to cheer their hero, General Leclerc, whose tanks were already within striking distance of the capital.

A man, roughly dressed in the uniform of a porteur

des baggages, merged with the crowds near the Tuilleries, his mouth curved in a grim smile of satisfaction that he had lived to see this day.

Buffeted by the throng flowing towards the Arc de Triomphe, too weary to quicken his pace, Pierre Lefevre remembered the way the war had started for him, as an idealistic young Air Force pilot eager to fight for his country in those fraught days of 1939, before France surrendered to the Germans.

A patriotic Frenchman to the soul, angered and humiliated, bewildered by his country's imminent defeat and badly in need of direction, a new sense of purpose, he had listened, with a dawning awareness of hope, to the exiled General de Gaulle's rallying broadcast from London to Frenchmen everywhere; his stirring words, 'Obedience to the government is not the only course open to you. Here is your chance to fight for the honour and glory of France'.

By the early summer of 1940, the Germans had overrun the Low Countries. Boulogne had fallen, cutting off the British Expeditionary Force near Dunkirk. It could be only a matter of time, days perhaps, before the Nazi Swastika flew over Paris. The Dutch had been ordered to stop fighting. Any attempt to reach England to join de Gaulle's resistance movement must be made now. Patriotic Frenchmen everywhere were flocking by sea and air to join de Gaulle. Pierre's compatriots, his crew, and fellow officers, were willing to take a chance. And so the decision had been made. They would leave their base at Chartres at dawn the next day.

That night he had lain sleepless in his bed, thinking of his family, his father, Gaston, his mother, Louise

Lefevre, and his three sisters, Hortense, Eloise and Gigi. The letter he had written to them was already on its way. In it he had made no direct reference to his escape plan, but they would realize his intention by his words: 'One day, perhaps, the phoenix will rise from the ashes. Remember me to "The Rose of Picardy". Tell her that I will try to uphold, with honour, all that she stands for.'

The Rose of Picardy, the single-seater plane his father kept as a proud reminder of his prowess as a First World War flier, had been named after the ballad to which he and Louise had danced at their first meeting, a song which somehow reflected the gentle blossoming of their love affair in that long gone summer of 1917.

Lying there in the darkness, awaiting the dawn, Pierre remembered his home in Normandie, a sprawling farmhouse near Falais. Saw clearly, in his mind's eye, the row of poplars flanking the drive leading up to the house; the hayfields, rich and lush beneath a summer sun; the place and the people he loved more than anything else on earth, and felt beneath his pillow for the rosary of shining blue beads his mother had given him at their last meeting.

She had been wearing a brightly coloured cotton robe at the time, her long, slightly fading blonde hair caught back with a tortoise-shell comb. Whenever he thought of her, he imagined her moving gracefully, fragrantly through life; possessed of that inate glamour of every true Frenchwoman; poised, calm and unshakeable, adored by her husband and children. He remembered going upstairs with her that last morning; the scent of the roses on her dressing-table, the tears

269

in her eyes when she had handed him the rosary; her words, 'This is very precious to me. It belonged to my grandmother. I want you to have it Pierre. Keep it with you always and remember, whenever you hold it, that you are not alone. That someday, God willing, we will be together again.'

She must have guessed then, that this might be their last meeting for a very long time.

Since his escape to Britain, he had neither seen nor heard of his family again. And yet he had been close to home so many times during the past five years . . .

A burst of machine-gun fire rang out suddenly from one of the boulevards near the Champs-Elysées: the dull crump of exploding hand-grenades. Volleys of shots quickly followed. Somewhere, close at hand men were dying as the Germans, cornered like rats, fought on for the glory of the Third Reich.

At least the enemy, and those Free French fighters, flushing out the German pockets of resistance throughout the city, fought openly with rifles and bullets. Pierre's own battles had been far less spectacular; fought undercover, his only weapons a pistol and a two-way radio transmitter; his mission to melt, chameleon fashion, into the background, to watch and listen, to glean vital information concerning enemy movements, and relay that information to the Allied Headquarters in London.

The sound of gunfire reminded him of that dawn crossing; of leaving the French coast; the brilliant flashes of bursting anti-aircraft shells; the cottonwool puffs of smoke, the sudden lurching of the aircraft as one of the shells found its target. Then, over the English Channel, they had encountered an impenetrable fog bank. From that moment, the instrument panel shattered beyond repair, the plane listing badly, with black smoke choking the atmosphere, they had flown blind, losing all sense of direction.

Now, swaying slightly on his feet, Pierre saw, with intense pity, bunches of flowers strewn on the pavement beneath a line of freshly made bullet holes. The splashes of dried blood told their own story: the public execution of innocent men and women lined up and shot by the Germans the day before. Christ! Would there never come an end to all the killing? The wanton waste of human life?

A longing for home, so intense, so powerful, that he could scarcely continue walking, suddenly overwhelmed him. The tide of humanity pushing past him, the glaring sky above, the heat of the pavement beneath his feet, the wild bursts of cheering as the first of Leclerc's armoured divisions rumbled into view, intensified that longing: his need for peace, the quietude of home, an end to war. But that was an impossible dream. Until this war was over and his mission accomplished, there could be no going back.

The sudden drone of aircraft in the skies over Paris, reminded him once more of that flight to freedom in the early summer of 1940; the gripping feeling of excitement in his belly as the fog had begun to clear and they saw the ground beneath their wings – rolling acres of deserted moorland, rain-drenched, under a pewter-coloured sky. England, he had thought. We have made it at last! Tears had tightened his throat as he circled slowly, and prepared to land.

While the British had felt let down, betrayed by the

French, after Dunkirk, those who had proved their loyalty to the Allied cause, who came to England to continue the fight, were given a hero's welcome.

Pierre remembered, with gratitude, the kindness and respect shown to himself and his crew when the police had arrived on the scene, following the report of a spotter who had witnessed their landing. But, to his amazement, he had not understood a word they said, he who had studied English to degree level at the Sorbonne. The police sergeant and his men spoke in what appeared to be a strange, foreign tongue. The reason why had slowly dawned on him. They had landed, not in England, but Scotland!

At the police station, a room on the ground floor of a stone-built cottage in a tiny hamlet, with rain beating against the windows, he and his crew had been given hot, sweet cups of tea laced with whisky; had had their papers checked to establish their identities. Then, young Jean Paul Ligny, the wireless operator, and Claude Dumont, the rear-gunner, had been whisked away to a nearby cottage hospital to receive medical attention. Later, Pierre, his co-pilot and the remaining members of his crew were escorted to the Proctor's house where they were fed a hot meal of cock-a-leekie soup, bannocks and bacon, and given beds for the night.

Next morning, after breakfast, they were driven to the Naval dockyard at Rosyth where they were handed over to a Free French Air Force officer, Armand Metiere – a man whom Pierre had instantly recognized as a former tutor at the Sorbonne.

'Ah, we meet again, mon ami?' Armand had wrung his hand, smiled charmingly, and escorted Pierre into his office. 'So you made the great decision? But then, knowing your background, your dedication to the cause of freedom. I would have expected nothing less of you.'

'All I want,' Pierre said eagerly, 'is a chance to continue the fight, to join the Free French Air Force here, in Great Britain.'

'I understand your enthusiasm, of course,' Armand replied sympathetically, 'but that may not be possible.' Lighting a cigarette, he narrowed his eyes against the rising smoke. 'Despite the number of French airmen who have flown here from North Africa, and others, like yourself, who have crossed the Channel, it seems unlikely that there will emerge a Free French Air Force, as such. The likelihood is that we shall amalgamate with the British.'

'But that is unthinkable!' Pierre said explosively, pacing the room. 'I came here with one thought in mind and now you tell me that we may lose our independence!'

Metiere sighed. Stubbing out his half smoked cigarette, he said, 'I understand your point of view. But has it occurred to you that there may be different, perhaps better ways of serving one's country?'

Pierre glanced curiously at his senior officer. 'What are you driving at?'

'Nothing. At least not for the time being.' Metiere laughed. 'We will discuss it later. Meanwhile, you must learn the art of relaxation. Which reminds me, there's a party in the Polish officers' mess tonight: lots of pretty girls, food, and drink. I'll pick you up around eight o'clock.'

Worried about his family, Pierre had never felt less

like dancing. Not that he disliked dancing, or girls. Far from it. In the previous weeks, during which Paris had fallen, there had been many such parties: evenings spent in the company of empty-headed young women who seemed unaware, as he danced with them, how much he longed for the quietude of his home in Normandie, the sight of a curving line of poplar trees beneath the stars.

One girl in particular, a Wren called Dinah Felix, had pursued him so relentlessly that he had felt inclined, at first, to refuse her invitation to attend a dance at Armley House, but that would have seemed churlish. And so, reluctantly, he had accepted.

Anticipating his arrival, the moment he appeared she had battened on to him like a leech, chattering away to him in her schoolgirl French, and sweeping him triumphantly on to the dance floor, as if he belonged to her.

But there had been another girl at that dance. A girl whose face he had never forgotten. Such a lovely face; heart-shaped, with blue-grey eyes and framed with soft golden hair. He still remembered the tune they had danced to: 'Stay in my arms, Cinderella', the way she had closed her eyes as he held her to his heart, her innocence and charm, her lack of pretension; the way she had later looked up at him, worried that she might trip over his feet; Her words, 'I'm not a very good dancer . . .'; the way she had blushed when he asked her name . . . 'Laura' she'd said.

'Laura. Ah, such a pretty name . . .'

Then the girl had been swept away from him as the Paul Jones continued. But he had meant what he said: 'I hope that we shall meet again,'

He had meant to contact her later that evening, to invite her to dine with him the next day. But, like Cinderella, she had simply disappeared into thin air . . . Then Dinah had twisted her ankle on the soap-flakes, and he'd found himself alone in the garden with the silly creature, disliking intensely her childish attempts to make him kiss her, her repeated references to the moonlight, to *Romeo and Juliet*.

'I mean, even you, a Frenchman, must have heard of Romeo and Juliet?' she had whispered intently, smiling up at him, placing her hands on his shoulders. 'Listen . . .

O, swear not by the moon, the inconstant moon,
That monthly changes in her circled orb . . .'

And all the time he had been chafing to find Laura again.

Next morning he had received orders to report immediately to Carlton Gardens, General de Gaulle's London headquarters. And so he had left Rosyth with a deep feeling of regret, as though something of vital importance had been lost beyond recall, swallowed up by the bloody machine that men called war.

22

After Rob died, Laura knew that she could not bear to stay on in Ringley. Memories were too poignant.

She found herself imagining, everywhere, his tall familiar figure – 'In the small café, the park across the way' – Strange that such a sentimental ballad could conjure up bittersweet memories. There had been no 'Children's Carousel', no 'chestnut tree', no 'wishing well' in their 'park across the way', and yet the song, 'I'll Be Seeing You', would never fail to rekindle memories of Rob.

Packing his personal belongings had been the worst task of all. What she would have done without her father's and Meggie's support, she could not imagine.

Will Prentiss had said nothing about his own troubles, but Laura could see for herself the effect they'd had on him. Curiously, her father's deep inner sadness had comforted Laura. No need of pretence between them. There never had been. By the simple acceptance of each other's sorrow, they drew comfort and strength from one another. Any unhappy situation, Laura realized, had always been made more bearable by her father's ability to say the right thing at the right time.

'It seems a pity having to give up your flat,' Will said quietly, helping Laura to pack the china teaset Meggie had given her for a wedding present.

'Yes. But only married couples are allowed to live out,' she explained, keeping her voice level. 'I just hope that whoever takes over will be as happy as we were.'

'I'm glad you were happy. It's comforting to know that.'

Laura said softly, 'I only wish that *you* were. Happy I mean.'

'I'm not sure that happiness is a prerequisite of living, at my age,' he said, 'at least not the kind of happiness that belongs to the very young. That kind of happiness rarely lasts.' He smiled. 'The important thing is knowing when you're happy: holding on to that happiness, the way I did, after you were born. At least that happiness has been ongoing.'

'What about Mum?' Laura held his hand.

'We're not rubbing along too well at the moment, but that is largely my fault. I never possessed the knack of making her happy. I'm not sure why. But I wouldn't want you to think that we haven't known better days. There are good times, and bad, in everyone's life.'

'Yes, I see what you mean.' She rubbed his hand against her cheek.

Will said, 'Believe me, Laura, you will find happiness again, one of these days. You are young enough to rebuild your life. And that is my wish for you. That, when this war is over, you will find someone else to care for.'

Grace and Ruth had travelled to Manchester together on compassionate leave. On their return to Ringley, they, and Laura, approached the commanding officer to request a posting.

Gantry listened sympathetically, understanding their

need to remain together if possible. 'I'll do what I can,' she promised, 'but don't bank on it.'

Later, she rang her friend, First Officer Phillips, in charge of HMS Grafton, a busy signals' station on the outskirts of London, explaining the situation.

Gantry however, had not extended heartfelt congratulations to Petty Officer Pritchard, when faced with the duty of informing her ladyship that she had been accepted as a trainee officer. Elevation to the crème-de-la-crème of the Women's Royal Naval Service was, in Gantry's opinion, an honour which Pritchard neither merited nor deserved. Someone had obviously been pulling strings behind her back to arrange Pritchard's promotion.

Shortly after that interview, Gantry received confirmation from Betty Phillips of McGregor's, Peters', and Maple's posting to Grafton. By an unfortunate coincidence, the three of them, and Dinah, were destined to share the same transport to Ringley station.

Not a word passed between them until, awaiting the arrival of the London train, Grace's anger had bubbled to the surface.

Confronting Dinah, who had elected to stand further along the platform, 'Before we part company,' she said in a voice harsh with emotion, 'I have only this to say to you, Dinah Pritchard. I shall hate you for as long as I live. The Mills of God grind slowly. I pray they'll grind you to dust. One of these days, I hope you'll be made to suffer as much as you've made other people suffer!'

'Don't, Grace, you're wasting your breath,' Laura laid a hand on her friend's arm. 'Dinah is not worth your anger, merely pity. I doubt if she even knows what you are talking about.'

That had happened two years ago, in the summer of 1942. Now the tide of war had turned at last. Paris had been liberated; the Belgian government had returned, in triumph, to Brussels; Antwerp had been recaptured by the Allied forces. With luck, the war in Europe would soon be over. And yet . . . despite her words on that station platform, Laura knew that she, too, would never forgive Dinah for denying her Rob's last hours on earth.

Looking out of the cabin window early one September morning, she noticed that the swallows were gathering on the network of telegraph wires strung between the aerial masts.

Since Rob's death, Laura had turned her thoughts to her new responsibilities as a Leading Wren, getting on with her life as he would have wished.

Yet, often, despite her efforts, the past came flooding back to her in unguarded moments, throwing her off balance. Such foolish things; the sound of rain at night; dance tunes heard on the wireless; moonlight; in springtime, the scent of lilacs; in autumn, leaves fluttering down from the trees; shadows on the grass, at sunset; a sudden laugh, a certain face which reminded her of Rob's. Now in the sight of those swallows dotted along the telegraph wires, in everything which led her to wondering what the future held for her, how it would be possible, when the war ended, to pick up the threads of her old life.

Scottie's death had plunged Grace into a miasma of

conflicting emotions concerning her religious beliefs. On that compassionate leave, after the loss of the *Rosie*, she had gone unwillingly to church with her parents, hating the cloying smell of the incense, the altar flowers, unable to join in the Mass.

Glancing sideways at her daughter, Mrs Flanagan assumed that grief over Scottie's death lay at the heart of her inability to join in the service. But it was more than that. Grace had known, standing there, that to pay tribute to a God who had not kept his side of the bargain, would be tantamount to uttering a blasphemy.

'If Scottie comes back to me, I will light a candle every day to Our Lady,' she had told Laura that night at the flat. Scottie *had* come back, and she had kept her promise. Now that Scottie was dead, there seemed no point in lighting candles any more. No purpose in giving thanks to a creator of life who allowed men to die in the full bloom of youth.

She had hated her father's constant harping on about religion, wanting her to go to confession. She also knew that if she opened her mouth to explain how she really felt, bitter, angry, resentful and disillusioned; that religion, as a means of comfort, had been tested and found lacking, her resolve never to enter a church again, there would have been a first-class row. And so she had kept quiet.

Afterwards had come news of her posting to HMS Grafton. How gladly she had packed her gear, seeing this as a new beginning. As much as she had loved Scottie, she had no wish to play the role of a grieving widow.

She had liked Grafton from the moment she saw

it – an older signals' station, far less raw and un-compromising than Ringley, within striking distance of the heart of London, which, despite the hammering it had taken during the Blitz was still the most exciting city on earth, possessed of a head-in-air pride and gutsiness which somehow reflected Grace's deter-mination to make the most of her life.

Scottie would have been the last person on earth to deny her the right to enjoy herself. And so, clinging to this belief, she had begun a relentless round of gaiety; dances, night clubs, and officers' mess parties.

But to Laura's way of thinking, Grace's warm-hearted nature had suffered an eclipse. Her laughter rang hollow, and that bubbling charm of hers, which had drawn people towards her, now seemed as brittle as glass.

Quietly observant, Laura regretted the changes she saw in Grace, who refused to even talk about Scottie, as though she had deliberately blanked out every memory of their life together at Ringley.

But what right had she to criticize? Hadn't she, too, tried to blot out painful memories of the past when Rob died?

Curiously, Ruth Maple had emerged the strongest of the three. It had seemed to Ruth, when she knew that Gavin could no longer be a part of her life – or of any other woman – that she had been absolved from the misery of wondering where he was, what he was doing. Jealousy, she had discovered, was an emotion which ate away the heart like acid, blotting out every decent, worthwhile emotion.

She had been afraid, at first, of returning to her home in Manchester, of seeing her mother and Aunt Ada.

Afraid of being questioned too closely about her 'accident'.

In the event, she had coped far better than expected, simply saying that she had been on the cliffs, too near the edge, when the ground had given way beneath her. Stonewalling the way she had done when Second Officer Palliser had tried to pump her she realized that her mother had lost the power to dictate to her. Seeing her as she really was – an over-bearing, self-centred hypochondriac who had made excuses not to visit her in hospital at a time when she, Ruth, had needed someone close to her, a warm, comforting presence, a shoulder to cry on – Ruth remembered that it was Laura's shoulder she had cried on, that it was she who had given her the courage to endure.

Afterwards had come HMS Grafton, far away from disturbing memories of the past, and her promotion to Leading Wren. It was at Grafton she had started visiting the lending library in Hampstead Village, paying regular visits to the hairdresser to have her lank hair cut and permed, wearing lipstick and nylon stockings – making sure that her seams were straight – concert-going with Laura, becoming a person in her own right. Standing proud and strong on her own two feet. Freed from the shackles of her former indecisive personality, Ruth was now a much stronger, more independent character.

In more reflective moments, she would think of Gavin; not with hatred, but a feeling of gratitude that it was he who had unwittingly taught her the most valuable lesson of her life so far – that sexual appetite had no bearing on real love; that jealousy demeaned the human spirit; that no matter how desolate the past, there was always the future.

One hot sultry September night when sleep would not come, Laura drew back the curtains of the cabin she shared with Grace and Ruth, and stared up at the full moon riding high among a constellation of stars.

What a marvellous concert it had been. Pouishnoff playing Chopin. How surprised and delighted she had been when Ruth, eyes shining, hands clasped, had risen to her feet to applaud the maestro – like a butterfly emerging from its chrysalis.

On their way back to Grafton, 'I had no idea you were so interested in classical music,' Laura said. 'You are a surprising person, Ruth.'

'Am I?'

'What will you do when the war is over?'

'There's only one thing I can do. Stay on in the Wrens. I could never go back to my old job in Manchester, my old way of life. I'm a different person now. But what about you, Laura? What will you do?'

'I'm not quite sure . . .'

Hopping aboard the bus, paying the fare to Hampstead, Laura changed the subject. She knew what Ruth said was true. There could be no going back. As much as she loved her home, her family, the magical days of youth were over and done with. The war had taken a starry-eyed girl and changed her into another person. A woman, a stranger in her own eyes, so that she neither cared nor loved as deeply as she used to.

In one sense, she was glad of this war which, despite its hardships, had given her a feeling of security in the day-to-day routine of the rising bell, lights out, making her bunk with the anchors pointing upwards, not down. But she worried about the decision making the end of the war would entail.

It happened suddenly, without warning, just as Laura and her watch were about to go off duty.

The sound that filled the sky resembling the buzzing of angry hornets.

Suddenly, 'Get your heads down,' someone shouted urgently. 'It's one of those German V-2 bombs!'

Then had come the terrible, fraught silence when the motor cut out, followed by an ear-splitting explosion.

23

It had seemed, to the romantically minded Meggie, a poor kind of proposal. George had not exactly swept her off her feet with his ardour. They had been walking round the town square in Ringley one Saturday afternoon when, nearing the registry office, standing for a moment or two to watch the emergence of the wedding party – the bride and groom both in uniform – George had said off-handedly, 'I suppose we ought to be thinking of getting married.'

'Huh?' Meggie felt her mouth sag open. She thought she'd heard George say something about getting married but she couldn't be certain. An Army lorry had rumbled past at that moment. 'Say it again, George,' she insisted.

'Say what?'

'What you said a minute ago.' They continued walking.

'Oh, you mean about us getting married?'

'Well, yes. Did you mean it?' she asked, anxiously. She might just have mis-heard.

'Yes, of course I meant it,' he replied impatiently, embarrassed because Meggie had stopped walking to stare at him.

'*Honestly?*'

'How many more times? Come on. It's starting to rain!'

'Are you – are we – going to choose the ring? Now, I mean. This afternoon?'

'Ring?' George looked startled. He hadn't thought about buying a ring. Women seemed to have engagement rings on the brain.

'*George!*'

'Oh, all right. Might as well, I suppose.'

'You might show a bit more enthusiasm.' Meggie sighed. Why couldn't he have bought the ring first, chosen a romantic setting, got down on one knee, and said, 'Meggie, darling, will you marry me?' Mind you, she couldn't exactly picture George on one knee. Men, apart from her screen heroes, had no sense of romance whatever, especially George. Still, any proposal was better than none.

Grabbing his arm, wasting no time, she hustled him across the road to the jewellers.

While George was having a quiet word with the assistant, Meggie stood near the counter staring at the fat, red velvet pads, catching the fire and dazzle of the expensive diamond and sapphire rings on display. One ring, in particular, a square cut diamond with sapphire shoulders, caught her eye. Oh, wouldn't it be wonderful if George lashed out, for once in his life, to buy her that ring?

At that moment, the elderly male assistant moved discreetly forward carrying three trays of rings which he placed on the counter for her consideration. Meggie leaned forward for a closer inspection. She had heard the phrase 'neat but not gaudy', but this was ridiculous. The diamonds appeared as pin-points set in tin. But no, it couldn't be *tin*. It must be platinum.

'What do you think?' George asked, anxious about

the financial side of choosing a ring, which he considered an unnecessary expense anyway.

If Meggie had said what she was really thinking at that moment, George would probably have left the shop in a huff. Her eyes strayed towards a pad displaying second-hand jewellery of Victorian design: semi-precious stones in gold settings. 'I'd like to look at these, if you don't mind.'

'Certainly, miss.' The assistant seemed pleased. George less so.

'Oh, isn't this one lovely!' Meggie's romantic heart lifted as she slipped on to her finger a half-hoop of opals; glorious, milky stones radiating a myriad of trapped colours. George gulped. 'I thought opals were unlucky,' he muttered.

'Unlucky? How could anything so beautiful possibly be unlucky?' Meggie smiled serenely. 'This is the one I want.' And if George hadn't brought enough money with him, she'd put something towards it herself.

George seemed relieved when he discovered that the second-hand ring would cost less than any of the microscopic diamond chippings. 'Ah, well, if that's what you want,' he said, more expansively, getting out his wallet.

Afterwards, they'd had tea at the Blue Bird Tea Shoppe, Meggie wearing her ring, glancing fondly across the table at her fiancé, sitting with her chin propped up on her left hand so the people at the other tables would realize that she was an engaged woman with a man to call her own. Not that any of them took a blind bit of notice.

'I'll have a white wedding,' she said dreamily, biting into a scone.

'A *white* wedding?' George frowned anxiously.

'Don't worry, you won't have it to pay for!'

'For heaven's sake, Meggie,' he said nervously, 'don't start on about the wedding now. We'll be late for the pictures if we don't get a move on.'

The film was *Casablanca*. 'Play it, Sam. Play "As Time Goes By" ', Meggie wept buckets; saw George as Humphrey Bogart, herself as Ingrid Bergman.

All that had happened over a year ago, during which time the capital 'R' in Romance had shrunk to quite a small 'r', due to George's reluctance to name the day; a hiatus which had caused more than one flare up between them.

'Anyone would think you didn't want to get married at all, George Butterworth,' Meggie had said accusingly at the time of their last battle royal. 'Well, do you or don't you? Because if you don't, you might just as well take this back!' Unfortunately, her grand gesture of flinging the ring in his face received a set-back when she couldn't get it off her finger.

'No need to be hasty,' George said. 'Why all the rush?'

'*Rush?* For goodness sake, George, we've been engaged for over a year now. If we don't do it soon, we won't do it at all! Or, perhaps I'm too fat. Is that it? Perhaps you don't really fancy me . . .'

'Of course I do. As a matter of fact, if you'd fancied me a bit more, we could have – well, you know what I mean. Remember, I *did* ask you . . . ?'

'What, and wear a white wedding dress, knowing . . . ? No, George, I've told you over and over again, that when we get married I want "it" lying down, on a proper bed, on our honeymoon.'

'All right, then,' he said desperately. 'Go ahead. Fix up the bloody wedding . . .'

'Right, I will! The sooner the better, as far as I'm concerned.'

At home in Wiltshire, on a month's compassionate leave, Meggie helped her mother with the thousand and one preparations necessary to the uniting of herself and George Butterworth in Holy matrimony, in the Hazelwitch village church.

With clothing coupons in short supply, what Meggie would wear on her day of days, had presented certain problems, until her mother had dug out her own wedding dress, slightly yellow with age, and far too tight to fit her more generously proportioned daughter.

'Never mind,' Lally said optimistically, 'I can let out the seams. There's plenty of spare material.'

Bang went Meggie's dream of floating down the aisle in a fairy-tale gown of white satin: a crinoline skirt caught up with bunches of pink rosebuds. She watched, with dismay, the refurbishing of her mother's wedding dress, and noticed that the let out seams were far lighter in colour than the rest of the garment. A dead give away.

All right, so what? she told herself resignedly. Everyone had to make do and mend nowadays. Perhaps she was daft in wanting a white wedding in the first place. Getting married in uniform would have presented far fewer problems. And, would Laura feel entirely at ease in the second-hand bridesmaid's dress she had seen advertized in the village shop window?

Meggie approached her wedding day with a host of misgivings. When her father told her, across the supper table, that he had killed a pig so there'd be plenty of roast pork sandwiches, sausages, and cold ham available for the reception, she had felt sick, excused herself, and rushed out into the fresh air.

The peace and quietude of the Wiltshire countryside, bathed in the light of a full moon, brought a modicum of peace to Meggie's troubled heart.

Leaning her elbows on the rustic bridge spanning the stream, the cause of so much contention between her father and Farmer Briggs, looking down into the water, being realistic, she wondered if she would be happy with George Butterworth or if she'd be better off as a single woman, content to fulfil her romantic dreams for the price of a seat in the stalls?

Perhaps some women, herself included, simply lacked the looks, the grace, the sexual drive, the ability and enterprize to enter into a life-long relationship with any man, particularly with an equally inept partner like George Butterworth.

George was *dull*! She knew that now. But, the day after tomorrow, unless she possessed enough wisdom and commonsense to break free, she would find herself saddled with George for the rest of her life. So what was the answer? Too late now, to break off the engagement.

That was the answer! God! And to think that it was she who had fairly bludgeoned poor George into marriage. Perhaps opals *were* unlucky, after all . . .

Suddenly, 'Meggie, is that you?' The voice seemed to come from nowhere.

'Who's there?' Startled she turned to see the figure of a man coming towards her across the bridge.

'It's me, John Smith. Do you remember? Sorry if I frightened you.'

'Johnny! What on earth are you doing here?'

Meggie's glance registered the fact that the boy she had talked to in the potato field, long ago, now had an arm missing.

'It's all right,' Johnny said quietly. 'No need to look away! No need to feel sorry for me neither. I lost my arm during the Dieppe raid in the autumn of 1942. So what? Lots of poor devils lost their lives. I count myself lucky.'

'But what are you doing here?'

Johnny shrugged awkwardly. 'Don't know, really, except I had a yen to revisit the old places; find out what happened to the people I knew. The times I've wondered if you'd married that black marketeer boy-friend of yours.'

'Fred Briggs?' Meggie said scornfully. 'Not likely. I told you there was nothing between us. But what about you and Mavis?'

'Mavis? Oh you mean that girl in the ATS? I wasn't really serious about her.'

'You mean, she wasn't serious about you?'

'Amounts to the same thing in the long run,'

'I suppose so.' Meggie looked up at the moon, remembering that day in the potato field. Suddenly she blurted, 'I'm getting married the day after tomorrow.'

'Married?' Johnny drew in a sharp breath.

'Why not?' Meggie stared at him defiantly. 'Did you think nobody would want me?'

'No! I never thought that!' Johnny protested. 'As a matter of fact you are the main reason why . . . I wanted to find out what had become of you.'

'Huh! You might have known, if you had bothered to keep in touch. Remember, you asked me to write to you once in a while? But you never even gave me your address.' There. It was out in the open at last.

'No, I'm sorry, I should have told you we'd be moving out soon. Perhaps you won't believe this, but I had a feeling I mightn't come back in one piece.' He laughed bitterly, 'Well, I was right about that at any rate.'

'What will you do after the war?' Meggie spoke softly, regretting her outburst. It was just that breaking his promise had niggled her ever since, had given her an inferiority complex.

'Oh, I'll be all right.' He smiled. 'I've been to a rehabilitation centre to learn office work. It's surprising what you can do with one hand. I just thank God it was my left arm. I must say, the government's been very good to me, and blokes like me.'

A sudden memory of Johnny standing in the potato field, wiping his forehead with the back of his left hand, brought tears to Meggie's eyes.

'Hey,' he said gently, 'none of that. You should be laughing. A bride on the eve of her wedding. Well, almost. He's a very lucky guy, if you ask me, this man you're going to marry.'

But Meggie, for some reason, couldn't stop crying. The water flowing beneath the bridge blurred suddenly. Johnny gave her his handkerchief. 'Here, blow.'

Meggie blew obediently, Johnny looked at her thoughtfully. 'You don't seem very happy, or is it just – nerves? I remember my sister cried almost non-stop for a week before her wedding.'

'I don't know what it is,' Meggie confessed, mopping her eyes. 'I just have the feeling that George doesn't really want to get married at all.'

Tilting Meggie's chin, 'Do *you*?' he asked.

'Yes,' she answered, too quickly. 'No. I *thought* I did, but I *don't*!'

'To this – George character you mean? Or is it just that you don't want to get married at all? Some women don't.'

'Of course I want to get married.'

'But not to George?'

'No.' Her lips trembled. She turned her head away.

'Leaving it a bit late, aren't you?' Johnny leaned against the parapet, looking down at her, thinking what a nice lass she was – warm-hearted, kind and unpretentious.

'What do you mean?'

'It's obvious, isn't it? Unless you do something smartish, you'll end up marrying the bloke whether you want to or not.'

'It's all very well for you to talk, but what *can* I do? Everything's fixed!' She looked at him, frowning, wishing him far away; turning up out of the blue, unsettling her mind.

'I know what I'd do,' Johnny said.

'What?'

Drawing in a deep breath, 'Tell George the wedding's off, and come to London with me,' he said.

'Are you out of your mind?' She stared at him in amazement. 'Have you the slightest idea what you're talking about? Apart from all the upset if I cancelled the wedding, why the hell should I go to London with you?'

'For a number of reasons.' He took a step towards her. 'Because I want you to. And, honestly, Meggie, you mustn't go through with this wedding. You'll regret it for the rest of your life.'

'That's all very fine.' She bridled, 'I might have known! So what if I were daft enough to do as you suggest? What then? I suppose I'd end up in some seedy hotel room, calling myself Mrs Smith.'

'If that's what you think, you had better go ahead.' Feeling as if he had received a blow in the face, Johnny turned away. 'Sorry I troubled you. Goodbye, Meggie, and – good luck!'

'No! Don't go! I'm sorry! Please come back!' Meggie's heart skipped a beat. 'Don't be angry! Oh, Johnny!'

Placing his right hand firmly about her waist, 'Then you will come with me?' he asked, knowing that this plump, warm-hearted girl was worth more than all the treasures on earth to him.

Meggie sighed. 'I guess so. I can't very well stay here. But what the heck shall I tell George, and my mother?'

'I'll come back to the house with you, if you like.'

'No. I wouldn't want you to do that. I must tell them in my own way.' She looked up at him, 'But what the hell *am* I supposed to say?'

Johnny laughed. 'Why not tell them the truth? That you are going off to London with a man you scarcely know, to find out if you care enough to marry him one of these days?'

24

Now she really had put the cat among the pigeons, Meggie thought, sitting beside Johnny on the early morning train to London.

She had thought poor George would expire on the other end of the telephone when she had rung up to tell him the wedding was off.

'What do you mean, it's off?' he shouted. 'It can't be off! What about the wedding presents? That engagement ring I paid for? You can't do this to me, Meggie! What about our honeymoon?'

'I'm sorry, George. Of course I'll return the ring. Well, you did say that opals were unlucky . . .'

Facing her parents had been a different matter entirely. Her mother had nearly thrown a fit when she knew that all her hard work on the wedding dress had been in vain. 'You must be out of your mind, Meggie,' she cried, wringing her hands. 'Cancelling the wedding at the last minute! What shall we tell the neighbours?' Appealing to her husband, 'You talk to her, Bob.'

'Now listen to me, my girl,' Bob said heavily, 'I've already killed that pig.'

'Oh, never mind about the pig, ask her about this man she's going off to London with. Who is he? What is he?'

Meggie said serenely, 'His name is John Smith. Surely you remember him? He helped us with the potato harvest in the autumn of 1942. In any case, whether you remember him or not doesn't really matter.'

'Doesn't matter? Of course it matters!'

'Don't you want me to be happy?'

'Yes, of course we do,' her mother wailed, 'but what about the neighbours?'

'I'm sorry, Mother, my mind's made up. I'm going to London with Johnny.'

Truth to tell, she hadn't quite believed it herself, until she had found herself sitting beside him in the railway carriage, jogging towards Paddington.

Later, walking along the Embankment, Johnny said, 'Look, Meggie, there's something you should know. Something I hadn't the guts to tell you last night. But I must. It might make a difference.'

Oh God, she thought, he's going to tell me he's married with five children. 'All right,' she said resignedly, 'might as well get it off your chest.'

'The truth is, I have to wear a – contraption . . .'.

Relief surged through Meggie. 'What kind of a – contraption?'

'A kind of – harness. It's a bloody nuisance really, though I can manage to strap it on without much trouble.'

'A – harness? Is that all?'

'It isn't just the harness,' Johnny said desperately, 'it's what's attached to it.' He wiped his forehead with the back of his hand. 'It's a bit primitive, really, which is why I prefer not to wear it at all if I can help it.'

'You mean a false arm?'

'Yeah, a false arm – with a hook at the end of it! A bloody hook, I ask you!'

'Well, that's not the end of the world, is it?' she said cheerfully. 'The main thing is, does it help you to manage better on your own? If so, what the heck does it matter what it looks like?'

'Oh, *Meggie*.' Bending down, he kissed her, uncaring of the passers-by. 'Trust you to say that. Oh God, Meggie, I love you. Guess I've loved you since that day in the potato field.'

Looking into his eyes, 'I love you, too,' she said.

'Then you will marry me one of these days?'

Meggie smiled mysteriously. Looking down at the River Thames flowing swiftly towards the sea, feeling the tug of romance in her soul, she said, unromantically, 'Of course I'll marry you, you chump!'

Suddenly it didn't matter a damn that she was plump and plain. She was loved – and that made all the difference.

25

Laura would always think of that fraught September of 1944 as a turning point in her life, a time of intense physical activity, a kaleidoscope of swiftly changing events, beginning on the day that V-2 bomb exploded on Hampstead Heath.

The girls had flung themselves to the floor when the motor cut out. None of them had known what to expect. They had simply lain there, waiting. The explosion, when it happened, was ear-shattering. Then came the aftermath; choking clouds of dust from falling plaster, rather like the earthquake scene in *San Francisco*, Laura thought afterwards. Someone had been playing 'Mairzy Doats' on the common-room gramophone before the blast occurred. Curiously, the record had gone on playing.

'Christ! That was a close call! What the hell will the bastards think of next? Are you OK?' The voice belonged to a young sailor who had been delivering messages to the T/P room when the bomb came over.

'I think so.' The sailor helped her to her feet, and she stood there, shakily, brushing the dust from her uniform . . .

The sailor grinned. 'What a bloody silly song.'

'Yes, isn't it?'

'The sooner we get away from here, the better. That ceiling doesn't look any too safe.'

Laura saw what he meant. Gaping holes had appeared in places, hence the clouds of grey dust choking the atmosphere. Meanwhile, the young sailor, a self-appointed Sir Galahad, was helping Ruth from the wreckage.

The incident imprinted itself indelibly on Laura's memory. In years to come, or whenever she heard that ridiculous song, 'Mairzy Doats', she would remember that day. The day Dinah Pritchard came to Grafton.

Laura had been on her way to the canteen when a taxi drew up near the front steps. At first she had taken no notice. The comings and goings of officers were a daily occurrence at a station the size of Grafton. In any case, she had been preoccupied with the events of the day. The damage caused by the V-2 bomb had left some of the cabins unfit for occupation. Grace, Ruth and she had spent the best part of the afternoon shifting their gear into another room, attempting to remove some of the dust from their belongings.

When the tea bell went, Grace and Ruth had gone ahead to bag a table and join the queue. Laura followed a few minutes later. The wide glass doors of the vestibule had been opened to let in fresh air; a squad of sailors were busy clearing the steps of rubble, otherwise she might not have glanced that way at all. Then, something about the officer getting out of the taxi had caught her attention. Dinah, she thought. Oh, God, it couldn't be. But there was no mistaking that familiar figure. It was Dinah, sure enough, wearing the uniform of a third officer.

In that split second of recognition, her many and varied emotions concerning Pritchard rose to the surface of Laura's mind – that last scene at Ringley

Station in particular, when she had seen in Dinah's face all the meanness and deceit of which she was capable. She had said then that she felt sorry for her, and this was partly true. Following Rob's death, she would have felt sorry for anyone incapable of loving. But there was more to it than that. God only knew how hard she had tried, throughout the past two years, to forgive and forget, to overcome her feelings of bitterness towards this girl whose arrogance had cost her the sharing of Rob's last day, but that was impossible.

Then Third Officer Pritchard walked up the steps, followed by the taxi-driver carrying her luggage. Laura had not shirked the confrontation, had stood there, curious to witness Dinah's reaction when their eyes met. She might have known what that reaction would be. Meeting Laura face to face, Pritchard's eyes swept over her contemptuously, dismissively, as they had so often before. Then, without a word or a sign of recognition, she sailed grandly along the corridor towards the duty office.

In Paris, billboards blazoned headlines of the provisional government's intention to place on trial those Vichy war criminals responsible for the surrender of France after Dunkirk.

Sitting alone in a bar near the Rue de la Paix, drinking a glass of lukewarm beer, staring at a copy of *Le Figaro*, Pierre Lefevre thought dispassionately that it was over at last, the relentless pressure brought to bear on people like himself who had worked in the shadows – a company of brave men and women whose real names he had never known, many of whom were now dead, who had faced execution alone and unsung, dying for their beliefs, their dedication to the cause of freedom, the liberation of their beloved France.

Early that morning, Pierre had received news of his recall to General de Gaulle's headquarters in London. Staring at his reflection in the bar mirror, he doubted if anyone at Carlton Gardens would recognize him. A stranger stared back at him; a man with tired eyes and greying hair, a silent, uncommunicative man to whom sleep no longer came naturally, as a benison, a respite from pain.

But how he longed for sleep. Sleep to wash away the heartbreak; to wake up in his own bed once more; to catch the fragrance of coffee and freshly baked croissants from the kitchen of the farmhouse at Falais; to feel the warmth of his mother's presence in his room as she drew back the curtains; his sisters' laughter from the garden below, his father calling the dogs to heel.

But all that, his enchanted boyhood, his urgent youth, his growing up in a world encompassed with security and love was over and done with. The farmhouse lay in ruins. He had seen its burnt out shell, the toppled chimney-pots and sagging roof; the weeds that choked the curving drive between the avenue of poplars.

What had become of his family, no-one knew, or pretended they did not. The villagers had been strangely uncommunicative, going about their business, turning their heads away, continuing to feed the hens, hoe the garden, peg out the washing, saying they couldn't remember. It had all happened a long time ago and they were suspicious of his motives, his questions. Even now, Pierre realized, these people lived in fear, remembering the time when to utter a careless word might have cost them their lives.

Then an old man sitting in the porch of a tumble-down cottage had raised a gnarled, beckoning finger. '*I* remember,' he said huskily, glancing over his shoulder to make sure that no-one was listening. 'The Germans found that plane of Monsieur's . . .' But someone *had* been listening. A young woman, possibly his granddaughter, had rushed out of the house at that moment.

'Be quiet, you silly old fool!' she snapped. 'Do you want to get us all into trouble?'

'But he's M. Lefevre's son . . .'

'Huh, so he says, but how can we be sure?' The girl cast a hostile look at Pierre. 'Good day, Monsieur. Ask your questions elsewhere.'

But there was no need to ask more questions. Pierre then realized what had happened. Discovering *The Rose of Picardy*, the Germans would have drawn certain conclusions regarding his family's dedication to the cause of freedom.

Oh God, it was unthinkable! Knowing, through bitter experience, the Gestapo's ways of extracting information from Gaullist sympathisers, Pierre imagined the ordeal his family must have endured at the hands of their inquisitors – his brave, uncompromising father, Gaston, his three pretty tender-hearted sisters and above all his mother, the lovely, gentle Louise.

Burying his face in his hands, he had vowed that one day he would return to Falais. When the war was over, he would dedicate his life to finding out what had become of his family, to the re-building and restoration of the house which meant so much to him.

One day in early September, Will Prentiss came home at midday to find Mary leaning against the back door, fighting for breath.

'What is it? What's happened?' He hurried to her side. Her face was flushed, contorted. Useless to question her. She couldn't speak. Acting quickly, decisively, he pushed a chair under her and went through to the front room to ring for the family doctor. On his way back to the kitchen, he saw his mother coming downstairs. 'Mary's ill,' he said briefly. 'She can't get her breath!'

'I'll fetch my smelling bottle.' Gran hobbled back to her room. By the time she returned, Mary had recovered somewhat from her frightening attack. 'No need to fuss,' she said, pushing aside the smelling salts.

'I've sent for Dr Soames,' Will told her. 'He'll be here any minute.'

'I don't need a doctor.' Stubbornly, Mary pursed her lips.

'You're seeing him whether you want to or not.' Will spoke more sharply than usual. Mary burst into tears.

'She gets herself into such a state, no wonder she's poorly,' Gran said huffily. 'She *makes* herself poorly if you ask me, cleaning up all day when there's no need. Anyone would think the house was hanging with cobwebs, the way she goes on.'

'That's enough, Mother. There's the bell.'

Will waited in the hall while the doctor made his examination. They had had a devil of a job persuading

Mary to go upstairs to her bedroom. 'I'm perfectly all right now,' she kept on saying, 'it's the warm weather, that's all. I always get breathless in the warm weather.' But Will knew it was more than that. God, what a time the doctor was taking.

A sudden memory of Mary standing on the doorstep of the boarding-house in Earl's Court, her hair in disarray, holding a bucket and scrubbing brush, invaded Will's mind; the way he had felt the night her mother died, when she turned to him in her grief, and he had held her close to his heart. If only she would turn to him now, as she had done then, if he only knew how to break through the barrier of silent mistrust she had built up between them these past two years. But nothing he could do or say made any difference. No matter how hard he tried to break through, the barrier remained.

'Mr Prentiss.' The doctor's voice broke into his reverie.

'Sorry. I . . .'

'Can we go somewhere more private?'

'Yes, of course.' Will led the way to the sitting room, and closed the door behind them. 'Well, doctor, is it – serious?'

'I'm afraid it is. Your wife is a highly-strung woman, but there's no need to tell you that.' The doctor, a humorous man with a down-to-earth approach to his patients, good in situations like this, patted Will on the shoulder. 'No need to look so worried, old chap.'

Resentful of the 'old chap' and being told not to worry when he was worried sick, 'What exactly is wrong with her?' Will asked brusquely.

'Your wife has asthma. Don't ask me why. I'm not

qualified to say more than this. Asthma is an allergic condition. To get to the root of the matter, you would need to see a specialist. There's a good man in London – Harley Street who could find out exactly what it is your wife's allergic to. But this much I *can* tell you, the asthma attacks which I gather have been gaining in frequency, have weakened her heart to some extent.'

'Gaining in frequency?' Will stared at the doctor disbelievingly. 'I didn't know. She never told me.'

'No? Well, that's understandable. I expect she didn't want to worry you. Perhaps that is why she moved into a separate room.'

'Oh, God!' Will brushed his hand across his forehead. 'Why didn't she tell me?'

'That is scarcely my business.' The doctor wrote something on his prescription pad, 'But take my advice, get her to London to see that specialist as soon as possible.'

'Yes. I'm sorry, doctor. I didn't mean to be so off-hand. It's come as a shock, that's all. May I see her now?'

'By all means, though she may be sleeping. I have given her an injection to help her breathe more easily. By the way, here is the address of the specialist.'

Mary asleep seemed more vulnerable somehow, Will thought, looking down at her, her mouth slackened, a tiny dribble of saliva oozing from one corner; those watchful, unforgiving eyes of hers closed against the world which gave her so little joy.

If only he could come close enough to tell her that his affair with Pat Dawson had been born of loneliness, his need for warmth and companionship at a crucial time in his life. Perhaps he had been afraid, had turned to Pat for reassurance. Whatever the reasons, he still thought of her every day, at some time or other, when something happened to remind him. Even the smallest things possessed the power to trigger a chain of memories; a woman walking past the labour exchange windows, perhaps, whose straight shoulders and springy step recalled to mind the way Pat had walked into Haldane Ward, head held high, smiling as she came towards him.

He thought, looking at Mary's face upon the pillow, that if she awoke, this minute, and asked him if he was still in love with Pat, he would have to admit that he was, and his words, 'But I love you, too, Mary,' would sound false, lame and futile, because she would never be able to understand that his feelings for Pat made no difference to their relationship. Mary was his wife, the mother of his child, and he honoured her as such. Mary was part and parcel of his day to day life. Pat nothing more than a shining memory tucked away in a corner of his mind.

At first, Mary pooh-poohed the idea of going to London to see a specialist. Will took no notice, he simply went ahead, made an appointment for her, and wrote to Madge and Herbert asking if they could put them up for a few days.

'Don't include *me*,' Gran said snappishly. 'I'm not risking those blessed buzz-bombs. When I die, I'd rather do so in my own bed, not buried beneath a heap of rubble. You and Mary go to London if you must. I'll stay here and look after Nell.'

Will breathed a sigh of relief. Later, he sat down and wrote to Laura, saying how lovely it would be if they could arrange a meeting, that Mum hadn't been at all well lately.

Reading between the lines, Laura guessed what her father was really trying to say; that time may be running out for Mum, that the rift between them should be healed before it was too late.

Putting down the letter, she drew aside the blackout curtains and looked up at the moon, a silver disc riding high above the treetops, shining down on the aerial wires.

On a night like this, she thought, Rob had held her in his arms, and she had believed that such happiness would last forever. But she was wrong. Happiness was a fleeting thing, and she was a different person from the girl who had travelled to Armley House in the Autumn of 1940.

If only it were possible to flick back the hands of time, which moments would she want to re-live over and over again? The day she and Rob were married? The first night of their honeymoon? That night he came to her in the hilltop park after the *Rosie* returned safely to harbour? Sitting beside Meggie in that cinema in Devizes, weeping into her handkerchief as Ronald Colman, in *A Tale of Two Cities* mounted the steps to the guillotine?

Suddenly, seeing her face reflected in the moon-silvered glass of the cabin window, a thin, pale face framed with neatly cut hair, a haunted face, unsmiling, robbed by time and anxiety of those soft pads of flesh which had once denoted youth and innocence, Laura knew that she had grown up at last. But oh, dear God, how she wished she had not.

26

Grace's anger erupted when she learned that Dinah had been put in charge of their watch. So far she had managed to avoid a confrontation with her sworn enemy. Now, 'I simply won't work under that bloody "kid glove killer",' she said heatedly. 'I'd sooner die. I'll ask to see the station commander.'

'If you do,' Ruth pointed out, 'the chances are you'll end up in the Outer Hebrides. *You*, not Dinah would be the loser. *You'd* be posted, and the three of us would be split up.'

Could this be Ruth speaking? Shy, negative Ruth Maple, who had seldom expressed an opinion before, and never so forcibly. Grace stared at her in amazement. 'Why are you so positive all of a sudden?' She laughed, her anger forgotten for the time being. 'Hey, it's not that sailor, is it? The one who picked you up off the deck after that buzz-bomb episode?'

'What if it is?' Ruth blushed. 'He's very nice. His name is Alan.'

'Not Alan Ladd, by any chance?'

'No, Alan Sundquist. His grandparents are Norwegian.'

'You don't say? Did you hear that, Laura?'

Laura looked up from the letter she was writing to her father. Absorbed in what she was doing, she had not caught the gist of the conversation.

'What's the problem, Einstein?' Grace perched on the edge of her bunk to tie her shoelaces, thinking that Ruth was right about Dinah, that if she started making waves, she might well end up being posted. Above all things, she desperately wanted to stay put for the time being.

'My parents are coming to London next week,' Laura said. 'Do either of you know of a decent restaurant? I'd like to take them out for lunch.'

'What about the King Charles Brasserie in Regent Street?' Ruth suggested. 'It's not bad, considering . . .'

'Considering what?' Grace broke in, buffing her shoes with a duster. 'Don't tell me, I know. I went there myself a couple of weeks ago. Half the items on the menu were "off", and the grub was slightly "off" too. Funky, to put it mildly. If you want my advice, treat them to lunch at the Hotel Royal in Grosvenor Street. It might set you back a bit, but the food is excellent, and there's a great band.' She added, shyly for Grace, 'I've been there with my new boy-friend a couple of times. His name is Philip Jamieson – he's a Seaforth Highlander . . .'

Laura had guessed that Grace was in love again. There was no mistaking the look in her eyes, the resurgence of her old ebullience and charm. 'Actually, he's quite a lot like Scottie,' Grace said. 'He has the same sense of humour . . .' She laughed dismissively. 'Hark at me, anyone would think I was in love with the guy!'

'And are you?'

'I'm not quite sure.'

'Has he asked you to marry him?'

'Well, yes, but . . .'

Laura knew what Grace meant. How could she be sure that this new love affair would last? But at least Grace had mentioned Scottie – the first time since she came to Grafton.

'I don't want to jump out of the frying pan into the fire,' Grace sighed. 'I don't think I could bear . . . Oh well, it's too soon to be thinking of marriage again anyway. I haven't known him all that long.'

How long did it take to fall in love? Laura wondered. Days, months, years? Or within the space of a few moments the way it had when she danced with the Frenchman, all those years ago. How curious, she had not thought about that incident for ages. Now came flooding back to her that undeniable moment of truth when their eyes met, and he said: 'I hope that we will meet again one day.'

She and the Frenchman had been destined never to meet again. But what if they had? The whole course of her life might have been different. There would have been different hazards to face; other kinds of heart-break. Heartbreak, she knew, was a part of wartime – the loneliness, the partings, the tears at saying goodbye. Then Rob had come into her life.

'If you love this Seaforth Highlander of yours,' she said quietly, 'I think you should marry him. Why risk a lifetime of regret?'

Studying her reflection in the wash-room mirror, Dinah saw, with dismay, the faint lines and shadows beneath her eyes. No wonder, working in an atmosphere thick with tension and cigarette smoke; her marriage on the rocks, Giles' threat to name Perry as co-respondent in the divorce case.

How Giles had found out about her affair, she had no idea until she discovered that he had engaged the services of a private investigator.

'So go ahead, divorce me. See if I care!' She'd flung at him defiantly. 'Perry and I are in love. Nothing you do could make the slightest difference to the way we feel.'

Giles said grimly, 'I wouldn't be too sure about that. When Lister realizes that he stands to lose his wife and children, he will drop you like a hot chestnut.'

'You're wrong. Perry would never do that. He is a gentleman, which you apparently are not.' She added scornfully, 'In any case, a man like you would never willingly admit, in open court, that his wife had found him so bloody boring in bed.'

'Bed, ah yes, that's what it all boils down to. Your refusal to sleep with me, to bear my child. Your adultery with Captain Lister.' Seizing her by the shoulders, he swung her round to face him. 'Why have you done this to me?'

Staring up at him, face contorted with anger, 'Because I feel sick whenever you touch me. I am not a brood mare. Now, get out of my room!'

'With the greatest of pleasure.' Pritchard smiled. Turning at the door, he said, 'By the way, Captain Lister's wife is pregnant with their third child, but I'm sure that he has already told you. Offer him my congratulations when next you see him.'

Staring at her blanched face in the mirror, it couldn't be true, Dinah thought wretchedly. Giles had made up the story. Perry had assured her that he and Stephanie no longer slept together, that he was not, and never had been in love with her, they had simply been thrown together, in the rarified social climate of pre-war Cambridge, where they had attended the same house parties, dinner dances, and Hunt balls. Their respective fathers had known each other at university, Perry had told her, they had rowed for Cambridge in the nineteen something or other Boat Race.

When he came down from university with a degree in economics, he had spent the summer of 1937 drifting aimlessly from one house party to another, playing tennis, riding, probably drinking far more than was good for him. And everywhere he went, Stephanie had been there, too, setting her cap at him. The upshot? When her father had offered him a job with his firm of business consultants, he had proposed to Stephanie, knowing that his future promotion and prospects relied on his becoming the 'old man's' son-in-law.

Avidly, Dinah had made him go on, wanting to hear more about his boring, ineffectual wife, building up an image of a weak-willed ninny incapable of satisfying her husband's sexual appetite. She loved this mental comparison between herself and Perry's wife, picturing the woman as a dowdy nondescript person forever organizing civil defence lectures, collecting old newspapers, serving tea at the Cambridge railway station canteen, dressed in WVS uniform, singing in the church choir, filling her days with countless dull, boring activities. Then, when she had heard enough, unsheathing her claws, she had run her nails tantalizingly down Perry's back and made little purring sounds, and she had known, triumphantly, that she had the power to drive thoughts of his wife from his mind; that, making love to her, he belonged to no-one else.

Remembering the times she and Perry slept together,

how could she believe that he had lied to her? She must see him, confront him. Oh, damn this bloody week of night watches. No possibility of seeing him before Monday. In any case, she wouldn't want him to see her looking like this, pale and tired. It was all the fault of Grace McGregor and that wretched Laura Peters. Laura, whose eyes she was half afraid to meet, in which she read both pity and contempt. How *dare* she look at her like that? To make matters worse, that stupid Ruth Maple, the cause of all the bother at Ringley, stuck to the pair of them like glue, so that whenever she went on duty, she found herself faced with McGregor's needling, Maple's dumb insolence, and Peters' accusatory eyes.

No wonder she looked strained and anxious, her skin like putty. Staring into the mirror, the words of a half remembered poem sprang to mind, something she had learned at school. How did it go?

But beauty vanishes, beauty passes,
However rare, rare it be . . .

With a smothered cry, Dinah turned away from the mirror.

27

The Hotel Royal had become one of London's most popular rendezvous. The Yanks especially loved the Victorian atmosphere; slightly faded curtains and wallpaper, tucked away smoking rooms, potted palms and polished brass, the lounge reminiscent of palm court orchestras, tea and cucumber sandwiches.

Presided over by a shrewd, elderly Greek, Andreas Poulos, the restaurant, leading from the hotel foyer, retained an aura of past splendour. Red plush booths adjoined the dance floor. The balcony area, approached by an elegantly curved staircase, had red-shaded lamps on pristine white tablecloths. Tall windows overlooked Grosvenor Street.

The bandleader, Benny King, a thick-set coloured man, resembled Dooley Wilson in *Casablanca*. His style of piano playing, allied to his warm personality and his signature tune, 'As Time Goes By', had caught the mood of wartime Britain, Poulos reflected.

A romantic at heart, the shrewd little Greek enjoyed seeing couples holding hands across lamp-lit tables. At the same time, he would keep an eagle eye on the waiters and made a point of remembering the fads and fancies of his regular clientele, whom he treated with exquisite courtesy.

Moreover, Andreas possessed an uncanny knack of evaluating people at their true worth. He knew, for example, that Captain Lister's titled girlfriend, despite her airs and graces, had the morals of an alleycat, that Lister, fair-haired, tall, with his smooth olive skinned face was a nobody, socially speaking.

The couple had often stayed overnight in the hotel. There had been some unpleasantness over that recently, when a private investigator, hired by the Wren officer's husband, had started making inquiries, thereby upsetting Alex, the hotel manager, who confided in Andreas that he intended putting a stop to their using the Royal for nefarious purposes.

Glancing at his list of lunchtime bookings that day in September, Andreas noticed that Lister had reserved a table for one o'clock, which meant that Alex had not yet spoken to the man, and thanked his lucky stars that he would have no part in that unpleasant confrontation when it happened. Poor Alex, so meticulous, so correct, anxious to uphold the Royal's good reputation, had confided in Andreas that he had no wish to become involved in an unsavoury divorce case.

Pierre Lefevre would have given anything to side-step the luncheon hosted by his friend, Armand Metiere.

'Oh come now,' Metiere said persuasively, 'you have had a tough war. One luncheon in pleasant surroundings, is that too much to ask? You, above all people, have reason enough to celebrate. It is not every day that one is awarded the Croix de Guerre.'

'You don't understand, Armand. I am in no mood to accept congratulations. I simply did my duty.' Staring out of the window at the park below, noticing the trees changing colour, he remembered those heroes of the French Resistance who had died alone and unsung.

Metiere thought how much Lefevre had changed from the eager young man who had flown to England in the autumn of 1940. 'In any case,' he said, the Ambassador, M. Abelard, suggested this affair in your honour.'

'Then I appear to have no other choice.' Pierre sighed, thinking that he would far rather have spent the afternoon walking alone in the park.

Mary and Will Prentiss had caught a train from Walthamstow to Liverpool Street Station. Hailing a taxi to take them to Grosvenor Street, Will knew, by his wife's attitude, that the meeting with Laura, his dream of a reconciliation between them, stood little chance of success.

At first, Mary had flatly refused. 'You shouldn't have told Laura we were coming to London,' she said bitterly. 'I shall never forgive all those harsh things she said. Telling me I'd poisoned her life.'

Entering the room at that moment, Mary's sister, who had caught the tail end of the tirade, attempted to pour oil on troubled water. 'Isn't it about time you let bygones be bygones?' she said calmly. 'For heaven's sake, Mary, the girl is your daughter, and blood's thicker than water. Besides, we all say things we don't mean at times.'

'She meant them, right enough.'

'So what? Try to look at it from her point of view. Weren't you making a fuss over nothing? The girl was in love, and she married the man, so it wasn't exactly a hole-in-the-corner affair. Now she's a widow, the poor kid. And I know how much she's looking forward to seeing you, because she told me so.'

'Laura's been here?' Mary looked shocked.

'Yes, why not? After all, I am her aunt, and I haven't forgotten all those holidays before the war, if you have. Another thing, with those buzz-bombs coming over day and night, we might all be dead and gone tomorrow. Life's too short to carry on silly quarrels.'

And so Mary had gone upstairs to put on her hat and coat.

'Thanks, Madge,' Will said gratefully.

'Thanks, nothing,' Madge sighed. 'You can lead a horse to water, but you can't make it drink. Frankly, Will, I can't think why you've stuck by my sister all these years.'

On the occasion of his twenty-third birthday, Philip Jamieson, a stalwart Scot, ruddy complexioned, with light blue eyes and a charming smile, had booked a table at the Royal by way of celebration – a luncheon party to which he had invited Grace, the girl he was in love with, Laura Peters, Ruth Maple, and Alan Sundquist.

'I'm sorry, Grace, that's the day I'm meeting my parents,' Laura explained, turning down the invitation.

'Why not ask them to join us?' Grace bubbled, wanting to be kind. Then, 'No, I guess you'd rather be alone with them. But you can send up a distress signal if the going gets tough.' A thought struck her. 'At least we could share a taxi.'

And so the five of them arrived at the hotel, laughing and talking, Laura feeling nervous, despite her determination not to spoil Phil's birthday party.

Suddenly, 'Oh my God, take a look over there,' Grace said pseudo-dramatically, dodging behind a potted palm. 'It's Dinah and that weak-chinned boy-friend of hers. Don't let her see me, that's all.'

Philip laughed. 'What on earth are you up to now?'

Parting the fronds, Grace pulled a funny face. 'It's that third officer I told you about. You know, my "Betty Norey".'

'So what? No need to fraternize with the enemy! Come out, you idiot. In any case, I thought you said she was pretty. She looks a bad tempered little so-and-so to me.'

'Yeah, come to think of it, she does look a bit put out,' Grace said, emerging from her hiding place. 'If looks could kill, that bloke she's with would be as dead as mutton!'

Smiling urbanely, Poulos walked forward to greet them.

'Good luck with your mother,' Grace said, squeezing Laura's hand as they parted company. 'See you later?'

'Thanks.' How odd, Laura thought, following Andreas upstairs to her balcony table, to be so nervous of meeting her own mother. At the maitre d's suggestion, she had decided to wait there instead of in the foyer.

'I will show your guests up to you the moment they arrive, mademoiselle,' he promised, keeping an eye on the time. 'Possibly they have been delayed by the traffic.' More probably, they had decided not to come at all, he thought, feeling sorry for the little Wren. Obviously, all was not well with her.

Dinah drew off her gloves with exaggerated care,

finger by finger, and laid them, side by side, on the table, the deliberation of her action underlining her displeasure.

Lister watched, frowning, wondering what the hell had gone wrong since their last meeting. He had never seen Dinah like this before, cold and angry.

When she said coolly, 'Tell me, Perry, have you thought of a name for your new child?' the colour drained from his cheeks. Someone had been talking.

Heart beating thickly, he began, 'Listen, darling, I can explain . . .'

'About The Immaculate Conception, you mean? Or was this child conceived in the normal way?'

'You don't understand. I did it to protect us, our relationship. I had to! Her father was breathing down my neck, Stephanie talking about a divorce . . .'

'And so you slept with her?'

'Yes, but . . .'

'You have, in fact, been sleeping with her all along? It's true, isn't it? All those lies you told me. My God, Perry, you disgust me!'

Benny began playing, 'As Time Goes By'. Grace and Philip got up to dance. Ruth and Alan looked at each other across the table, aware that they had fallen in love.

'It's no use, Will, I can't face all those stairs! What was Laura thinking of to book a balcony table? In any case, what kind of place is this? I expected to have lunch in a quiet restaurant, not a dance hall.'

'Please, Mary, keep your voice down.'

'Pardon, madame, monsieur, I could not help

overhearing.' Andreas stepped forward, smiling. 'I am certain that I can find you a downstairs table. If you will follow me, I will ask your hostess to join you.'

The poor little Wren, he thought, no wonder she had seemed ill at ease. This mother of hers was a harridan.

Oh God, not another toast, Pierre thought distractedly, glancing round for an escape route, hating every moment of this boring luncheon party; the men from the embassy in their correct grey suits and gold cuff-links, smiling and nodding over their glasses of wine.

It was then he noticed the maitre d' speaking to a girl in Wren uniform, and imagined his eyes were playing tricks. It couldn't be Laura. But he knew that it was . . . Rising quickly to his feet, 'Please excuse me, Armand,' he muttered briefly, 'there is someone I must see. Now! It is very important!'

Following his friend's glance, Metiere said smoothly but firmly, 'For heaven's sake sit down. You cannot possibly leave. Affairs of the heart must wait!'

'I'm sorry, Armand, they have waited long enough!' He had lost Laura once. He could not risk doing so again, and yet to leave the table so abruptly would, Pierre realized, seem a grave discourtesy to his fellow guests.

Sitting down reluctantly, he summoned a waiter. Scribbling a brief note to the bandleader, 'Please see that he receives this as quickly as possible,' he said, pressing a substantial tip into the man's hand.

Would Laura remember the tune, he wondered.

She approached the table nervously.

'Hello, Mother.'

Will stood up, heart in mouth, willing a miracle to happen. But miracles were few and far between, in his experience.

'Hello, Laura,' Mary said grudgingly. 'I can't think why you booked an upstairs table. Your father told you I have asthma, I suppose?'

'Yes, I'm sorry. Have you seen the specialist?'

'Mother had her first visit yesterday,' Will explained, smiling at Laura. 'He hasn't discovered the cause of it yet. It's some kind of allergy . . .'

'Huh, so *he* says, but *I* know better. It's worry, that's what it is.' Mary angled her shoulders. 'Well, aren't you going to sit down?'

Benny began playing softly, 'Stay in my Arms, Cinderella'.

'What's the matter? Why are you looking like that?' asked her mother.

Laura had tilted her head. Listening intently to the music, memories flooded back: memories of another time, another place. A basement room, hot and stuffy, a dance floor sticky with soapflakes, the coloured lights of a radiogram. The Frenchman . . .

'Well, are we going to have something to eat, or not? The sooner we get this over, the better. I'm sure that waiter put us near the dance floor to annoy me because I refused to climb those stairs.'

Looking at her pursed up mouth, Will's patience snapped. Tired of her uncompromising attitude, 'For God's sake, Mary,' he said harshly, 'is nothing ever right for you? Of all the ungrateful women!'

'*Will!*' Mary's eyes opened wide, her mouth trembled. 'To speak to me in such a fashion . . .'

Laura was not listening. Her eyes were fixed on the staircase, and the man walking down it, searching the room with his eyes, looking for her. She would have known him anywhere, even though his dark hair had silvered at the temples. Suddenly, he saw her. An expression of unutterable relief and joy washed over his face as he moved towards her.

Mary glanced up fearfully. 'Listen! It's one of those flying bombs!'

Dinah picked up her gloves. 'I'm leaving.'

'No, please don't. We have to talk.'

'What is there to say? I refused to listen when Giles told me your wife was pregnant. I thought you were in love with me.'

'So it was Giles the jealous husband?' Perry laughed unpleasantly.

'I might as well tell you, Perry,' Dinah said coldly, 'he's starting divorce proceedings. Naming you as co-respondent.'

'Oh, my God! But that means . . .'

'Yes, it rather looks that way, doesn't it? Your precious wife will find out what a pathetic little rat you really are!'

Getting up, she began walking towards the door. With a muttered curse, Lister snatched up his belongings, and followed her.

The dance floor was crowded. Some of the women, on leave with their husbands, had dressed in civilian clothing, brightly coloured dresses, and unrationed hats trimmed with veiling and artificial flowers, to grace the occasion. Other couples, in Navy, Army and Air Force uniform, waltzed serenely to the music. The scrape of shoes on the maplewood floor, the laughter, the hum of conversation, effectively masked the drone of the V-2 engine. In any event, most people had become inured to the sounds of wartime London. But not Mary, who was staring up at the ceiling, breathing rapidly, her face white with terror.

'Will,' she whispered hoarsely, 'for God's sake, listen! The motor's cut out!'

Scarcely stopping to think he pulled her to the floor, and covered her shaking body with his. 'Laura,' he cried, in desperation. 'Laura! Take cover!'

Suddenly the ground rocked beneath them with the force of the explosion. Metalwork twisted, windows shattered, the ceiling crumbled, beams crashed down, the balcony stairs collapsed. The air was filled with a suffocating pall of dust. All was darkness and confusion.

Captain Lister died instantaneously. Sheet music fluttered like snowflakes in the wind. Benny had fallen forward, his hands still resting on the keyboard.

A cascade of tables and chairs, cutlery, uneaten food, silver covers, and broken wine bottles slithered from the crazily tilted balcony. One woman, who had managed to cling on to a scrap of buckled metal, hung suspended above a twenty foot drop, until her fingers gave way and she plunged, screaming, to the floor below.

Laura blacked out momentarily from the searing pain in her left arm as a sliver of flying glass, as sharp as a knife, embedded in her shoulder.

Recovering from her faint, she felt the warm seepage

of blood dripping from her fingers. Biting her lips, she felt for the splinter with her right hand. Blackness threatened once more as she pulled it slowly from the wound, and felt its serrated edges cutting into her flesh like a saw. Then she began crawling forward on her knees, and on one hand, leaving a trail of blood behind her; coughing, half choking, inching her way forward slowly, unable to think clearly, half blinded by the suffocating clouds of dust, losing all sense of direction, hearing the screams and cries of people trapped beneath the wreckage.

'Mary! Mary! Are you all right?'

Will couldn't see her face; simply felt the grasp of her fingers on his sleeve, and heard the harshness of her breathing.

'It's all right, love, I'm here,' he whispered, holding his wife in his arms, unaware of the tears coursing down his cheeks.

'You have always been there, Will,' Mary murmured drowsily, 'whether or not I deserved you. Poor William, what a burden I've been to you.'

'Don't talk so daft. We'll be going home, soon.'

'Just one thing, before we – go home. Will you tell Laura I'm sorry? I do love her, I always have. I love you, too. I just couldn't find the words to tell you how much. There never seemed a right time for me.'

The fire started in the kitchen, when spilling fat from an unattended chip pan bubbled over on to a flaring gas jet. At the same time, the naked wires of a blown out fuse box whiplashed suddenly, showering sparks.

As the fire spread, an acrid smell of burning, smoke and flames, gusted through the swing doors.

Crawling through the wreckage, Laura heard a faint

cry for help, close at hand. A woman's voice. Someone was trapped beneath a fallen beam heaped with masonry. Clenching her teeth, ignoring the searing pain in her shoulder, uncaring of the blood gouting from the wound, she began delving frantically with her bare hands, wincing as her fingers came into contact with the pile of rubble and fallen plaster, hearing the roar of the encroaching flames, realizing that soon the entire building would be engulfed by the fire. Then she heard the sweetest sound she had ever heard in her life, the clamour of fire-engine bells.

And now the woman's left hand had emerged from the wreckage. Clasping hold of it, whispering words of encouragement, straining with all her might to pull her from the masonry, as the firemen broke into the building, emitting the light of the world outside, Laura realized that the hand she was holding was Dinah's. There was no mistaking that flawless diamond engagement ring of hers. She also realized that the enmity which existed between herself and Dinah did not matter a damn, now; that nothing mattered in this crazy, war-torn world, except forgiveness. That, without forgiveness, and love, the whole of the human race might as well be buried alive.

28

Grace entered the church of the Immaculate Conception.

Rays of evening sunshine slanting from damaged stained glass dappled the nave with stepping stones of faded colours. Slim candles shining about the statue of Our Lady created haloes of light where the shadows lay thickest.

A trickle of people had already begun drifting down to the crypt where they would spend the night. The priest in charge welcomed each as a friend, especially the very old people who moved more slowly than the rest.

Choking back tears, Grace lit a candle to the Madonna, remembering her vow never to light another candle, never to enter a church again for as long as she lived. Within the space of a few hours, she had changed her mind about a great many things.

Bowing her head, she thought that this war, which she had once treated as a joke, was nothing of the kind, and never had been; rather a banner raised to the courage of ordinary people who had fought and died to create a better world.

Ordinary people like Laura who had risked her own life to save Dinah's. One of the ambulancemen had said gruffly, 'This little lady deserved a medal. She might have bled to death, but she wouldn't leave her friend. Careful with that stretcher. As for her friend, the poor little devil. It's a damned shame . . .'

Watching the ambulance move away, Grace had stood there helplessly on the pavement, Philip beside her. When he asked quietly what he could do to help, 'Nothing,' she said numbly, 'I just want to be left alone.'

Knowing that he was hurt, bewildered by her brief dismissal, she watched him go; wishing she had known how to express her feelings, her need to come to terms with herself, and God.

'Holy Mother, forgive my foolish stubbornness and pride,' she prayed, tasting the hot, salt tears of regret on her lips, remembering the many times she had turned her back on her faith, careless of the consequences, the enmity she had nurtured between herself and Dinah, to what end? What purpose?

Sick at heart, she recalled that shock of horror when she had caught sight of Dinah's face on that stretcher. A face cut to ribbons by flying glass.

Alan and Ruth walked together beneath the trees in Hyde Park, deeply shaken by the restaurant bombing. 'That was a pretty close call,' Alan said. 'I thought we'd had it.'

Ruth shivered, thinking how lucky they were to be alive. Others had not been so fortunate; Benny, Captain Lister, many of the couples who had been dancing together when the ceiling collapsed. Thank God Grace and Phil had been near the edge of the floor when the bomb struck.

Her heart had gone out to Laura's father as she watched him climb into the ambulance beside his daughter's stretcher. What must he have been feeling at that moment, knowing that his wife was dead, Laura seriously injured? As for Dinah, how would she feel, regaining consciousness, seeing her face in a mirror? All she had ever had was her beauty. With that gone, how would she survive a grim, unlovely future?

Alan said, 'Know what I think? If we two are destined to spend the rest of this bloody war dodging flying bombs, we might just as well do it together.' He paused. Holding Ruth's hand, 'I'm asking you to marry me.'

Ruth looked at him, startled. 'But you don't know anything about me! The kind of girl I really am.'

'Go on, then, tell me.' He did not believe that her revelations could be all that shattering, not in his present state of euphoria at being alive.

Knowing she risked losing him, taking that risk, Ruth said haltingly, 'I – I had an affair, you see.'

Screwing up his eyes to watch a squirrel performing acrobatics from branch to branch, 'So you had an affair?' he said lightly. 'That's nothing unusual in wartime.'

'I thought you might be – angry.'

'No, why should I? What really matters, have you got him out of your system, or are you still in love with the guy?'

'I know now that I was never in love with him,' Ruth said. 'In any case, he's dead now. But it seemed very important to me at the time.'

Leaving the squirrel to its own devices, smiling at her, 'Well, that's all right then, isn't it? Not that the poor bloke is dead, I don't mean that. Oh hell, how can I put it? What I'm trying to say is, I'm glad this affair of yours wasn't just a one night stand. We all

have to learn from experience. Here, blow your nose.'
He gave her his handkerchief.

Ruth blew obediently.

'Well are you going to marry me, or not?' he asked.

'Oh yes.' Smiling up at him, Ruth thanked God that
experience had taught her the value of true love.

'Great! That's settled then.' Alan breathed a sigh of
relief. 'Now, let's go and have a cup of tea, shall we?'

Walking out of the church, Grace thought that if her
life were to have any meaning at all from now on, it
must be at the cost of her own pride, her empty-headed
approach to living.

Was she in love with Philip, or not? She couldn't be
sure. So far theirs had been a light-hearted, laugh
a minute affair. What kind of maturity could she
possibly bring to their relationship? In any case, how
could she be certain that he would want a more mature
relationship?

Possibly real love, that overwhelming love she had
felt for Scottie, happened only once in a lifetime. And
perhaps she would never know if Phil really cared for
her or not. After being sent away so abruptly, he might
not want to see her again.

Crossing the road, dodging the traffic, suddenly she
caught sight of him standing on the opposite pavement, waiting for her, unsmiling, hands outstretched
to greet her.

'I thought you'd gone,' she said breathlessly. 'I saw
you catch the bus!'

'Yes, well, I got off at the next stop.'

'Why?'

'Need you ask? Because I couldn't just leave you to

go through all this heartbreak alone, I love you too much for that. No, don't say anything, not now, it's too soon. I just want you to know that I'll always be there, if you need me. But that's up to you.'

Saluting, he turned abruptly, and strode away from her along the crowded pavement.

It was then Grace realized that her prayers had not been in vain. 'Philip,' she called after him. 'Philip! Wait!'

Will scarcely knew how to break the news of her mother's death to Laura. The past days had been a torment, faced with decisions about Mary's funeral, visiting the hospital, sitting beside Laura's bed, anxiously waiting for her to regain consciousness, yet dreading the moment he would have to tell her the truth.

Talking things over with Madge and Bob, he felt he had done right in deciding that the funeral should take place in London. Mary, after all, had been born there, and it seemed pointless to have her body taken back to Scarborough. It would be a harrowing experience for Gran.

He had not expected his mother to take the news of Mary's death so badly, but she had broken down and cried on the telephone, adding to his worries. An old woman alone in a big house, even though he had arranged for their next door neighbour to keep an eye on her, and do her shopping. But Gran had stubbornly refused the woman's offer to stay with her at night. 'I'll be all right,' she'd said firmly, 'the dog can sleep in my bedroom. Besides, I don't want the woman next door to see me without my teeth in.'

In the event, Will was spared the ordeal of telling Laura that her mother was dead. It was Meggie who broke the news to her, on the day of Mary's funeral.

Johnny was waiting for her when Meggie emerged from the hospital. Knowing that she was too upset to talk just then, he walked her along to the nearest café and ordered a pot of tea. When she seemed calmer, he asked her gently what had happened.

'Well, at least I've got it over with,' Meggie said, drying her eyes. 'When Laura came round long enough to speak, she asked about . . . well, you know, about Uncle Will and Auntie Mary. I just sat there, not knowing what to say, then she must have known by my face there was something wrong, so I plucked up my courage and – oh, Johnny, I couldn't help crying.'

'How did she take it?'

'I'm not sure. She didn't say much. I expect it hadn't sunk in properly. She was still very woozy. Then a nurse came and said I'd better leave, and not to worry, she'd be all right, they'd look after her.' Meggie blew her nose. 'I expect the poor things are used to it by now – getting people over shocks like that. I expect they'd give her something to make her sleep. Poor Laura.'

Meggie was wrong in supposing that Laura had not grasped the fact that her mother was dead. But there had been no words to express her feelings, even to Meggie. Poor Meggie whose tears and stumbling sentences had somehow heightened her grief, the despairing thought that it was too late now to make amends, too late for that longed for reconciliation with Mary, too late to say she was sorry.

Just before Meggie stood up to leave, Laura held

out her hand, and whispered, 'Thank you for coming. For being here.'

'Shall I come back tomorrow?' Meggie had asked uncertainly, believing that she had mismanaged the situation in her usual incompetent fashion.

'Yes. Please.'

Glancing anxiously at her cousin, Meggie saw that Laura's eyes were closed, tears trickling down her cheeks. Then the nurse had come to take charge, and Meggie had walked out into a grey September afternoon to find Johnny waiting for her.

Watching daylight fade slowly from the sky, hearing the beating of the rain upon the hospital windows, the clatter of the trolleys, seeing a young nurse drawing the blackout curtains, Laura lay quite still, feeling the now familiar throb of pain in her left shoulder, the even more familiar pain of sadness in the region of her heart.

Unconscious, there had been no pain, simply a great tunnel of darkness, leading nowhere. Conscious, the pain of memory flooded in on her: memories of the restaurant bombing, that dagger of glass gouging into her shoulder, gouts of blood spurting from the wound, a choking pall of dust; mounds of rubble; the crackle of the onrushing fire.

And before that? Before the bomb exploded, she remembered standing near her parents' table, listening to her mother's carping criticism, and then . . . then she had heard the music of a half forgotten song, had turned her head to see the Frenchman coming towards her. The Frenchman!

Then, the world had seemed to tilt on its axis as the bomb struck, robbing her of that feeling of joy when his eyes met hers, when she had believed, for one ecstatic moment that miracles were still possible.

Now she knew better. And this was the silent agony she must endure from now on, this realization that there were no miracles left in a world of death and destruction. Her mother was dead and buried. For all she knew, the Frenchman might also be dead.

Closing her eyes, she saw him clearly, in her imagination, moving across the dance floor towards her, smiling, hands outstretched, an unutterable expression of relief in his eyes that he had found her again.

Then their brief moment of joy had ended when the bomb exploded.

Now the sound of rain against the windowpanes invaded her hazy drifting into the oblivion of sleep.

She dreamt that she was walking in the rain, her father and Nell beside her, running along the seashore, laughing in the rain, throwing sticks for the dog, hearing the comforting sound of the sea breaking over the rocks of Scarborough's South Bay.

In that dream, she was young once more, the laughing, light-hearted girl she used to be, in love with life, carefree and happy.

When the dream ended, she opened her eyes to see her father sitting beside the bed. Suddenly, she remembered that her mother was dead.

'Dad,' she cried, reaching for his hand. 'Oh, Dad!'

Holding her hand, Will said, 'I just wanted to tell you. Your mother's last words: "Will you tell Laura I'm sorry? I really do love her. I just never knew the words to explain how much".'

'Mum said that?'

'Yes, and she meant it.'

'What will you do now?' Laura asked, eventually.

'Stay here with you.'

'But what about Gran? You mustn't leave her on her own. Poor Gran. She'll need you now, more than ever. You must go home.'

'But what about you?'

'Don't worry about me. Meggie's coming in to-morrow, and there'll be other people, too. Grace and Ruth . . . Aunt Madge and Uncle Bert.'

'I wish things might have been different,' Will said. 'Strange, isn't it? I never realized until I told Gran that Mum was dead, how much she really cared for her, despite everything.'

'I know.' Laura remembered Dinah, the way she had felt pulling her from the wreckage. Whatever their quarrels of the past, old grievances had been forgotten when the chips were down.

'I think Gran enjoyed the cut and thrust,' Will said. 'Old people are like that.' He smiled sadly. 'I don't want to leave you, Laura, but if that's what you want. I'll write to you every day.'

'Goodbye, Dad. Give Gran and Nell my love. Tell Gran I'll be home soon.'

Kissing her, Will wished he could say something to bring a smile to her lips, rekindle the light of happiness in her eyes. She seemed so sad. This was only natural, he supposed, having lost her mother. But there was something else, a deeper sadness, a look on her face he had noticed only once before, after Rob died.

Thank God for Meggie, he thought, walking slowly down the ward, turning at the door to raise his hand in a final gesture of farewell, if anyone could bring comfort to Laura, it was Meggie.

Head bowed, deep in thought, not looking where he was going, he bumped into a man, with heavily bandaged hands, standing near the reception desk.

'I beg your pardon,' the man said, 'there appears to be no-one on duty.' He smiled. 'But then, I am not even certain that I have come to the right place.'

Glancing at the man's hands, 'Possibly you want the out-patients' department,' Will said kindly, 'that's down the corridor, on the left.'

'Oh no, monsieur,' the man said quickly, 'you misunderstand. I am looking for someone – a girl.'

'Oh, in that case,' Will said, 'I'm afraid I can't help you, but the receptionist should be back in a minute, she'll be able to help.'

'It might be easier,' the Frenchman said despondently, 'if I knew the girl's surname. But all I know is her first name – Laura.'

'Then you don't know her very well?' Will asked, keeping his own counsel, curious to hear more.

'No,' the Frenchman admitted, 'all I know is that she is the only girl in the world for me, that I shall not rest until I know what has happened to her.' Running a hand wearily across his eyes, 'I have searched everywhere, visited every hospital in the Greater London area, but there has been no word of her. This is my last hope, the last hospital on my list. If she is not here, then I must renew my efforts to find out what became of her.'

Studying the man's face, Will liked what he saw – the face of a young man etched with the lines of experience, as if the war he had fought had not been an easy war. A kind, compassionate face.

Suddenly he knew, with an instinct older than time,

the love of a father for his daughter, that he could safely hand down the torch of love into this man's keeping.

Smiling, Will said quietly, 'My daughter's name is Laura.'

THE END